SHIPWRECK OF HOPES

Angela Reich

Shipwreck of Hopes

ISBN: 978-0-578-41620-5

Library of Congress Control Number: 2018913054

For Mom

Acknowledgements

With much appreciation to those who read and commented on my early drafts, for their kindness and encouragement: Judanna Lynn, Katherine Reich, Diane and George Nichols, Arlene Soranno, Boris Stiglitz, and Vince and Denise DeGiaimo.

Special gratitude goes to my son and editor, Brendan Reich, who with his sharp wit and sharpened pencil, patiently emended and helped to shape all the many drafts of the manuscript.

In addition, a great debt is owed to the scholarship of Margaret Fuller's biographers, primarily that of Megan Marshall, Charles Capper and John Matteson.

With gratitude for the unending support of Dave Griese, administrator of the Fire Island Lighthouse and staff, including Patti Stanton, Amanda Vaskas and Bette Berman.

Special thanks to Arlene Stephani and the staff at the Long Island Maritime Museum historical archives and to Gordon Fleming for generously sharing his specialized maritime knowledge. To the Bayshore Historical Society for abundant access to its library, to Roger Seebald of the Bayshore Brightwaters Public Library for assistance and support with its fine Long Island History Collection. To my research "yoda," Ned Smith of the of the Suffolk County Historical Society, to Jonathan Thayer, keeper of the historical records of the Lifesaving Benevolent Association, Maria Molestina of the Morgan Library in NYC, T.R.Dring, Commander, USNR- Retired, expert on the history of the US Lifesaving Service, Gina Piastuk of the historical archives of the East Hampton Library and Heather Cole of Harvard's Houghton Library for access to the Fuller family papers, and to Henry David Thoreau's notes on the interviews made of local residents on Fire Island after the wreck of the *Elizabeth*.

And finally to my husband, Rudy Nolfo, whose steadfast encouragement supported me throughout this project, without which this book would not have been possible.

PART I

1

Hannah and Smith Oaks
Fire Island, Long Island, New York
circa 1842

Hannah Oaks stood alone atop the highest dune. The sun shone bright on her tanned skin as the wind swept back her long blonde hair, let loose. Arms, toned from toil hung idle, legs stood strong and apart, feet firmly set, bare, calloused, upon a new growth of sparse wild grass. Her cotton frock whipped backward and between her legs, revealing her youthful shape. Here she faced the mighty sea, its jagged surface gleaming like glass in the sun.

She remembered a life that seemed so long ago, distant, yet still visceral. An impenetrable shadow remained, though time blurs the edges of memory. This about a young girl, unsuspecting. Taken by surprise, and helpless.

So despite the passing of the years and across the miles, haunting memory-dreams would not release Hannah. They kept her prisoner, chained. Startled awake many a time from deep slumber by a flash of awareness, then she'd know it again all at once. That once upon another time, there was a child who died. Who Hannah buried, deep and forever.

"But here," atop the dune, she thought, "I am away from that place. This island keeps me captive. This island keeps me safe."

*****

A ramshackle farmhouse. A rotting fence surrounding a dirt yard. A broken gate, jammed open halfway. The house stood out of habit. The house spoke its own sadness.

There were the last throes of mother's illness, blindness and disease progressing, she lingered painfully. Toes blackening, then feet, extremities lost one by one. There was no help for it, no cure. It was for Hannah to take over the care of the family's daily chores. The appetites of her brothers and father, labor upon them, they arrived home always with their rough ways and demands.

"Hannah, what the *hells*'a matter wit' ya' settin' there? Make some use o' yerself! Whata'ya been doin' all day anyways?" her father bellowed as he staggered across the threshold, home from the mill late again, whiskey on his breath.

"Sorry Papa."

She'd learned not to argue with him after her mother died. That was all she'd say, "Sorry, Papa" though tears of frustration stung her eyes, blurring the needle while she, in the parlor, mended their threadbare linens.

As it was, her days started before dawn. First, she'd select the driest logs and coax them gently to flame in their small kitchen hearth. Then when they were snapping sharply alight she, with two tin pails empty, made her way out, behind the house, past the small graveyard, down the gully, muddy and dank, slipping and sliding to the back stream.

There she'd step into the cold flow to carefully fill each bucket. Heavy the metal buckets were, her small hands calloused already from daily labor. Shoulders aching from the weight of the load, thighs scraped from the rusted old buckets that no matter how carefully balanced, splashed their contents all the way back to the house. Each day, water had to be hauled for washing, cleaning and cooking. Many hard trips would it take to fill the tubs needed to run the house.

If only Mama were here, she thought. If only Mama didn't leave me.

Each day was assigned its own chores. Baking day to produce all the breads needed for the week. Washing day, water boiled, lye soaps for heavy clothes and linens then hung to dry on rope lines tied to trees. Ironing day, metal irons heated on red-hot coals. Then for marketing, a day's walk to and from town for necessary supplies. Cleaning day, floors to wash, all rooms kept swept and dusted. And then there's the garden in season, and in all seasons tending the chickens and the family graves.

For Hannah, the days and weeks rolled by in numbness and exhaustion.

*****

Now, atop the dune, she watched the wash of the waves that left a sparkle on the sand shimmering like diamonds dropped by a benevolent spirit. And capping all, the sky, moody, blended land and sea, horizon indistinct. All elements swirled about Hannah in movement; wind, sea, sky. All movement to her seemed motionless, captured and eternal. Hannah caught the scene in her mind's eye. Memories swept in like old companions from the past who come to visit, at once familiar when arrived, as if they'd never left.

She remembered that day long ago, when she made her way home, the dusty walk from town seemed even longer with the hand cart loaded with provisions for the larder. She hummed a tune for company, observing the sunlight through the trees, the sway of the upper branches in the breeze.

Down the quiet lane, Hannah's farmhouse came into view.

Now, the cart to unload, she approached the back of the house. She saw the kitchen door was inexplicably left ajar. She entered. "Papa?" she called out. But no answer came. A quick glance out back showed the pony gone, the shed empty.

Yet, Hannah entered the house and sensed a strangeness there. Something amiss; like a vague disturbance. Curious, she followed the puzzling feeling through the house, like one in a trance.

Then, the baffling sight of large muddy footprints leading down the hall. She followed them to her bedroom. There she saw unfamiliar boots on the floor, rumpled quilt tossed aside.

Stepping into the room, the unexpected, but familiar face. He was waiting for her. One from town who always leered; lingered too long.

Now, his expectant smile turning sneer when he saw her dismay.

She stepped backward toward the door, still facing him, edging away, but he too fast, too strong.

Then the attack, the torn dress. The rough shove downward. The two as one. His brawny sun-browned form covering her pale flesh, his head thrown back, eyes closed; she, eyes wide, blinded and benumbed.

After, she ran out of the house. Ran to the back stream and bathed in its clear waters, her tears mixing into the running flow.

*****

Yesterdays blend with todays on this barrier beach, time as indistinct as the shoreline; tides that change the island's borders from day to day and from storm to storm. The sea and the wind, all malleable, changeable motion.

Look, who's to say how past and present intermingle? Who's to say what shapes our future? Who's to say how our minds present dreams, feelings, thoughts. Isn't it all as one, then? Time, memory, action? Isn't it all of a piece? Our lives lived on the edge, the threshold of worlds colliding.

Now, years and miles from that memory, she knew that on this barrier island was the real, the eternal. From here would her being lift and become whole. This place of freedom and of power immutable, the wild Atlantic shore.

Here she would see scenes of wonder – a moment's gleam- perhaps the glint of the sun on the sea as she weeded the small garden patch; or, while hanging laundry, the fleeting wave of the sea grass on the dune as she turned to face the warm breeze.

Then, in the quiet evening, she'd use a charred stick from the fire and scraps of paper, whatever wasn't needed, and in her small parlor, she would sketch the landscape, scraping the image in her mind onto the rough paper. She'd create, contouring, with changes of pressure or motion, her fingers playing, coaxing the scene from the crude instrument, bold definite lines, or delicate soft shadows. Her strokes portrayed power wild, or softness tranquil, nature's moods. In this, her vision, expression, complete.

All details lovingly recorded and finished to her satisfaction, she'd place the drawing carefully into the fire to watch it catch. First, the edges would curl, then the paper would singe from the middle, then the flame would break through and she'd watch it glow briefly, then die into black ash - some that would crumble, some that would sift through the logs. A lucky glowing cinder might fly a moment, swivel about in the updraft as if to escape, then blacken and fall to her feet.

"Just a bit of paper and coal, that's all it was," Hannah would think while she watched her work become part of the embers for the next day's fire. "Nothing of any worth, anyway." She would stay and watch her work burn to ash.

2

She'd grown up just outside a bustling little shore town named Patchogue, about sixty miles east of New York City. Though the local tribe had left the town its name, it was the children of the first settlers who had the town humming with business, mills and small industry.

Hannah was the fifth of eight children left alive: four dead in infancy. As a young woman, Hannah would visit the little cemetery out behind her house. It was only in the family plot, beside the graves, where she found peace and solace. She'd tend the rosemary on the graves of her siblings, infants never grown. Next to them, her mother's grave had a wild beach rose which Hannah had taken from the dunes and transplanted, keeping it trim and in flower.

Then there was the other grave, unmarked, but for a small bayberry plant that she tended in secret. Hannah's child, when no more than a child herself. No one else knew about any of it. The child, born of violence, came and passed in silence, unknown.

Already at her young age, Hannah knew there was no air enough to fill the lungs of the bereaved, the suffocation of loss. She knew the hunger that would not be satisfied, the hunger for the departed ones, whose impressions flash before her mind always. There she mourned mother and child. There she knew the loss of innocence.

She, alone in her haze of shame and guilt.

*****

The years spun out in sameness. Hannah kept the small farmhouse tidy; clothing washed and mended, meals ready for her hungry ungrateful family.

After her father died, the household slowly broke up: her brothers moved and drifted away.

She cared for the old house, falling further into disrepair. She knew every creaking board and loose nail. Every leaking window where the wind blew in. Every drip from the roof during pounding rainstorms.

Of course, the neighbors talked. They passed by, knowing her as solitary. "Hannah who is alone." Or, "Poor, lonely Hannah," they would say.

Occasionally, she would be called upon to do some sewing. Her stitching was artful and patient. She was known to do beautiful, delicate work.

"It's not good to be alone, Hannah," the ladies would say as she measured a hem or stitched a bodice.

"Yes ma'am," Hannah would reply absently.

She kept house. She tended to the few chickens in the coop out back. She kept the vegetable garden. She mended and sewed for the ladies in town. She existed.

But opportunities arise unexpectedly, even in these small shore towns. She began to notice a man when she went into town for errands. He noticed her, as well.

"Smith Oaks," she was told.

"Poor Hannah, all alone," he was told.

"Arrived here from Ohio about a year ago," she was told.

"Lives outside of town," he was told.

"He sails here from the barrier island. Takes people out fishing and hunting," she was told.

"Her parents died, her brothers gone. Keeps to herself," he was told.

Each, always in town alone. At first, furtive glances from across the road. Then their gazes met. A nod. A smile. Their looks lingered longer, until Smith Oaks asked for her hand.

It wasn't long before she left her home in Patchogue among the hunters and farmers and mill workers for the barrier beach as the wife of a sportsmen's guide.

3

1840 - Ohio

Smith Oaks had been drifting many years since leaving his home in the rugged mountains of western Virginia. Hunting, trapping and fishing, he lived in the wild until he reached the Ohio border. Then, odd jobs on farms. He made few ties; petty thieveries both sustained him and forced him to move on.

Finally, he found a town that suited him, and decided to settle. He became apprenticed to the village blacksmith. He liked the work, physical, tough and steady. He liked the horses, mute beasts he could control and tame.

But Oaks soon found himself restless there after an accident at the forge left his left arm weak from the shoulder.

"Can't be trusted to handle horses and molten metal with that weak arm," he was told. "Ain't no place for you here nomore."

He walked away from the blacksmith's barn where he had put in his time, learning the trade. "Arm's not s' bad. Arm'l be jes' fine in a while. I jes' know it." Angry and hurt, he spat in the dust of the street. "Somma bitch nev'r liked me anyways," Smith muttered aloud, furious that he'd been fired.

The glare of the sunlight was cut off as he entered the dark saloon. "Man gits thirsty here," he said loudly, taking a seat at the bar. "Whisky. Double."

"Whad'r you doin' here so early?" came the voice from behind the darkened bar.

"Non o' yer damned business, barkeep," Smith replied. "Jes' keep 'em comin'."

"As ornery as ever, even in daylight," replied Jesse as he poured for his friend.

"Somma bitch fired me. Said it's 'cause o' my arm," said Smith Oaks. "Jes' an excuse to git rid o' me. Never liked me anyways..."

"Ahhh. Yep," Jessie commiserated. "He's a tough 'un. But don' worry. You'll find somethin'. It's a big world out there."

*****

At first, Smith Oaks felt disoriented and adrift. A man without purpose, he wandered about the town, wasting his days. But, with some time, he felt his mind take ease.

He eventually came to realize that he was now free. No longer an apprentice to a grueling business that would never be his. No more of the forge's suffocating heat that singed the hair of his face and arms. No more of the deafening clang of the driving hammer that made sparks fly from the heated metal. No more would his sweat mingle with that of the horses: both man and beast of labor joined.

Then, he began to recall the enticing tales told by travelers whose horses he shod while on their way to claim their piece of America's expansion westward. They told of the east coast from whence they came, of miles of sand beaches, of fresh clean air that swept from clear across the sea, then sliced through the grassy dunes, of water as pure and blue as the skies. They told of ships and sailors and pirates and the ghosts of all those who haunted the desolate dunes, making the native grasses sway wild with the wind that carried haunting ghostly moans into the night.

Oaks realized now that these need not be faraway tales of adventure: that he was free and that all was now available to him for the seeking.

Smith Oaks decided, then went east with the morning light.

4

1841 Brooklyn, NY

"That you, Smith?" An astonished voice rang out in the evening twilight as Smith Oaks found his way to New York, then to a small neighborhood in Brooklyn and to the block of row houses and the sign that read, "Andrew Oaks, Cabinetmaker."

"Wa'al! Looks like yer doin' alright fer yerself here! Nice business…cabinets.. is it? All'as was good with yer hands. Do ye live here too?"

"Coulda' writ you were coming…"

"Wuz kinda a last minute decision, he said with a grin. "Offer a brother a drink?"

They sat at the kitchen table, bottle of whiskey and old troubles between them.

"How long you out here for?" Andrew asked.

"Stayin'. New York's my new home."

Andrew's face did not conceal unpleasant surprise.

"But not here," added Smith with a sly grin. "Headin' east to the beaches where the air's clean and the breezes blow."

What a relief, thought Andrew. Always trouble following this one, remembering their early years, and their worried mother, and the litany of his petty offenses that kept the local sheriff at their door.

"Could use a job fer some travelin' money, though. Ran out already."

"I run my own shop here, don't need no help. Bed down for the night, anyways. I'll think of something in the mornin'."

5

Smith Oaks was at the car barn of the New York and Harlem Railroad on the next day.

"Heard you was openin' a new rail line up t' Williamsbridge, thought mebbe you can use some help," said Oaks.

"Can you drive a horse upon these new rails?" asked the Stationmaster.

"Sure can. An' did some blacksmithin' too, so I can do yer metal-work...horseshoein', rail, car repairs."

"Good." He sized up the new man. Looked weathered. Wiry. Strong. "Be here tomorrow just after dawn."

As the weeks went by, Andrew was amazed at the change in Smith. He was up and out before the sun, arriving home nightly, late and exhausted. Never much for conversation anyway, his brother always went straight to bed. He seemed no trouble at all.

But Smith Oaks was busy. He knew opportunity when he saw it, and he made the best of it. He made himself indispensable at the rail line to an overwhelmed and exhausted stationmaster with his knowledge both of horses and of metalwork. He could fix the horses' harnesses as easily as a car's broken axel. He shod the horses while whistling a tune, and could drive a team along the rails like he was born to it.

A man's man, the rest of the crew took to him easily. He spun stories in the station house after work, easing the men's exhaustion from the day's labor. Hearty laughter, men's laughter, rang from the open windows, as Smith was always ready with a joke, or tales from the west, yarns of mighty deeds improbable and amusing.

One evening, after feeding the horses, Oaks closed up the barn. A nightly habit, he stopped by the office to check in with the stationmaster who was busy deciphering a dispatch, just in from headquarters.

The door struck the jamb with its familiar bang as Smith stepped into the small room. Without so much as lifting his eyes from the paper, the stationmaster exclaimed to Oaks, "Dang rail line's growin' like crazy!"

The stationmaster, spitting his tobacco juice expertly into the urn near his desk, continued, "I got my hands full already, and here they are planning new rail lines to the north now, and every two years followin'!" He threw down the paper exasperated, and stretching his long frame, got up to stand at the window.

Oaks, attentive, sensing weakness. His predatory instincts took over. The frustrated stationmaster continued, "We barely get one station operational, when right away the next one is suppose' to start up! How do they think all that work's gonna git done? Dammit! And I ain't been home t' supper in a month o' Sundays. Wife's beginning to fergit what I look like!"

Smith listened, and knew this was his moment. Avoiding eye contact, he turned slowly so that they stood next to one another. Shoulder to shoulder they gazed silently out of the same window.

"Mebbe you kin take some time away with the wife before construction starts on the new line," suggested Smith. "Take yerself some time off...." He let his voice trail off casually, gently.

The stationmaster then turned toward Oaks, taking stock of his newest employee. Smith returned the scrutiny with an expression of confidence and ease.

Then like an old friend, he suggested, "Jes' sign the work schedule fer me; you know I can handle everythin' here. What's broke, I can fix. The horses are fine. And the men r' reliable."

"Mebbe I will take some time. Mebbe I'll do just that..." the stationmaster replied.

6

Andrew's woodworking shop door stood open for some relief from the heat of the day. He worked in the half-light and the humid air, sweat mingling with the sawdust and shavings, putting finishing touches on the dresser he was to deliver by noon.

His mind was on his brother, wondering where he was. He has been keeping long hours with his boss's time off. And he did not come in at his usual hour last night. Though no bother, Andrew became used to hearing the creak of the stairs when his brother arrived home. He knew from the past that changes in habits at home usually meant bigger changes ahead for Smith Oaks.

I'll go into town to see him when I'm done here, thought Andrew. I'll have nice bit o' change here for this dresser. Mebbe we could get some supper together tonight, he thought. Catch up on things.

Andrew rode into town later that day to see quite a bit of a crowd gathered on the street near the car barn where Smith worked. Onlookers curious, in the street milling about, necks craned to see. Maybe an accident. Human nature sure loves misery, thought Andrew. Then, remembering his brother's prior accident at the forge, his heartbeat quickened with concern.

He tied up his horse, dismounted, and ran across the dusty street, pushing his way through the men, sweaty and rough, only to see a semicircle break in the crowd, distance given, respect for the police who were busily interviewing the employees of the rail line.

"What's going on here?" Andrew asked a fellow onlooker, his eyes anxiously searching the crowd for Smith.

"Robbery," the man replied. "Earlier today. Office door locked on the outside. When they broke it in, there's the safe wide open, cash box cleaned out."

"Any clues?"

"Don't know yet. Searchin' for the new man. He's the only one of the crew missing."

7

Barrier Beach: *Fire Island, NY*
1841

Smith Oaks made his way from Brooklyn further east onto Long Island, a narrow strip of land no more than 120 miles long and 50 miles at its widest point. There, natural beauty featured forests and hills and high rocky cliffs on its north shore, and opposite, long, flat sandy beaches on the south. A series of barrier beaches separated the main island from the Atlantic Ocean on the south shore, with a shallow, pleasant bay between. Oaks settled on one of those slim, desolate barrier islands called Fire Island.

His days were spent ocean fishing. Blues and bass abundant, nearly bounding into his boat as if in some mystical spirit of cooperation. The bay behind offered no end to shellfish; oysters and clams in beds patiently waiting; and overhead flocks of mallard, merganser and canvasbacks flew and landed in the marshes on the bay side. And, above it all, the osprey, falcons, and hawks dipped and swept and hunted, while the gulls and terns ruled the sandy shores on the Atlantic side.

Pure and pristine was the sand that captured currents careening in from distant shores, places exotic and wild, across the miles to him, it seemed, just for his pleasure.

It was a land of plenty, an island on which he felt a rough, natural happiness that he had never known before. He built a shack on the beach, and lived.

8

Patchogue, NY

When Smith Oaks needed supplies that he could not catch, hunt for or make himself, he would sail across the bay to the bustling shore town of Patchogue. Here, the town buzzed with activity. Industrious hands made the most of the natural resources available to provide for themselves, and for the building boom going on in New York City.

Just sixty miles west, its harbor swelled with new commerce since the opening of the Erie Canal; ships filled with bounty from the Midwest now had ready access via the Hudson River out to the sea and away to international ports. In turn, the offerings of the wide world became ready and available; ships returned from foreign lands to New York Harbor bursting with exotic goods easily sold in this growing country of the free and the brave.

So, despite its remoteness, the town prospered. Its location, between two rivers, provided ample power for industry: a mill for lumbering and one for paper, fed by the nearby forests; a grain mill just west that provided good flour from local farmers; another mill where wool was brought to be carded, spun and woven into cloth and blankets.

South of the village sat the bay, which supplied ample clams and mussels that were in demand for the city's restaurants and kitchens. All these products had easy transport, down rivers, out of the inlet westward awaited by the city's eager merchants.

And just as these goods all found their way to markets west, vacationers from the city traveled eastward to Patchogue via a railroad line whose recent expansion, like tentacles extending, reached further and further into the verdant countryside of Long Island.

In the summertime, the trains brought along those who wanted to get away from the crowds, the heat, the bustle and grime of the growing metropolis. The rail lines brought those who sought the wild shore; adventure seekers who fancied themselves hunters and fishermen. They came and supported a growing industry of hotels and inns bayside, the local innkeepers all too happy to accommodate and welcome visitors.

As always, Smith Oaks made the best of new opportunity. He spent some time in town to survey the possibilities. He made himself known when he came in for supplies. He took a moment with the local merchants who wanted to hear of his off-shore fishing exploits. He tipped his hat to the ladies, and escorted them across the dusty street when needed. He strolled about, acquainted now with local businessmen who were eager to refer their customers to him as an expert sportsman's guide.

*****

On this day, he brought his purchases to the front counter of the dry goods store, where the proprietor could always be found perched on a three-legged stool. The spot gave the owner a view out of the front window onto Main Street so he could keep track of all the comings and goings; and with just a quick turn of his head, he could also maintain a clear view of all his customers and merchandise in the store.

There, to the front counter, Oaks brought a new pair of pants and suspenders, five boxes of rifle ammunition, a pot of dry crackers and a sack of dried beans.

"Need some coffee along with that?" the proprietor asked him.

"Nope. Not t'day. Got plenty," replied Oaks. "But come t' think of it, I could use a couple o' your good cigars."

"Oh yeah?" came the casual remark as the owner selected two of his best from the humidor behind the counter. "Celebratin' some-thin', are ya?"

Oaks knew this man kept a mental catalogue about everyone who came into his store. Their purchases told him if they lived alone, or had family. If they have company staying with them and for how long. He knew if a baby was born or if someone died. He knew his customers' finances if they bought on credit or paid cash. If they bought in bulk or just what was needed for the day.

"Wa'al. Sort of," replied Oaks. "Guidin' business been pickin' up. Got me some satisfied customers this week."

"Yep. Season's comin' in now," he said as he made change for Oaks from the cash box. "You doin' good fer a newcomer, too. Folks comin' back from the island sayin' they git a good haul o' bass fishin' with ye."

"Yep. It was a good week," he replied. "An' pickin up two more t'day at Roe's, aimin' t' do some duck huntin' in the marshes."

"Good," replied the merchant. "Good business fer one is good fer all o' us."

He sized up his customer as he wrapped the purchases in paper and tied them with twine. His discerning eye missed nothing. Lean, rug-ged and tough was this area's newest sportsman's guide. Pale grey eyes, quick, that took in his surroundings. Straw colored hair, unkempt, but face clean-shaven. Clothes well worn but presentable. Frugal. An air of mystery, despite his outward friendliness. Seemed uncomfortable in his boots; everything about him for a purpose, he surmised. To make an impression, maybe. Calculating and careful with every word he spoke. He let out only what he wanted to be known, and always for a purpose.

"Need some help with the bundles?" he asked Oaks. "I got a boy t' carry."

"Not yet. But mebbe' ye can hold 'im here fer me while I go t' meet the stage over t' Roe's place."

"I'll send 'em with the boy to the town dock when yer' done."

"Thank ye. Thank ye kindly."

The proprietor watched Oaks out of his front window as he made his way down the dusty street near the busy four corners area to Roe's Hotel.

Oaks climbed the wooden steps of the town's busiest inn onto the friendly porch, replete with rockers for the guests. The screen door opened easily into a warm and friendly reception area, wide pine floorboards creaking as he stepped toward the front desk.

"Got some need for sportsmen's guide I hear?" he asked old Mr. Roe.

"Wa'al, if it ain't Smith! Been waitin' fer ya."

Oaks had to wait for his eyes to adjust to the dim interior before he could read the message proffered to him from across the wooden counter.

"Yep. These two fellers is return business. Had them out fishin' once before. Now they want to try the marshes fer some duck."

"That's what we like, young feller. Keep em' comin' back fer more," said Mr. Roe breaking into a wide grin.

Smith Oaks stepped outside to wait for his customers who would arrive in the coach from the railway station. He leaned against the hitching post next to a dozing pony, reins loosely looped over the rail.

Oaks mused about his good fortune to have landed in such a place. Such easy work had never come his way before. To simply take these slickers out for a good day duck hunting to his favorite spots, or out for a day's fishing where the water teemed with catch was a pleasure. Gregarious when needs be, he was a natural guide, putting the customers at ease, entertaining them with tall tales, detecting the desires of his customers, and surmising which of his secret spots would satisfy.

An expert outdoorsman, he was also quick of mind with a talent for reading people; he could ascertain his customer's skill level, tolerance for adventure and for danger. But most importantly, he understood what they desired most to take home with them: not fish or fowl, but bragging rights and tall tales of adventure. Oaks made sure his customers would have plenty of feats and escapades off shore and in the salt marshes. And he reveled in the fact that he was getting paid good cash for the things he did as naturally as breathing.

But standing there outside Roe's, he noticed how steady was the flow of visitors to the town's inns. Why shouln't I be makin' this money, he thought. I could have 'em stayin' at my place after a day's huntin' 'stead of sailin' em back here t' stay. Could have 'em with me fer days, then.

He knew then that instead of his sportsman's shack on the beach, he needed to build a proper house, and to have someone there to cook the catch and prepare the bedding. He knew then that what he needed was a wife.

9

The Barrier Beach
Fire Island 1842

Here, upon the bold and rugged Atlantic shore is where Hannah settled with Smith Oaks. Hannah now upon the high dune on the barrier island, the sea at her face, her back to the main island from whence she came. She lived upon that wild edge, where the fury of the sea first touches land.

Called the Great South Beach by the original European settlers, this desolate sand bar protected the main island from storm surges from the open ocean. In generations before, Native Americans would go there to fish, and, when the gods granted them a gift, to drag the occasional stranded whale ashore.

There, with bone-tipped spears, they would kill, and with their axes and razor sharp boat spades, harvest the beast. Blubber was stripped and taken, then boiled down for its precious oil. Meat was cut and distributed to the tribe. Bone and baleen were taken for their many uses to make tools and implements. Then, carefully, the tail and fins were removed for use of the shaman's great religious ritual of thanksgiving to Paumpagussit, the deity of the sea.

Elaborate ceremony and song welcomed the whale's spirit to thank it for giving itself to the people, reverence paid for its selfless sacrifice.

Connection between the earth and the spirit world reaffirmed, reassurance that man was being provided for by a great mysterious force. Tail and fins were carefully roasted and consumed as first offering, then all gifts from the land that the tribe had prepared. All sang songs of joy and danced in gratitude, for the sea, and its deity, provider. Here they lived with the forces of nature, the sea and land as source.

This simple strip of sand has faced the ravages of time, its shape formed and re-formed by storms and tidal surges. It has provided for the tribes that have come and gone, and was named and renamed by the the Dutch, then the English who brought their own customs, habits, languages and politics.

Despite which peoples came and went, the barrier island remained rugged and desolate: the sea immutable – there, ready for anyone with the nerve to live with nature's mighty force, at times either gentle and generous, or brutal and deadly.

10

Domination

So, on Fire Island, Hannah and Smith Oaks, newly married, made a home. Hannah, shy, did her best to please her husband. She knew how to keep a larder, but now had to make do with what small supplies they had on the barrier island. She tried to make a pleasant parlor with some things of her mother's from her childhood home. A teapot with pink flowers on it. Some lace curtains her mother had made when she was a bride. She brought from her farmhouse some worn cushioned chairs that had been embroidered with a floral wreath design all around the perimeter. And a wooden rocker that creaked, the arms and seat worn smooth by years of use, and a crocheted coverlet for the marriage bed that Hannah had made by her own hand.

Hannah tried to make a comfortable home for them both. She, open and innocent. But, over time, a dark foreboding overcame her, a feeling of wariness that she couldn't explain. Smith became to her a puzzle she could not solve. Over time, it seemed an invisible blanket descended upon Hannah's spirit. She, suffocating slowly, the feeling of his hand over her mouth.

Smith always seemed distant, unhappy. Was it she? Was it how she prepared the meals? Or how she kept the house? Or was he unhappy with her in the marital bed? She became worried that any word or gesture she made was causing his displeasure. She was made to feel off-balance, unsure of herself.

At supper, Smith Oaks would sit across the rough wooden table from Hannah. He'd stay in his work clothes, remaining unwashed from his day's labor. His lanky body hunched over the dish, he would eat his meal in one fell swoop, guarded, as if someone might try to take his food from him. His eyes, grey and indistinct, distant. A one word answer, or a blank stare would be the reply to her attempts to make conversation.

But Smith's moods were mercurial. There were some days he was buoyant and full of words.

Joyful at these upturns and hungry for company, she was first flattered with his confidentiality. Hannah would listen, attentive, hoping that this was a signal of his acceptance of her.

But any rejoinder she tried to make would be met with sudden anger. "Can't ya jes' *shut up* a minute, Hannah? *I'm* doin' the talkin'!" Hannah, taken aback. Then silence, or a gruff "nevermind," or "fergit it."

For speaking, she would be punished with his dark anger and silence. Fearful, she'd retreat, and heaviness would overcome the mood in the small house. Hannah chastised, as if she were a child, overstepping.

Over time, Hannah realized he used the ceaseless talk or the dark moodiness to control and dominate. By then, she sat nightly to endure either his manipulative silence, or his endless stories about himself and his day's encounters. She'd hear his versions of every incident of the day, featuring himself as hero of every story, the rescuer, or the leader of all worthy action.

His stories were stories of others, imagining endless competition in his mind with those around him. How others don't measure up to his high standards. Their sails poorly made; their boats not as swift; their houses not as strong; their workmanship shoddy; their materials poorly chosen; their skills not as sharp.

He featured himself as the undeserved victim of imagined wrong-doing. He'd report in detail the latest conjured-up insult he had to bear from a chance meeting, or from a store clerk across the bay, or from a fellow guide. He, the innocent victim of all wrongs from every walk of life, unfair treatment seemed to find its way him. And despite the frequency of his imagined victimizations, he'd never think to search his own part, that each story's end might have been inflamed by his own actions. No…he'd never question is own blamelessness.

Sometimes, she'd quietly attempt to raise the other's viewpoint. But that was, to him, an act of defiance. That required violence to control.

"That Selah Strong," Smith one day complained, "he watches all the comin's an' goin's on the island. He can't be trusted, I say. Jes' can't keep his nose out of anythin' happen' onshore."

"But, Smith, isn't that his job? I mean, as the lighthouse keeper…" Hannah once innocently remarked.

"Don' need no snoopin' round *here!*" Smith shouted suddenly, his fist banging the table, causing a clattering of dishes and glassware. Hannah jumped and started back. Breath caught in her throat, tears sprang to her eyes in surprise.

Her reaction betrayed her fear. Knowing he had her, he let his anger rise and shift against *her* now. "*Don'* need his knowin' any o' my business," he snapped, moving his face in close to hers, she felt his spittle hit her skin, his visage a grisly ugly snarl.

She, shocked, afraid; silent.

"An' don' need *you* tellin' none o' our business neither," he added with a grimace, afraid she'd confide in idle chatter to Susan, the lightkeeper's wife.

Or, another victim of his complaints, their nearest neighbor… "That Dominy ain't much of a sportsman's guide, neither. It's his lucky day if he kin bag a deer in one shot," he'd say, malice unbidden.

Felix Dominy was his closest competitor for business, so was under Smith's constant scrutiny. "I got me a six pointer last season. *He* ain't had one o' them in years. Usin' them old guns, he is. Can't sight worth a damn, anyways!"

"Of course you do very well," Hannah once tried to respond, "but Felix has experience, too. Anybody can have a bad season," she tried to point out.

Smith exploded then with deep personal insult. In one swift movement he rose, and toppled his chair backward to make great drama of the clatter. His strong hands suddenly shoved the table toward Hannah, pinning her against the wall.

He leaned toward her across the rough wood, and using his height, into her upturned face, his voice, shrill and pitched, "What kind o' wife *are* ye?" eyes flashing. "How come yer all'as takin' *their* side!" he, shouting accusation.

Trembling, intimidated, she shifted her head down, avoiding. "*Look* at me!" he shouted. "Don't you disrespect *me!*"

Her position, in the chair, trembling. She obediently looked up at him, tear filled eyes, childlike.

He rose to his full height, and with bitter indignation, flung his chair in a display of force, shattering her favorite memento, her mother's water pitcher.

Afterward, for days, a stony silence. A disgruntled seething anger, now directed against her. Emotional treachery. Mind games meant to demean and control.

Of course, he counted on Hannah's isolation for his tactics to work. He would intentionally clear out others who might befriend Hannah. Like the innkeeper's wife...

"And that Phebe Dominy. Thinks she's superior 'cause o' she's got the *big* inn on the island. Nosy interferin' woman if I ever seen 'un. Less I see o' her, the better. Don' want her comin' round here neither."

Her nearest friend, over two miles west, Hannah counted on Phebe for some conversation. Though she was only on the island in- season, her occasional visits were a soothing balm to Hannah.

But Smith's jealousy stained any visit of Phebe's for Hannah. She knew that when Phebe'd come round, there'd be hell to pay afterwards.

Smith would be taciturn, threatened by a stranger in his midst, wary, distrustful and silent.

Over time, Hannah gave up, to stay within, silent.

She learned that their marital relationship was never truthful or authentic. She came to realize that when he did talk, Smith always had purpose, hidden agendas that Hannah never fathomed, she, easy victim. He, ever suspicious, would ask a question he already knew the answer to just to test her truthfulness, or to ascertain her powers of awareness. No talk between them was ever uncontaminated with his distrust.

In all these ways, he trained Hannah away from herself and into fearful silence. Thus she became implicated, complicit in his doings. It is for him, her most important role, to be his quiet witness. A wife mastered, like a beast in the barn.

Now she, obedient, unsure and afraid.

*****

Hannah, alone on the barrier island, atop the dune, watches the sea.

Too late, Hannah realized that she was responsible for her own undoing. With this marriage, she had traded herself away for what she thought would be safety, security… and escape from her haunting past.

Instead, now she lives with daily dread. She would do anything not to confront him, whatever it took to avoid his anger, the unspoken threat of retaliation from Smith Oaks, if he thinks her disloyal to him.

Hannah's hand works the charcoal from the evening fire onto small scraps of paper, whatever is not needed. She contours and creates, shading so intricate, lines so fluid, with tools so crude.

A stick. A coal. Her fingers move without command. They see and create from her mind's eye. In these moments, her soul sings, speaking a freedom she knows not in daily life. Perhaps, perhaps she thinks, I can capture the wind.

These, her creations, seen by no one. Not worth keeping, she would think. What worth could my work possibly have? She burns the paper, adding to the ash for the next day's fire.

11

Oaks' Childhood Home
Western Virginia: 1831

Smith Oaks' wrists were cut open from the harness leather wrapped tight, dug in. He silently traced the blood streaming downward toward his elbow, crimson rivulets bright. It dripped silently onto the barn floor.

Then another crack: was it heard or felt first? This one hit hard, he, too exhausted to arch his back from the pain, Smith swung from the rafter like a dead deer, gutted.

"Ye ain't worth *nothin*," the shout delivered with the last lash. Josiah Oaks' spittle sprayed through the gaps in rotted teeth. He, panting from the effort of the beating, now dropped the whip onto the floor, worn wooden planks and dusty hay.

Smith Oaks hung there mute. He knew if he spoke, more pain would come. He knew if he just waited, Josiah would get tired and sit on a bale of hay and have a smoke.

His body revolved slowly from the rafter of the hayloft. He looked up and saw the late day's sun stream in through the roof cracks, dust particles swirling. He saw their movement, free and unbound. Glittering almost, like the stars.

Smith could hear Josiah beginning to move now below him. He'd caught his breath and reached for his tobacco pouch to roll a smoke.

He heard Old Josiah muttering to himself now, barely audible. He soothed himself with the story that Smith has heard told to him all his sixteen years of his life. As if any of it was his doing. As if he plagued this man with his presence on purpose.

"Yer Ma' *tricked* me. Married me pregnant a'ready. Where's yr *real* Daddy? Heh? *Heh?*" Josiah's gravely voice vibrated with the thick phlegm pooled deep in his throat. He hacked heavy and long, then spit out onto the floor.

Satisfied, he wiped the saliva from his mouth with the back of his hand, he went on, "Took'en off, he did. Yer Ma sez he's dead. Sez his name's John Smith. Ha! Made up name if I ever heard one. Made up story he's dead too. Took'en off he did, took'en off like a jackrabbit thet sees a hungry hunter."

Josiah was rested enough now to build up some steam. He looked up at the lad, raising his voice. "Thought she'd trick me int' raisin' ye. Give ye his name too. Ha! *Smith*! Heh?"

He took a moment to strike a match, then to inhale the smoke deeply. Now in a voice resonant with resentment, he continued, "Wa'al I'm raisin' ye alright. Ye got a roof over yourn head? Ye got food t' et? And still ye ain't worth a damn aroun' here. Lazy somm' bitch ye are. Chores is chores. Ye better *earn* yer *keep!*"

Josiah arose now and stood, squinting up at Smith. Tobacco smoke curled upward and reached Smith's nose. The smell half revived him. Smith knew to say still and silent. The boy at sixteen was tall, lanky, and strong. Survived by his wits in this atmosphere of violence and hatred for as long as he could remember.

Josiah bent to pick up the whip. He used the butt end to poke the boy's body into swinging around so he could survey the damage he inflicted on the boy's back. The harness leather twisted into Smith's wrists cutting deeper. Smith bit his lips shut so as not to utter a sound.

Josiah peered at the wounds. Satisfied with the blood and welts, he turned on his heel and stomped off toward the daylight, leaving him.

Smith knew that someone would come to cut him down. He knew to wait in silence.

*****

"Wuz 'e drunk when he did it this time?" young Andrew asked Smith after he sliced the harness leather that held his brother to the rafter. He stood aside as Smith, exhausted, toppled onto the wooden planks.

He lay still, breathing hard. Then he made his way to a bale of hay to sit and gather his wits. He took a moment to answer.

"Ain't no difference," replied Smith finally. "He don' have t' be drunk to be mean."

Andrew, junior by two years, now sat behind him on the bale so he could swab some vitriol on his brother's wounds.

"Whad ya do this time?" he asked.

"Nothin'. He don't need no real reason."

Andrew hesitated a moment, then said, "He told Ma you were stealin' ag'in. You were caught by the sheriff."

"Yeh. What of it? *He* steals alla time. Don't nobody beat *him* fer it."

"Yeah, but sheriff sez next time yr goin' t' jail."

"So that's why the beatin'! He ain't gonna have me t' do his chores if I'm in jail."

"He sez yr no good anyways."

"He sez alotta things, Andy. "He sez he feeds us. But we only git meat when I got time fer huntin.' And there's only soup fer us 'caus Ma works 'er garden patch."

Andrew continued to work carefully on his brother's back, peeling away the strips of shirt that had become embedded in the wounds. Then he cleaned the open flesh carefully, each stripe of the whip, one by one.

Smith winced with the pain. His mind now clearing, and the throbbing in his shoulders began to ease.

"He sez I got a roof over m' head. Look, it ain't no more 'n a one-room shack that leaks in rain. He continued, his pain now turning to anger. "An' this here," Smith looked up at the rafter from which he'd hung, "ain't no right barn neither, it's nothin' more n' a shed."

"Ow! Damn! Stop it now!" complained Smith. The vitriol stung the raw wounds. "That's enough doctorin' from ye."

"But yer still bleedin' in places."

"Don' care. That's *enough*!" Smith twisted painfully now to face his brother.

"Look Andy. You belong here. Y'r his own. I ain't his an he nev'r lets me fergit it. This ain't no place fer me."

Smith patiently endured Andrew's help to put on the fresh shirt his brother brought him.

He attempted to stand now, but blackness nearly overcame him. Andrew then saw Smith's hair matted with blood from the open bruise on the back of his head, where Josiah took him down from behind, probably with a shovel. Surprise attack, no doubt. It's the only way he could have gotten Smith tied up.

Andrew handed him some strips of material from the shirt shredded by the lash to wrap a bandage around his head.

Smith used them, then said, "These mountains 'closin' me in any-ways. I aim t' follow the river. I'm gettin' outta here." He then ripped into the last of the shredded shirt to bandage his torn wrists. He, still unsteady, but now ready, arose from the bale.

"No! Don't go!" Andrew's voice shook with desperation.

Smith looked down on Andrew only mildly surprised at the boy's reaction.

"I got t' leave here, Andy. Next time he'll beat me t' death, he will."

Andrew looked astonished. He never considered that Smith could leave. That anyone would have the power to change things around here. In his young mind, all things were permanent. His mother's helplessness; his father's rage, his older half-brother on whom the rage was afflicted.

"Whre'll ye go?" Andrew asked.

"Anyplace. Anyplace's bettern' here. He looked at Andrew, hatred for Josiah still glaring in his eyes.

Smith pointed out toward the last of the sun's rays. "Goin' north. North and west, I reckon. Got to be somthin' out there more'n this. We hungry here anyways. Gotta' be somthin' better'n this."

He looked at Andrew. Young, fair, blue eyed. He knew it was Andrew that told on him. That he could trust Andrew no more than he could a trapped snake. But Smith needed to be cut down from the rafter, and he needed a shirt, and Andrew delivered both out of guilt.

Smith knew it wasn't really Andrew's fault. He lives in terror of the day that these beatings will fall upon him. Slight and often sickly, he'd never survive Josiah's wrath.

Josiah will know who cut Smith down. And he'll grill Andrew, close in to his young face with that foul breath and threatening eyes. He'll trap him and terrify him, and in fear for his life, all that Smith said to him will be delivered to Josiah.

Smith knew it was time for him to leave. He picked up his knife and hunting rifle, saying to Andrew, "Ya know *he's* the one who's worthless. Either drunk or sleepin' it off. Ye kin tell 'im that fer me."

He turned, and with nothing more to say, Smith made his way, through the rough mountainous country where he was born, sticking to the narrow valley of the River Kanawha, a river much like himself; a river that flows wrong. That leaves the mountains northward, on its own path, to unexpected places.

12

Fire Island

In this marriage, Smith and Hannah brought a daughter into this world. She was named Marietta, Hannah's best concern and companion. Marietta, a willing and loving girl, so innocent and fair.

From the moment of her birth, however, Smith was disappointed that Hannah had given him a girl child. He averted his eyes from Hannah's when she held the child, newly born. He stayed only a moment in the room.

"Son's what I need, Hannah. What goods' this 'un gonna do me here?" he said when he saw his girl born.

Time was his testament. He stood by his word. Smith had never held or embraced the child. Nary a glance did he give her while Marietta was in her infancy.

Marietta had been born in July. She came prematurely, so no preparations were made ready for Hannah in her home.

The pains started, severe. Hannah cried out as her water broke. "Smith! It's happening!" She clutched her swollen belly, and staggered. He grabbed her roughly about her waist and helped her to their bed.

She moaned, then cried out in pain. Smith panicked. He had never seen a baby born before and knew not what to do.

"Phebe!" cried Hannah. "Go get Phebe!"

Smith ran all the way to the inn, leaving Hannah alone.

It was Phebe who comforted Hannah in her pain. It was Phebe who guided the baby into this world. It was Phebe who helped Hannah to learn how to nurse and care for the child. It was Phebe who comforted Hannah in her tears.

"What am I to do?" she wept, holding Marietta in her arms. It was weeks since the birth, and Smith barely looked in on Hannah. "He doesn't want her." The new mother, distraught, gazed through tears at her sleeping infant.

"What will you *do*?" Phebe answered in disbelief. She repeated her words for emphasis. "What will you *do*?" She busied herself straightening out the coverlet on the bed unsure what to say, gathering her thoughts. She knew there was trouble here, but wanted to calm poor Hannah, a young innocent in a loveless, puzzling marriage. She paused a moment to look at her young friend, hair disheveled and unkempt. Eyes swollen from tears and sleeplessness. Skin sallow, face bony and thin.

At length and with calm, she answered, "You will take care of yourself so that you can take care of your child. You will be her *mother*. You will care for her and protect her. And you will thank God for the birth of this beautiful healthy baby," answered Phebe. Then she added, "And you will be patient. Smith might just come around when she's a bit older."

Hannah heard her friend's motherly advice, then continued, "I knew it would be an adjustment… to be married and all. But I never expected this."

"Never expected what?" she asked. Marietta stirred. Phebe took the infant from Hannah and held her close.

Hannah sounded desperate. "I never expected a man like this. He scares me. There is a side to him that I cannot fathom."

"Many men are like that," Phebe responded, trying to sooth her.

"You don't understand," pleaded Hannah. "You can't possibly. Phebe, he is not the man everyone sees about town, so friendly-like." Hannah spoke sadly and slowly, as if a great exhaustion hampered her speech.

"It's like he just endures me. As if I don't belong here. Why did he ask for my hand if he does not want me?"

*****

The seasons passed, and as Marietta grew, limbs lanky and long, she scampered upon the beach, or happily helped Hannah with chores, or intensely concentrating, learned to stitch. She was Hannah's delight, her reason for joy and her source of love. Yet Smith's only reaction to the child would be an occasional grunt, or a look. His only words to his daughter were to give orders for a task that must be done.

Marietta learned to be wary around him. As far as the child was concerned, this man was a stranger who lived among them, entering the house most evenings, blustery and hungry, smelling of the day's activity; fish or gunpowder. Mostly moody and hungry, the source of chronic anger in the house. On those days, Marietta and Hannah were silent in their every move. His darkness permeated the very walls. He would eat sloppily and voraciously, pleased that he dominated them with his seething disposition.

Mother and daughter spent those evenings in fear of an explosion at an errant look or accidental gesture. Then what relief for them when he fell into an exhausted sleep by the fire, the day's labor his master.

Or other times, he'd arrive home ranting, accusing and blaming others of some infraction. And, as if no one were in the room with him, he asked and answered his own questions. Referring to himself in his stories by his own name, as if he were a character in a narration. On those days, Marietta looked at him with wonder, Hannah averted her eyes and went about household business in silence.

Uneasy was the atmosphere of the house on the lonely shore. With the passing of time, Hannah had learned Smith Oaks' true nature too late. Unknowable, dangerous and dark was the man she married.

*****

Hannah now isolated on the barrier beach, no guests during winter to lighten the daily feeling of dread. In winter, the loneliness spoke loudest to her.

Her only opportunity in those months to express herself was in her sketches. In them, she tried to capture the wind that howled in the day and in the night, that shook the house and made its way into its small cracks, no room secure and warm. The beach grasses on the dunes, lonely witness, bent forever inland by the force of the wind relentless, looking as if a heavy burden weighed them down. The swoop of the fervent gulls, whose strong wings patient rode the air currents, then in a momentary lee, took control of their direction, and dip, or career sidewise, carving their way through the element fierce. Sand, blown into hills gathered, then scattered by the next stronger gusts fierce, or swept out to sea by currents controlling the shape of the coast.

How can I capture it, the power of all I see here? The wind unceasing. A force invisible, except by what it builds or destroys.

13

Fire Island
The Wreck of *THE LOUISA: 1844*

Captain Michael Baker was feeling the years bespoken by the white hairs in his beard. Waiting for hours on the *Louisa*, stranded on a sandbar off Fire Island on a cold February day for high tide to free her, had not done the aches in his bones any good.

Wearily, he sat now on the rail coach swaying noisily through the flat lands of Long Island toward the west on his way to Atlantic Dock in New York to report the salvage of his vessel to the Maritime Marine Office. They must have a full accounting for what was saved and what was lost, the report to be transmitted to the investors and their insurers.

He watched the landscape out of the window absently, still a bit benumbed. He reviewed in his mind the events of the grounding. The freak storm, appearing out of nowhere. No time to outrun her, too close to shore to tack away, the violent wind and tide slammed the ship onto a sandbar just east of the Fire Island light.

The *Louisa*, he mused, a good ship. She had always been strong enough under pressure of time and tide. And this, my last voyage. What a way to go out! This was supposed to be a simple run... Just unload her, pick up my final paycheck, and settle in with the cousins who live here in

New York. But I should have known, there are no simple runs… Never expected my career to end this way, though, making a salvage report.

Ah, well…could have ended much worse, he realized. She held together, she did. And very little of the cargo ended up in the drink.

Well, at least the surfboat made it out from the rescue hut as soon as the seas settled enough, and made quick work of bringing in the crew and the cargo. She held together well, and after all, the gale was abating by the time of the grounding. That, at least, was a piece of good luck. Lucky for us all. Especially me. 'Cause this time I brought all my worth, the best of the treasures from all those years sailin' the seas. Cashed in, they'll set me up in my new life here. He thought of the kind of home he'd buy, near his cousins in Brooklyn. That near his family he'd no longer lead such a lonely life.

Captain Baker shifted his gaze now away from the passing land-scape. He closed his eyes wearily. His life as sea captain put him at the mercy of the elements, weather, wind and tides; he was used to that. But now, he thought, all those years of living by instinct, responsible for ship, crew and cargo… all those years culminated now in nothing more than a sheaf of papers, scrawls of signatures, and inked rubber stamps.

*****

Next morning, Captain Baker returned to the wreck site. "Who's in charge here?" he asked one of his crew whom he saw sitting idle.

"Man called Dominy, Sir," came the reply as the seaman awkwardly rose. "Agent of the underwriters, Sir."

"Wa'al…" he drawled, ignoring the seaman's discomfort. Baker's eyes scanned the beach. "Where is he now?"

"Don' know, Sir. Ain't seen 'im since early this morning. Was talkin' with the lightkeeper 'bout the list o' wreckers who helped with the salvage. Seems some trunks gone missin.'"

"Drat!" Captain Baker scowled. "Can't turn my back for a second!" He thought of the revisions that would have to be made to the salvage inventory he just signed in New York. "Land pirates, ya' think? Everything was covered overnight, wasn't it?"

"Yes, Sir! And a guard put to the night watch, too. I relieved 'em early this mornin'. Two locals, names o' Benaja Wood an' Daniel Jones. Seemed friendly 'nough t' me. Odd jobbers from the big town onshore. Both gone back to the main island a'ready."

"Yeah. Lot o' good that. Puttin' locals on to guard cargo! These guys make a livin' o' stealin' salvage from wrecks. No more n' pirates on dry land, they are."

Captain Baker felt drained. Haven't there been enough mishaps that will need explaining? He added, "Damn fools! Puttin' their own on overnight watch? Ha! They're all in cahoots with each other anyways."

His eyes scanned the piles of trunks and boxes, stacked in the make-shift salvage tent. Most in good condition, he thought, some stove in, contents destroyed. To the innermost of the rows of cargo he made his way, for before he left the beach for the city, he dug a hole and buried his personal trunk wrapped in a canvas, then covered it with crates of cargo marked COAL, stashing his worldly goods away from all eyes to see.

Captain Baker's frown transformed into a scowl as he approached the hiding spot, for he could see boxes and trunks had been moved and replaced sloppily. He quickly began clearing the area. The strength in his arms redoubled as his suspicions mounted, fearing the worst.

Standing now, panting from exertion, he searched the area for what he knew should have been there. Then his eyes beheld, where his trunk had been buried, the canvas he'd carefully laid over it was tossed carelessly, covering now only a sandy, empty hole.

*****

Soon after the Captain's trunk was reported missing, Smith Oaks approached his house nearing dusk, and noticed large sandy footprints left on the path. Immediately suspicious, he snarled under his breath, "Who all'd be here? At *this* hour?" His eyes narrowed, and shifted from left to right, scanning his property, alert to the potential danger of intruders. He readied his rifle in one hand, the other hand on the door handle.

He flung the door to the little house wide open. The sudden cold gust of wind caused the crashing of the wooden door inward to the small parlor.

His eyes beheld the U.S. Marshal and two of his men seated with Hannah in the warm glow of the fireside. He stood, the cool of the evening air dropping the temperature in the room. Instantly, he raised his rifle to ready position, trained on them, trigger finger poised.

Shocked, the little group turned in his direction, and all eyes focused on the barrel of Smith's gun.

The Marshal recovered first, and addressed him.

"Mr. Oaks," he said with forced calm, "We have a warrant writ out…"

"I don' care *what* warrant ye have! Or if Jesus *hisself* writ it." Oaks voice, steady, throaty and low commanded the room. "Ye ain't comin' here int' *my* house!"

Smith, positioned in the doorway, rifle steady in hand, pointed menacingly toward the Marshal and his men. He stood, mostly in silhouette, the sun's waning rays behind; the shadows helped his lanky frame to seem to fill the doorway.

"Sir, put down that gun!" The Marshal spoke with cool authority. "Mrs. Oaks here graciously invited us in with our inquiry."

Hannah sat in the small parlor, paralyzed with fear. "These m-men came to ask some questions," she stammered to her furious husband.

Hannah knew the room was filled with danger. She recognized the change in Oaks' face. The hardening of the jaw, the set of the lips, the coldness in the eye. He felt the rush of adrenaline from confrontations past, retaliation, a gush of blood, his enemy's head reeling backward from the force of his fist, or the figure stunned still with his bullet's true aim. Hannah knew and took this all in instantly, leaning forward to rise and speak, hoping to diffuse his impetuous anger.

But, just at that moment, a sound from the left, a shuffle of small feet, a sniff of a runny nose. Marietta appeared from the bedroom, wakened by the voices. She came out slowly toward the parlor, her favorite blanket dragging, sleep still in her eyes, unaware of any danger.

Hannah's blood froze. She thought, I must, *I must* protect Marietta.

"Stay, Marietta," crooned Hannah with forced calm. Hannah sat back slowly, keeping her seat. She strained to keep the fear out of her voice, cajoling the child. "Papa has to talk to these men. You go back to your bed now."

Marietta looked at the gathering, not really registering the scene. She stopped, still stupefied with sleep. She could just as easily take a step forward into the parlor, as she could turn away, thought Hannah, as she watched helplessly.

The Marshal did not take his eyes off Smith, and repeated his directive. "Gun down now, Mr. Oaks. No need to frighten the child."

"Ye can't come in *here,* in *mine own* house an' tell *me* what to do with *mine own kin,*" he sneered. Then, the rifle still leveled, eye squinted into the sight, he ever so slowly twisted his trunk toward the sleepy child so that the rifle now was pointed at her.

"No!" shouted Hannah, rising instantly from her chair toward her husband. Then she stood, feet frozen to the floor, arm outstretched, beseeching.

The men, too, started forward in their chairs, then stopped motionless, afraid to breathe, their jaws dropped, mouths agape, eyes wide with terror. All in the parlor frozen in an eerie tableau vivant.

Marietta, innocent toddler, still blind with sleep, now turned slowly away, nothing of interest to her among a group of adults in the parlor. As if in a dream, wordlessly, she hesitated, then shuffled slowly back to her bed, not ever aware of peril.

Smith Oaks saw the relief on the faces of his wife and the men. His grey eyes sparkled in glee, and his cracked lips pulled back showing tobacco stained teeth as he cackled a gruesome laugh.

He reveled in the fear that he'd caused. He relished the terror in his wife's eyes and savored the tension of the Marshal and his men. He delighted in his power over them.

Dominance established, he knew then there would be no inquiry here.

*****

Hannah, guileless, not a half-hour before, had let these men in. An inquiry, they'd said. There's nothing to hide here, she'd said. How can I help? she asked.

She realized now that she should have turned the Marshal away. That Oaks fortifies against others; the very island his own territory. So Hannah was surprised that he took up with Dominy's inquiry to help organize the cargo on the *Louisa* wreck site. But he knew opportunity when he saw it. This *Louisa* incident was filled with possibility.

"A day's work in slow season."

"No sportsmen's guides needed in February," Oaks agreed. "I'll oblige."

Hannah had been pleased that he took up with the salvage effort. Maybe he's changing, she thought.

She should have known better.

*****

Heaviness, palpable in the small parlor, like the atmospheric change in the aftermath of a vast explosion. Smith stood his ground maintaining a stony silent stare, rifle now trained back on the men.

Hannah still stood, not a muscle moved since Marietta left. Dumbstruck, she watched her husband's eyes for a sign of what he might do.

Finally the Marshal cleared his throat, trying to regain some authority. He still had his duty to perform.

Addressing Oaks, he said, "Been some trouble over at the *Louisa*. I hear you were there workin' for the underwriter haulin' cargo."

Oaks offered no reply.

"Trunk's gone missin'," the Marshal continued, determined. "One marked *Captain Michael Baker*."

Now Oaks' head inclined slightly deeper into the rifle's sight. "Git outta my house," came the low husky growl. He then moved his body slightly sidewise of the doorjamb, leaving a narrow exit path.

The men looked at the Marshal. All in a heated standoff now.

Then slowly, deliberately, Oaks' finger pulled the hammer from half cock to full, ready to fire. That slight movement and steady aim, his only reply. Smith squinted into the sight in anticipation. He stood firm.

The Marshal hesitated, then sighed a deep sigh. He yielded, conceding defeat. He took his hat from his lap, turning toward his men, "Let's go. Nothin' here for us to see."

Then rising from his seat, his eyes on Smith, he slowly and deliberately made his way toward the door, saying, "Mrs. Oaks, a good evening to ye," with staged politeness.

Oaks remained in the open doorway, the rifle now lowered, barrel supported in one hand, butt of the gun on the floor next to his leg. He said nothing, not moving to make way, causing the men to shuffle awkwardly out of the house sidewise, heads lowered, sheepishly making their way down the front path, and through the garden gate.

Then Smith turned to his wife, a deep silent glare. She could see now his pants legs were wet at the bottoms, dune grass and sand caked to them and to his boots, traces of where he'd been. His eyes fixed her, the wordless threat understood between them, and then he retreated into the evening.

Like a good guard dog, he checked his property. He patrolled outside, sniffing and scouring, until satisfied, sure his perimeter was secure.

PART II

14

Massachusetts 1810 to Rome 1848
Margaret Fuller

Across the sea, a woman, far from her native land, stood upon Monte Pincio above the bustling, tumultuous city of Rome. This verdant setting provided some respite, a quiet place for her to reflect and to think. Not long ago, it had been her place of joy – of her romance with her beloved Giovanni- a peaceful spot away from the noise and crowds of the city where they felt free. Here they could picnic, stroll the gardens, inhale the clean air - and love, feel and be, and plan their times ahead.

But, oh, in such a short time, how their lives have changed! Now they face forced separation, loneliness, uncertainty. Their world breaking apart before their eyes. A time of political upheaval in all of Europe. Unrest, protest, bloody revolution. The people's desire for representation in government rule, to break the control of the monarchies. And here in Italy, that sentiment developed into a war of national liberation.

On this afternoon, Margaret took some time for contemplation. Here, thoughts of her life flew by her in fragments, like scenes from chapters in a long book that lay open, exposed to the wind, pages ruffling, her past streaming before her mind's eye. She recalled her life in Boston, then New York, the long ocean voyage that took her on her

European journey... England, Ireland, France, all leading to this place, this moment, in Rome.

All now seemed an inevitable trajectory that led her here, and to this place in the time of the Italian Revolution, where danger, treachery, and the stink of death became her daily life.

Fitting, though, in a way, thought Margaret, as she recalled the course of difficulties in her life, starting with her earliest memories. There remained for her the puzzle of her New England youth and severe upbringing, her stern father's demands that somehow still shaped her, haunting even her quietest moments. The feelings of those years had become encapsulated; preserved. Her current accomplishments and her fame notwithstanding, those early experiences left an empty space in her emotional world; a void that she could not name.

And now, her world at war, the very earth seems to move under her feet, current uncertainty reawakens fears and uncertainties of the past; her memories reemerge in her dreams, otherwise contained and buried.

On Monte Pincio, still shaken by last night's dream, her formative narrative unearthed, and recalled in child-like cadence her early understanding of her world:

I love Father more than anything, so to please him, I learn and learn. No matter how hard it is, no matter if the sun is shining outside and I want to play in the creek.

"No, Margaret, you may not play," says Father; "you must finish your lessons."

"Yes, Father."

I must obey. I have no time for skipping rope or playing house, either.

At bedtime, the headaches come, starting in my eyes, and then moving around to the top of my head. It feels like the top of a tent with the pole sticking out. I wish it would just blow off in the wind so I could just sleep. I am always tired.

There is so much to learn about. There are such important stories that I have to read. They were told by people who lived long, long ago who lived in a different land. There were monsters that tore people limb from limb. There were kings who killed princesses, and killed babies. There were terrible plagues and much suffering.

Sometimes, people had to go down into hell and see all the suffering, then come back up to earth because they learned a lesson. They were privileged to have learned so much, and they were obliged to tell all the people so they would learn too. What they saw in hell was most horrible tortures that had to be endured for eternity. People must be warned.

"These are the epic stories upon which empires were built."

"Yes, Father."

"They must be read in their original language to be understood."

"I will, Father."

So I have to learn the languages, then memorize the stories, which isn't hard to do because they are my dreams at night. I could see all the blood, and entrails, and hear the screams in my dreams. I dream of trees that drip blood.

Sometimes I would see the other girls at church on Sundays. I remembered who they were even though they stopped calling for me to go play with them. Now when they see me, they don't smile at me with their eyes, but instead just turn sidewise and start to talk among themselves. I wonder what they are talking about.

I talk mostly to grownups. When people come to my house for supper, sometimes I am asked to sit at table with them.

Father would call attention to me, then ask, "Margaret, please tell our guests about Dante's Inferno."

I would recite in Italian. The grown ups would listen with surprised looks. Then I would see that this made Father proud. He would ask for a kiss on his check, then send me to bed, after I curtsey to the guests at the table.

Then, as I grew older, Mother began to feel sorry for me, but I don't know why. I liked my home and my library. I was not lonely with all those books to read. And now there were other studies, too...mathematics and the sciences.

But I heard Mother say to Father that I should be with other girls my own age. That being so solitary was not good for me.

I was growing older.

Mother indicated that now, as a young lady, I should begin to think of having a beau, and that when guests come to our home, I should dress properly and remain in the parlor. That I should talk and play the piano when asked.

Mother helped me to learn about how to talk about the fine weather, and other things of no consequence. She helped me to learn that not everyone wanted to hear about Plato and Virgil and Dante in everyday conversation.

Of course, I complied.

Then, I began to listen to the discussions that the adults had. About the mistreatment of slaves in the South. About the tremendous growth of the cities and industries. About the railroads and the increased transportation. About the terrible conditions in jails for the criminals, some of whom were insane and could not help themselves.

These were interesting topics to hear about; and they made me think of many of the philosophers I had read, who also pondered similar topics. What is a man? What is our duty toward one another? What is the role of governance? What will this country say about itself in the laws it passes?

I began to read and think about the condition of mankind, and of our civic duties in earnest. This country is growing, and new laws are being passed every day. How do we know these are the best laws? How do we shape the way others are thought of, and treated? It is imperative to get this right.

I began to write essays on such topics of importance. Many of Father's friends liked them, and allowed them to be printed in newspapers and pamphlets so others could think about these topics.

I knew then that Father was pleased.

And he *was* pleased, Margaret knew now, proud of his work, his life's accomplishment through the reputation of his daughter, considered among Boston's intellectual elite with her writings and lectures. But even so, Margaret was looking for more. She had a yearning to step away from the world she knew, to a new place of life and growth. She felt hampered there in Boston, and dreamed of creating an identity of her own.

Margaret was ready for opportunity when it arose. She took a leap of faith and moved from Boston with a job offer to write for an up-and-coming newspaper in New York City. Her world expanded in this city of frenetic growth, so different from proper, formal, established and stuffy New England.

Margaret's fame grew across the nation with the acclaim of her latest book, *Woman in the 19th Century,* that attention now fortified as literary and social critic in her front page newspaper column.

And through her editor, Margaret became part of a new social circle. She welcomed new friendships, especially that of like-minded liberal thinkers Rebecca and Marcus Spring, who were active in the causes of abolition and feminism.

She became a frequent guest in their home. And with their friendship came an invitation to travel with them to Europe, an opportunity never before available to her.

In August of 1846, Margaret sailed with the Springs from New York with an advance from her editor to act as an international correspondent on her travels through Europe, to be published as a first page column.

She eagerly embraced all these developments, the opening of the new life she had wished for. The beginning of a new Margaret Fuller.

15

Rome, Italy
March 1847

Her arrival in Rome was on a brilliant day of wide blue skies. The sun shone brightly into her rooms, long white muslin drapes pushed aside by the breeze let in from the large windows overlooking the piazza. Rebecca watched her with curiosity while Margaret deliberately stood still a moment to breathe in the air from her open window. She wanted to inhale the feeling of Rome, its people and their passions, their everyday zeal for life.

She felt alive here in Italy. She felt the movement and color below her windows, the vibrant shouts, expression spirited and unrestrained. She compared this to the life she had known in Boston. These feel like my people, she mused privately... more akin to me than those stiff New Englanders of my childhood ...

Rebecca waited patiently, watching Margaret deep in her thoughts, taking in her new surroundings. Finally, she pierced the quiet of the room, asking, "Margaret, dear, what has you so enchanted that you stare in silence out of the window so?"

The reverie broken, Margaret turned toward her friend, and including her in her thoughts with a gesture toward the piazza, replied, "Notice here, Rebecca, in with the clear breeze floats the voices of the shopkeepers selling their wares to the women; and the laughter and squabbling of the children ringing rhythmically in their musical language. It is so unlike our American English," she observed. "Its fluidity, even its structure, denotes the culture of Italy. The very sound of the language is a song."

"Oh my! You have become such a romantic on this trip!" exclaimed Rebecca.

"Whatever do you mean?" Margaret asked.

"Of course, my dear one, you *do* know that your New England practicality was given an airing when you moved to New York. But here, even more, you seem free as a bird!"

"I could see why you would think that," replied Margaret. "But as for New England, you know I had been ready to leave for quite some time. I felt so stymied there. Then, when along came the offer to write for the *Tribune,* I was ready!" Margaret's eyes sparkled with the memory. "All in one blow I left stale, stuffy Boston for a growing, exciting metropolis. And instantly, my readership increased with the newspaper's national audience!"

"Yes, all that *is* true," replied Rebecca, "But don't forget the most important part; New York is where *we* became friends!"

They smiled at each other, appreciating their friendship.

"Now it is time we get started," said Rebecca, gesturing toward Margaret's traveling trunks all piled into one corner of the room. "It will take us some time to get you unpacked and settled in."

But before they started, Margaret added thoughtfully, "Rebecca, my friendship with you and Marcus is one of my greatest treasures. And your invitation to travel here with your family was a dream come true for me. Because of family obligations, I was never afforded the opportunity for European travel before. And now to visit England, France, Germany, Italy…to experience the genius of the European cultures I have studied all my life!"

And even more important, was the timing of this journey. Back in New York, Margaret's newspaper office was downtown, not far from the bustling harbor. Margaret would walk to the piers to watch the ships come in, the new immigrants disembark, some with their trunks and bags, some with only what they had in a rucksack. She heard them in the streets, in the cafés where she sat to hear their stories of life in their native lands.

She heard first-hand their accounts of personal hardship, of political unrest spreading throughout Europe, capital cities awash in protests, demonstrations, and uprisings against their aristocratic rulers. The people of Europe discontent, knowing of the freedoms that America had achieved, and now they, too, wanted a say in their governments.

Now, with this opportunity for travel, Margaret could be on the precipice of a great movement for political change. A change she was ready to witness and to report on for her readers back home. And, Margaret was ready to experience life as she had never known it before. Her own journey of personal growth awaited, and she welcomed that with an open heart.

"Rebecca," said Margaret a bit formally, "thank you for asking me to come with you. I would have never been able to travel like this without you and your family!"

Margaret embraced her friend. Rebecca responded in kind.

She added, "Well, Marcus certainly is *thrilled* you are with us! You have added a great deal of excitement to our journey with your letters of introduction to the literati in England and France. He can't seem to stop writing home to friends of the salons of the famous writers we have visited."

"Now, then," Rebecca continued, not willing to let go of her original observation, "I was saying that this is a *romantic* you! Not the same woman I knew back home! Here, in Europe, with each country you have visited, I see more and more of a side of you I never knew you had."

"I suppose the demands of my labors had made me very dry," assented Margaret, "especially in Boston after Father died and the weight of the household finances fell to me."

Rebecca sympathized, "That is true, I am sure."

Conversation flowed easily between them as they busied themselves with the unpacking and organizing of Margaret's personal things in her new rooms for their three-month stay in Rome. But Rebecca wanted to know her friend more intimately, and she seized this opportunity of quiet time together to do so.

Back at home, Margaret was firmly established as an icon in the literary world and as a bastion of Cambridge's intellectual elite. And more, she was a voice for human rights as she sought to influence the political decisions made in this newly formed country. Her sharp intellect and strict classical education served her individuality and unique vision.

Margaret could see with a keen eye the direction that young America should take in shaping policies that would affect the well being of all citizens. She took on the causes of those who had little influence, those who were overlooked. For them she wrote and published, to trumpet awareness of the plight of those neglected by society. She became the voice for universal suffrage, for the end to slavery, for improved conditions for the mentally ill and for those imprisoned. She saw her country as an extraordinary landscape to be tended and fashioned carefully, for *all* of its citizens. And she saw it as her duty as outspoken social critic to enlighten as she could.

And enlighten, she did. A doubled edged sword, though because her notoriety as a liberal idealist served against her socially. Busy was her life, but excruciatingly lonely. Margaret had no female intellectual equal. She could converse with any of the great male intellectuals, but socially, she did not fit in. Men marveled at her accomplished intelligence, but their wives saw her as a threat. And the "available" men who accepted her intelligence could never accept her as a prospect for marriage. This was the public Margaret, the persona everyone knew.

But here on this European trip, Rebecca had some time to learn about Margaret's early years; and she felt there was still more to learn.

What early experiences formed the singular woman she had become? Rebecca yearned to know.

So on this day, as she helped Margaret arrange her rooms, she seized upon opportunity. Rebecca pressed her inquiry further. "But dear, what about *before* your father's death? From what you have told me, all your *life* has been a labor. Your father was an unmerciful tutor."

"Unmerciful is a strong word, Rebecca," said Margaret, her eyes immediately turning misty. But I *would* say he was stern... yes."

"More than that," returned Rebecca, "if you are being honest. He took up all of your childhood, your years of youthful whimsy with strict learning. What young girl translates Virgil from Latin at the age of six? You *had* no time for friends and because of that, and later, no skills to attract a social circle...or suitors."

Margaret moved across the room, uncomfortable now with the direction of the conversation. But Rebecca was relentless. "You've said to me that you'd like to experience motherhood. So what do you do now, Margaret, to attract a man?"

An awkward silence ensued. Rebecca sensed that she might have pushed too far, so she laid the dress she was unpacking carefully on the bed to turn to look Margaret in the eyes. "Be honest, now, Margaret. Do you leave any time to socialize? Can you even dance a quadrille?"

"No," she admitted, her countenance downcast. "I am awkward with movement and rhythm. I have studied the patterns of the dance, but am not very good at executing them."

"Of course not! How could you be?" Rebecca said compassionately. "No time for a social or personal life. Your father trained that Harvard education of his right into your brain from your earliest days. And to think," she added with a huff, "when you were of age, those Harvard 'scholars' wouldn't even let you attend their college... But it was fine for *you* to work tirelessly teaching and writing to earn the money to send your *brothers* there."

"Oh *come* now, Rebecca," returned Margaret abruptly.

A sharp look from Rebecca caused her to realize her tone had become defensive, so she softened her approach. "It is lovely of you to be so protective of me, but don't forget that eventually Harvard did afford me the honor of being the first woman to conduct research at their libraries."

Rebecca relented, and perched at the edge of the bed, face upturned toward her friend.

"And…" Margaret continued, "concerning my brothers, as the eldest sibling it was my *duty* to attend to them after father died."

The last trunk was emptied and they had spoken frankly, openly. Margaret realized that Rebecca's judgment of her history was correct, but hearing it stated so bluntly felt hurtful and harsh.

Margaret folded the last of the linens, and turned to face her friend, now wanting to conclude the conversation with cheer, "So now that my brothers are settled and on their own, I can strike out a bit, I suppose. And I have! Here I am now, with *you*, in Rome!"

"Yes!" agreed Rebecca, relieved. She did not mean to hurt her friend with her bluntness. She added smiling, "And there is so much to see here, in this ancient city… starting tomorrow!"

Rebecca rose to join Margaret in one last approving assessment of their afternoon's work, as they moved arm in arm toward the door.

"So now," said Rebecca, "you can make the finishing touches on your own. We meet for supper later."

But Margaret was unwilling to let her friend leave just yet. She felt unsatisfied with the way in which their conversation about her family ended. She realized she had gotten a bit oversensitive, and wanted to recover her closeness with Rebecca before she left.

"Rebecca, wait." Margaret detained her with a gentle pressure on her friend's arm. Rebecca looked into Margaret's' troubled eyes. She waited.

"I want to say something more. It *is* true what you said about Father. He was very strict; and my childhood was very difficult and lonely. But, now, as an adult I can appreciate that it is because of all those years I spent studying I was able to support the family when it was needed.

You know, he left this world intestate, and now my uncle is in control what little father had. And he is neither generous nor kind to us. And mother has always been so sheltered in the ways of the world, she did not know *what* to do."

"I am so sorry. I did not realize. How difficult for you! Of course, you were a great help to your mother."

But Margaret felt she still owed Father some further defense.

"And the education Father gave to me was an unusual gift for a young girl. But you see, he believed in me and in my intelligence. He felt that a female's capacity was equal to that of a male's...and he wanted to prove that through me."

"But, dear, such a great burden to be put upon a child!"

"It *was* a great responsibility, and at the same time, a great compliment. But my young days were terribly difficult and solitary," Margaret admitted. "And the hardest was when Father's business called him away to Washington for weeks at a time."

"Those were the years in the House of Representatives?"

"Yes. I had not even him, then. 'Public duty above all,' he had said. It was his calling."

Margaret now realized that the cries of the street vendors had gone, and the day had waned before them. The quiet of the late afternoon infused the atmosphere in her rooms with a solemnity, a kind of peaceful beauty.

"I can see, Margaret, that you loved your father very much."

"My life was completely dedicated to him. And now to his memory."

"I realize, now, Rebecca," continued Margaret with gratitude, "that all of my labors did, after all, lead here, and to this moment."

She turned to face the late afternoon sun's rays streaming through her window.

"And ... I feel so *comfortable* here. I feel as if I have come home, more than I feel like a traveler to a foreign land."

Margaret allowed her excitement to break through in her voice. "Rebecca, tomorrow we see it, taste it, experience it all! Oh! Tomorrow!" she exclaimed, "To Rome!"

16

St. Peter's Basilica
Rome
(Holy Thursday April 1847)

The weeks Margaret had spent so far in this ancient city enraptured her, she, absorbing the culture and customs, the ways of Italy.

On this day, she and the Springs were to visit St. Peter's Basilica to witness Vespers on Holy Thursday, the prayers that would usher in the celebration of Easter Sunday, the most important holiday of the Catholic faith.

The folds of her green taffeta skirts swept the geometric pattern of the Basilica's marble floor from side to side, as Margaret turned to and fro, and round and round, almost dazed, at her attempt to see it all. "Oh! There is too much! Too much! For all my senses increase, then blight with the grandeur!" she gasped, clutching Rebecca's sleeve.

"Yes, Margaret," Rebecca replied. "We have arrived early enough before the service to enjoy the marvels of St. Peter's. But try now to be still, to take it in slowly, and we shall meet again at the entrance after Vespers. Try not to be late, bec…"

The advice became lost in the rustle of echoed whispers, as Margaret glided away, transported by the vastness and beauty of St. Peter's, a beauty she had only read about in books. Now, enchanted, dazzled, she progressed alone along the nave as if drawn by an unseen force toward the central altar.

Under the majestic dome, her eyes filled with the splendor impossible to behold all at once. Great fluted and cabled pilasters that seemed to reach the sky; marble of greens and golds in swirls and patterns served as backdrop for statues of martyrs and saints, the founders of the faith. Everywhere angels and cherubs soared among the slants of light let in by the alabaster framed window in the apse, the sun's beams seemed sent as if from heaven itself.

The immensity of the building belied the attention given to every available surface to archive Catholicism's temporal history, yet still declaring the essence of the heavens, mysticism pervaded, claiming the earth as its rightful expression.

Margaret so powerfully felt the spirit that enfolded the sanctuary that a sudden telescoping of the senses occurred to her. The hushed voices of hundreds of visitors, so many whispers uncontainable, crescendoed in the vast vault like a wave to its crest in the massive marble chamber, engulfing all, muffling the sound into a haze, a soft gossamer descending.

Then, there seemed to Margaret's senses, a swell of murmurs from an unknown deep, like voices of the past, a rising tide to enfold her. There she remained, in the heavy air of the afternoon; heat and fatigue striking suddenly and holding her; while in her mind, history now seemed timeless, present and past intermixing, she swooned slightly as she stood.

Before Margaret silent, stood *The Pieta*, Michelangelo's masterpiece. The Virgin Mary so beautiful, seeming alive. *Mother of Sorrows,* she thought, remembering the painting she kept next to her desk in New England, the *Mater Dolorosa*, having, since her youth, a sympathy for the concept of sacrificial suffering.

But here, in St. Peter's, Margaret beheld the Virgin Mary's countenance on the *Pieta*, youthful and sweet, face turned sideways as she, in marble pure and white, holds her beloved son's crucified body on her lap, across the voluptuous folds of her garments cascading.

The sculpture seemed aglow in the afternoon light.

Michelangelo's masterpiece swallowed up Margaret's own senses, her body now rigid, muscles tense as she observed Mary's features, delicate, seeming submissive, eternally young, eternally the Virgin child, Virgin mother incongruous. Incongruous also, the scale, Mary's body immense, garments commanding in size, drapery of dress and veil, enveloping the corpus of her Son, as if absorbing his form. Her left arm and attitude not embracing, but open to the world, that hand free, fingers long. Palm outfacing.

Now, the heat of the afternoon began to moisten Margaret's brow – her attempt to blink away the sweat only had it settle in her lashes, increasing the effect of the glow of the late afternoon's slanted sun's rays on the Virgin face. To her impression, the statue's dimensionality faded, shifted, and blended with the mad swirls of the marbles behind, a wreath of laurel seemed to descend upon the virgin's delicate head.

Mary, Virgin Mother, now appearing to Margaret like an heroic apparition, a glowing celebration of the eternal virgin, a slanting sunbeam now streaming across the veil – the cool marble face appeared to manifest the boundless acceptance of her sacrifice.

Time seeming still, all the while she stood, observing this figure of stone, Margaret's eyes agaze and wide. Now, her body trembling and weak, she became aware of the sound of the voices, the sea of murmurs that engulfed her, which arose, echoing a still and infinite truth.

17

At length, sounds of earthly voices clear and distinct broke her reverie.

Margaret started abruptly from her trance, aware now of her surroundings. She breathed a deep sigh, then turned, and saw that the crowds had mostly dispersed. Time had passed, the day had grown long, and the shadows had lengthened.

She searched to and fro, eyes seeking her friends among the remaining groups who chatted amiably; she saw the trailing couples, students, visitors, now exiting into the late afternoon's slanted rays. Her friends nowhere to be seen, long gone she now supposed, the realization occurring to her that she would be alone and unescorted in the streets of Rome. This, for a woman, she knew, was at the least unseemly; and at most, a danger.

She stood alone in the piazza, vulnerable.

There, a young man of noble bearing, in the shadow of a pillar, leaned against the cold marble, observing. He perceived her mounting dismay. Approaching slowly, carefully, he introduced himself; Giovanni Angelino Ossoli, a regular worshipper at St. Peter's, he said, adding that his family villa was not far from the Basilica. He then asked politely if he might offer some aid.

Margaret explained in her halting Italian that she had lost her friends.

"May I escort you home safely?" he asked, offering his arm, with a stiff slight bow from the waist. His eyes, deep and serious. His comportment formal and respectful.

Margaret hesitated, unsure at first whether to accept. She looked past him and saw the gathering dusk, the streets nearly empty now, gloom pervading. Then with sudden decisiveness, she accepted. She took his arm, welcoming his assistance with relief.

He had some English, and she, imperfect Italian, yet they made their way, playing their parts in the twilight: a halting and uncertain gallant offering aid to a damsel in need.

Margaret took him in as they strolled easily toward her rooms. He was youthful, tall and slender. Athletic. He instinctually adapted his long strides to match hers, the attitude of a comfortable companion. There was attentiveness to her that she'd never felt from a man before. He was bred as a gentleman. Considerate, protective, caring. His easy confidence relaxed her.

"Margaret Fuller. From America. First from the state of Massachusetts, then New York."

"Ah! *Margharita!*" he replied with a sweet smile. "Such a name of beauty. It becomes you."

Uncharacteristically, she accepted the compliment. It seemed delivered with such sincerity. "*Grazi*, Giovanni," she replied with a blush.

He delivered her, shyly, with little conversation, to her doorstep. In that short time, a comfortable companionship seemed ready to form.

"May I see you again, Margharita? This city of Rome has much to offer. May I escort you to see our ancient wonders?"

The charms of a Roman evening had taken its effect on them both.

Margaret agreed, then proffered her hand in thanks. In a gallant gesture, he gently brushed the back of her hand with his lips, so lightly Margaret wasn't even sure she was touched. She, evidently pleased, left him on the street gazing up at her as she climbed the stairs to her door.

After that chance meeting, Giovanni became her daily companion, accompanying her to see the city's many splendors. And in that, a deep friendship grew.

They walked and talked. He aiding her halting Italian; she supplying him with words in English to assist. They were both amused, and often laughed with the thought of what they must sound like to others overhearing their fractured conversations.

They grew together. Their walks a source of warmth and joy for each. Weeks became months. Eventually, they openly spoke of their childhoods, their families and backgrounds for which they shared sympathy and support, for their emotional sensibilities were aptly matched.

"My family is very old," remarked Giovanni one day. "We bear the title of *Marchese*. We trace our lineage for centuries, listed in the Golden Book of Italian Nobility by our full family name *Ossoli della Torre*, originally from the north near Lake Garda. But when the family was honored to be called into the service of the Pope, the family acquired the castle of Pietraforte in the Sabine Hills and the Palazzo you see in Rome, which is now our family home."

"But what of you, Giovanni? Where do you stand in your family now?"

"My mother died when I was a child. I have three elder brothers. They, as my father before, serve the Pope in the Vatican. My elder sister Angela raised me."

"And still, Giovanni, what of you?" she asked again.

"My father and I, with my sister and her husband live in our family home. The care of my father, now old and ill, falls to me. I attend to family properties with my uncle."

"And the title of *Marchese*? To whom does *it* fall?"

"My father's eldest brother inherited the title. Then when he died, passed it to his son, my cousin Pietro. But we are all of the blood of a *Marchese*. All in our family, in the book of royals, fall third in rank below Princes and Dukes. Called *Nobile di Marchese di Lombardy* officially. All males in the family have the possibility of attaining title in the event disaster falls to other family members. As such, we retain our rights in whatever title and fortune that may befall us."

They had walked a long way on the Via Del Corso, one of the principal roads of old Rome, past piazzas and palaces. Margaret wanted to see the work of the architect Sabi on the famous fountain of Trevi. Giovanni guided her off the Corso along some side streets to the sight of its pure waters glittering in the afternoon sun.

"The fountain of the Virgin," Giovanni recounted. "A maiden who took pity on some tired soldiers of Rome on their journey back to the city after fighting in a campaign. She directed them to a local spring, their town's water source. The Roman leader, Marcus Agrippa, ordered an aqueduct to be built there to direct this fresh water supply to the city, and here, this fountain is its termination."

"The story from 19 B.C." Margaret recounted from her own readings. "Agrippa was Octavian's brother–in–law."

"And still the fountain flows, centuries later, under the careful watch of the statue of Oceanus."

Margaret's imagination was held by the sight of this purely Roman celebration of the arrival of pristine mountain waters into the city, made to cascade from carved sculptures of gods, men and monsters, the dramatic noisy gush ultimately gathering benignly into a large pool.

At length, she turned her attention to Giovanni, saying, "Italy is a place of ancient stories. Of titles and properties and duties passed from one generation to the next. It seems that your family story follows suit."

Then, recalling her own home cities of Boston and New York, and further, America's great landscape of the west, she continued, "For us in America, all is new. All is being formed. Our government in its infancy; our laws our peoples in a new journey of formation."

Giovanni agreed. "Your country is an example of freedom to the world, he said with admiration. "Where anything can befall a man, no matter his birth or station in life."

"Yes, Giovanni. My birthplace, Cambridge in the state of Massachusetts, is by American accounts, old. My father's family among the first to cross the Atlantic for America. He served in the government, as voice for our state, the House of Representatives."

Margaret told of her family and its history, ending with her own personal responsibility.

"After father's death it fell to me to support my younger siblings."

Giovanni took it all in. He mused, "We both are caretakers, Margharita. Our families are of the public, and serve the larger causes for the people. But we... we serve our families."

Their stories, memories and delights, sorrows and losses transcended their differences in language and culture. They shared much in their common humanity, and each understood, and felt compassion for the other.

*****

One evening, after supper, Rebecca asked Margaret about her young man. "You *do* spend a great deal of time with him, Margaret. You have had been months now of his daily attention!"

Margaret's only response was a blush of color to her cheeks.

"Ah! I see his effect on you," Rebecca teased with a laugh.

Then she continued, "Therefore, my dear, Marcus and I must meet him!"

Margaret did not answer immediately. She thought of her private relationship with Giovanni becoming part of her friendship with the Springs. She hesitated a moment, but then assented with a nod.

"Good! May we expect him this Thursday? We can serve a typical English tea at four o'clock, as we did in London. Perhaps Giovanni would enjoy a taste of the British Isles?"

When Margaret proposed the meeting to Giovanni, he felt quite pleased to be presented to her friends. His easy reception of the invitation eased her mind. All nervousness dropped from her care. After all, she thought, why wouldn't my friends like and admire him as I do?

On the appointed day, Rebecca, Marcus and Margaret waited in the parlor for Giovanni. He arrived exactly at four, and was escorted to the parlor by their housekeeper.

Marcus rose from his seat to welcome him; Giovanni proffered his hand in greeting. Marcus grasped his strength, immediately taking in his youth. He noted the shy smile on Giovanni's unlined face, the slight stiffness in his bearing, tall, thin and straight. He glanced protectively at Margaret and wondered at their difference in years, she the elder, her frame slightly stooped from years bent over book and pen.

Rebecca, on the other hand, thought of none of this. She seemed charmed, and passed an approving glance to Margaret while the men were otherwise engaged.

Once seated, conversation began easily, as Margaret and the Springs recalled for Giovanni their first meeting and fast friendship in New York. He took it all in, eager to learn more about Margaret in her homeland.

Giovanni cleared his throat. "And what of your travels here, in Europe?"

Rebecca answered at length about their adventures in England and France before their arrival in Rome. She then spoke of their intended travel, revealing that soon they were to leave Rome to continue touring north, the lakes, the mountains, then on to Germany.

Giovanni's expression shifted from interest to a look of concern. Their daily walks seemed a permanent part of his life now. To him, their friendship seemed intimate. Why had Margaret not told him that her intention to leave Rome was so close at hand? Registering now that Margaret's time in Rome is coming to an end, he became a bit taciturn. The atmosphere in the room had changed. Rebecca exchanged a look of puzzlement with Margaret, then made an effort to draw Giovanni back into the conversation.

"Have you been to England ever?" Rebecca asked him.

"No, I have not travelled much outside of my own land," he answered shyly.

"Well, do you know the English writer Thomas Carlyle?" she pressed further.

"Yes. I know of him. The name, but not his writing," Giovanni explained.

"Well, thanks to Margaret's letter of introduction, we had tea with the Carlyles at their home in London. And there, we met one of your countrymen, the brilliant philosopher and thinker, Giuseppe Mazzini," she explained proudly.

"Oh! Mazzini! A *great* man!" exclaimed Giovanni. His enthusiasm overtook his otherwise quiet demeanor, surprising both Rebecca and Marcus.

Giovanni continued, "Mazzini founded the 'Young Italy' movement, which I much esteem. It has been years since he has been exiled from this country for his liberal ideas."

Noticing the attentive look from Marcus, Giovanni explained further, "The Austrians declared membership in his 'Young Italy' movement as high treason, punishable by death. They fear the power of such a cause. It is a threat to their control of our northern territory."

"Yes," added Margaret. "We spoke at length of the politics in Europe during that visit at the Carlyles. And we continue our friendship in our letters. I do admire Mazzini so. He is a man of vision and of genius."

"I have followed his ideas for years," agreed Giovanni. "He believes in the liberation of Italy from the tyranny of foreign governments. I feel he is right! Our culture has great achievement and its own great history. Why, because of a European treaty, are we carved up among European kings as prizes for them to rule and control? The Italian peninsula must be reunited politically and under our *own* rule."

"This is surprising of you, Giovanni," interrupted Marcus. "Aren't you of noble birth? Haven't you a lot to lose if Italy becomes a republic?"

Rebecca shot Marcus a sharp glance. His question seemed direct and rude.

However, Giovanni was nonplussed. He answered simply, "Do you see our land, Marcus? The north is ruled by the Austrians and the French; the south by the Spanish. Only the Papal States remain protected by our own Italian Pope. Ask yourself, why do foreigners, and not Italians rule our land?"

Giovanni continued, "We, as a people, have been dominated by others for too long. A great leader is needed to unite all of Italy. To answer your question directly, Marcus, I am in favor of this cause for the greater good of the people. I am not interested in personal gain. And this is the time to act, now, when all of Europe rebels against their monarchs."

Margaret already knew of this selfless side of her friend, one of the causes of her great affection for him. She stepped in to support Giovanni's reply, adding thoughtfully, "Mazzini would like to see Italy united and self governed. His is a voice for freedom, but his vision includes the causes of freedom for all. He sees the human family as one, and beating with one great heart. He is not merely a politician. He is a man of great thought and spirituality."

"I see," admitted Marcus. "The cause for freedom does extend beyond 'Young Italy.'" Marcus' gaze shifted directly to Giovanni. "It is true, there is great unrest brewing on the continent. Time is fertile for change."

*****

Afterward, Margaret walked Giovanni to the door. The afternoon's talk only increased his admiration for her. Conversation with the Springs revealed to him more about Margaret's accomplishments: her publications and lectures and her position as writer for a national newspaper, and her commitment to use her public voice to serve the cause of human rights.

He had never known such a woman before. To him, Margaret was the living representation of the freedoms of *America*, and of what a future united Italy could yield. The political and the personal cemented their friendship, kindred spirits, both.

Giovanni's walk home was slow and sad, however, his mind now disturbed. He found in Margaret a wondrous gift, a woman of fortitude, wisdom and quiet passion. Nary a sunrise to sunset for months had he passed without her company. And now, looming before him was the sad knowledge she must soon take up the rest of her European tour with her friends; her time in Rome were nearly at an end.

*****

Meanwhile, Rebecca sat in the parlor as the housekeeper removed cups and saucers, trays and linens. She awaited Margaret's return.

"This is a singular gentleman you have found, my dear," she remarked casually when Margaret entered the room.

"Yes, a marvelous friendship, a treasure found unexpectedly and in a most unexpected time and place," she agreed. "It is a delightful refreshment, to talk with one so pure of mind and heart. A young man so genuine and caring; gentle and strong."

"Indeed. But do you think that's what Giovanni feels? *Friendship?*"

"What are you implying?" asked Margaret with surprise.

"Oh come, now. Even you can't be so blind!" chuckled Rebecca.

Margaret sat silent, looking at her friend, waiting for an explanation.

Rebecca continued, "I saw him look at you. He sees more than a friend, my dearest. This man harbors an unfailing passion for you. Might I even say, *love…?*"

"Oh, you exaggerate, Rebecca!" replied Margaret, impatiently. "The passions of Rome have affected your judgment. You are speaking of what you *wish* for me, not of what exists."

18

May 1847

For days, Giovanni tried to consider his life without Margaret. The void seemed impossible to behold. She had become the center of his joy and his sense of renewal. Her womanly warmth gave new purpose to his life. He reasoned that if Margaret were to leave Rome with her friends, he might never see her again. He concluded then that he must press the moment.

During one of their twilight walks, in the soft light of the waning sun, they strolled arm in arm, hearing only their own footfall on the deserted Roman street, and felt refreshed by the sweet mountain air that drifted in from the west. Their contentment came from each other; tranquility, a surety in the confusion of life, as if all before led up to this moment they now share. Time passed peacefully.

They strolled lazily through the triumphal Arch of Constantine. It was here, as they passed through the central arch, flanked by Corinthian columns and myriad relief sculptures, that Giovanni took his great leap, a daring chance. Now, in the brightness of the moon that shone against the dark sky, against the moonglow on the fragments of the ancient Colosseum, he asked.

Margaret's breath caught in her throat. Her steps stopped still.

She was unaccustomed to bafflement. Though astonished, she reacted with calm. Immediately, and, with little explanation, she graciously thanked him, and asked for time to think about his proposal of marriage. Her response was formal. Cool.

Giovanni walked her safely home, as usual, but now a nervous silence accompanied them. He wondered if he pressed too soon. He felt a quiet desperation. But he forced himself to be patient. To allow her judgment to take hold. They parted, as usual, at her doorstep.

Invulnerable now, in the quiet of her rooms and alone, she had the opportunity to react to the shock of his marriage proposal. She experienced a wild confluence of emotions. The whole notion of marrying this young man had her flabbergasted. She was all at once flattered, afraid, and tempted. This young Giovanni was handsome, attentive, kind. She knew he admired her; respected her; loved her. He would be her helpmeet. A strange opportunity for Margaret. Could this be *happiness* knocking at her door?

She pictured what their lives would be like together. He, a man of quiet dignity. Noble. Humble. His daily kindnesses, thoughtful gestures. Nary a demand would he make upon her, he declared. He could not see his life without her, he said sincerely.

Margaret considered. Alone, in her rooms, she pondered.

She became immersed in imaginings of his singular devotion. Of a life of contentment. Perhaps, this, a chance for a family of her own. A dream she had dared to dream, and express only to those most close to her. A dream nearly forgotten, until now.

Then, in the midst of the pleasant daydreams, without warning, a world of memory-feelings over-flooded her very being. A familiar heaviness overcame her, a sad focus, as if something broken that was carried inside had become unearthed. Emotional residue.

Father's stern demeanor came before her, cold blue withholding eyes. A father-love of demands and conditions. Confusion in a child's mind of what love means, what it should feel like. An imprint that remains.

And Mother. Margaret's witnessing her sad and mournful sighs. Her increasing quiet withdrawal to Father's power. A wife that could not please his standards.

Margaret shook herself free from this reverie. New England practicality overtook her considerations of Giovanni's marriage proposal. Suddenly, all she could see were the differences between herself and Giovanni brought into sharp relief. She, older by ten years. She, a liberal intellectual, a Protestant American; what chance had she to be accepted by his family, ancient and noble, Catholic and severe?

No, she concluded. This was too impulsive. Not thought out. The details, too messy. Impossible! Flight would be her only defense.

It was on their next walk that Margaret told Giovanni that a marriage between them would only provide difficulty and strain for them both. She refused his offer, then added that she must continue her European tour with her friends.

She will leave Rome with the Springs, as planned.

Disappointed, Giovanni accepted her choice with quiet dignity. Although Margaret's refusal of marriage stung, his heart told him it would be temporary, for he felt that she loved him as much as he did her. He decided he would wait.

*****

The departure from Rome went smoothly. All trunks packed and loaded, arrangements planned carefully, the party traveled northward together.

But as the days wore on, Margaret felt unusually irritated with the Springs. She expressed displeasure in the itinerary. The timetable felt too tight, though before they left, they had agreed to travel to Assisi, Perugia, and Arezzo before reaching Venice. It seemed to Margaret they never spent enough time in one place. Or they took too much time in places of little interest or artistic merit.

Margaret's time in Rome had been spent as she'd pleased. But now she felt hemmed in, under the control of others adhering to this schedule that no longer seemed relevant. She felt an impatience not usually known by her toward these, her intimate friends.

However, even in her frustration, she came to realize that her irritation was not truly with them, but with herself. She carried with her, since Rome, a restlessness in her mind that caused her dissatisfaction. That caused sleeplessness. That caused her short temperedness.

It was fear. A fear she'd adopted and carried with her ever since she had refused Giovanni's proposal of marriage. A fear that gripped her more with each rutted road that took her northward. With each city they visited. With each mile that carried her further and further from Giovanni.

She knew even more now in their travels, that as good and kind as the Springs were, she would never truly belong with them. She could never be a part of their family. She was welcome, but would always be an outsider. And in this situation, day after day in transports and carriages, small pensiones, shared meals and living spaces, experiencing an intimate insider's view of their family life showed her even more plainly that she was in fact, alone.

She realized that she had left behind her last chance at true human connection. Intimacy. Love. At perhaps even having a child, a family of her own. At the feeling of belonging, and of happiness.

And similarly, back in Rome, Giovanni's own heart burned, his mind filled with great trepidation. His days were filled with worry. What if my Margharita does not return? What if I have lost her forever?

He wrote to her faithfully as she travelled. To keep him in the forefront of her mind, so that she does not forget him with time and miles between them.

But, knowing her independent nature, he made sure the tone of his letters were not cloying. That his letters were accepting of her decision to be away from him. He cheerfully inquired about what she has seen and enjoyed on her journey. About the Springs, and about any new acquaintances she may have made.

He filled his correspondences with news of his family, and with the latest news of Rome, their common interest in politics, the people's yearning for independence. He posted these and prayed for her replies.

Margaret waited hungrily for his letters. She found that she began to look forward more to them than to visiting the next church or library or historic building. Despite all the places she visited, all the marvels of history and of art that she saw, she felt most the void, the emptiness in her life without Giovanni.

She missed him. The kinship they had formed. The unmistakable richness of sharing new experiences with a loved one. She found that thoughts of him surrounded her wherever she went. What would Giovanni think of this? ...Or, would that here were here to see that with me... or this. Or, he would walk with me now, and he would say....

She thought often of those last glorious evenings spent with Giovanni. There they sat near the fountains in the Piazza del Popolo, and it seemed the rising moon would shimmer in the waters just for them. Or glimmer on the surface of the river when they walked the banks of the Po, quietly, arm in arm.

There they wandered about, amid the ancient ruins, the old walls and marble columns. There, their love seemed contained in a magical timeless embrace. She felt a beauty, a softness, a feeling of voluptuousness when she was with Giovanni that she had never known before.

And at their inevitable parting, immeasurable pain for them both. Hers, she kept quietly in her heart. His was evident in his countenance, his posture, his liquid eyes. With their last embrace he whispered, it seemed more to himself than to her, "*You will return, Margharita,...to me.*"

Weeks had passed thus, Margaret's mind preoccupied, recalling their intimate moments together, and their pain-filled parting.

Thus the summer was spent. Margaret and the Springs now in Venice, the city of waterways; this their final city to explore in Italy before travelling to Switzerland.

On this, a day bathed in brilliant sunshine, Margaret decided to hire a gondola out on her own for the afternoon. Seated in the rear, she felt comforted by the lazy motion of the boat, rocking gently from side to side with the gondolier's rhythmical rowing, strong and steady. The flowing waters calmed her. In those moments of peace, her irritation floated away, and she could think clearly.

She saw couples and lovers walking together on the banks of the canals. The closeness of their bodies seemed casual as they strolled; the unconscious inclination of their heads tilting toward one another spoke of warmth and affection.

All the world for her seemed contracted now to this one longing. For all that she had accomplished, all the places and people she had known, she could only feel this one absence in her life. She recalled those moments of beauty with Giovanni in Rome, as they walked arm in arm, feeling each other's warmth and desire.

His absence now felt to Margaret like a tearing away of an essential part of herself. A lack she felt in her every fiber. She knew then what she must do.

*****

"Rebecca, Marcus," she addressed her friends in the early evening after supper, "I must tell you both ... of a change in my plans."

Marcus politely replied, "Thank you, Margaret, but you will have to excuse me, I will leave the details of the planning to you ladies while I take my evening walk."

"Of course," replied Margaret.

Rebecca smiled at him with understanding. Marcus strode toward the humidor for a cigar, then to the hallway for his hat and walking stick, off to enjoy the night air.

Left alone, they made their way to the parlor. They sat comfortably now on soft chairs, covered in vivid floral tapestry. Portraits in gilt frames covered the damask walls. Volumes of histories lined bookshelves. On prominent display was an ancient bible, leather embossed.

Rebecca did not seem surprised by Margaret's declaration of a change in plans. She felt her friend's unhappiness of late, and had no doubts as to why. Rebecca, however, stayed silent, and waited attentively for Margaret to continue.

Margaret began. "I feel I must not leave Venice with you and Marcus. I must stay here a bit longer. I know you both must go on as planned. But there is more here that I must study. The art and the architecture demand more of my attention."

"Oh. I see." Rebecca replied calmly, casually to her friend, casting a knowing, friendly glance.

"Truly, Rebecca," continued Margaret, "I am not yet ready to leave Venice. And the rest of our plans to visit Switzerland and Germany hold less interest for me now. There is much more for me to see and experience here in Italy."

"Of course, dear," said Rebecca. "There is so much more that can be studied," she added wryly. She leaned forward in her chair to face Margaret directly. "I am sure, for example, that Rome deserves a second look. There is so much more to that city than we had time to learn of. Perhaps, even a certain *someone*...." she allowed her voice to drift off with a smile.

There was a complete understanding between them.

Margaret now felt relaxed, grateful.

She confided, "When in Florence, I visited the workshop of our American sculptor Hiram Powers. I wanted to see his statue *The Greek Slave* that had made him so famous."

"Yes. That sculpture made quite a splash on its tour of America. A life-sized full nude of a young Greek woman, stripped and chained and for sale by her Turkish captors at a slave market. Art critics claim it is an allegory of our own struggle to free the slaves in America."

Margaret continued, remembering, eyes averted, as if talking to herself. "And for all that I have read about its successful reception there; and for all I have written upon the subject of emancipation, all I could see…all I could think of when I saw her…were her hands. I could only focus on her hands."

"Why, Margaret? Why focus on them?"

"They were in chains, bound. Her hands, delicate and smooth. No laborer, she. One hand was bent to protect her virgin parts from the prying eyes of the men in the marketplace. The other rested on her robes, cast aside on a post, as she, naked stood."

Rebecca could see Margaret's eyes beginning to brim with tears. She reached forward to touch her arm, protectively, encouragingly.

Margaret continued, "All I could think of was the tyranny of it. She stood captive, bound, enslaved. Her life and her very being, taken from her by forces beyond her control. She would never be free. She would never know her true self."

Margaret placed her hand upon Rebecca's now. She turned to face her, accepting the comfort of her friend. She drew a deep breath. "I must be free, Rebecca. I must seek out my own destiny."

Rebecca saw the pain in Margaret's eyes. She nodded in agreement, and added encouragingly, "You have grown and changed since our first days in Rome, Margaret. And Giovanni is part of that growth. Here, in Italy, is where you belong. Go to him. Only you can decide what is right for you."

The two women sat for a moment in the comfort of the small parlor, knowing the impact of this turning point for Margaret. Then they arose, and faced each other, each reaching out for a warm embrace.

"I will miss you, Rebecca."

"And I, you," she replied.

But wanting to put on a brave face, Rebecca stepped away with a deep sigh, then a smile. "Go with our blessings, Margaret," said Rebecca to her friend, "and find your happiness."

*****

Swaying and reeling down the rutted country roads toward Rome, her carriage piled high with her trunks, she gazed upon the rolling farms lush with fruit trees, their branches laden to bursting. The earth willingly gave its gifts, nature's bounty.

She saw the soft hills, undulating, seeming alive. Margaret imagined the countryside animated, offering pear and peach, luscious fig; fecund soil and earth beneath providing nutrition for their gifts. The air itself carried sweet fragrances in the gentle breeze. All alive seeming generous and warm.

Traveling alone through the countryside thrilled her with anticipation of her reunion with Giovanni; with desire, and excitement.

Again, to Rome!

To begin anew in this ancient and noble city steeped in history, culture and art. And at this time, the city now simmers with the energy of a rebirth into its own, political independence, to fuel the identity of a free Italy. An Italy, finally ready to claim her own identity.

And this, just as she, truly liberated for the first time, felt filled with the joy of a homecoming of her own making, born of a pure desire she had never known before; a passion awakened in her by this young man she now chose freely to love.

PART III

19

Fire Island-July 1847

First of July, and Oaks was busier than ever with city visitors. The years that have passed since his arrival from Ohio have secured his standing as a sportsman's guide. And this season has topped all others in numbers of parties he has guided out on the bay, the ocean, and the marshes. His reputation spread far and wide, he was quite in demand.

On this morning, Hannah could see he had been preparing to take out a hunting party; and now he was on the bay side, readying the catboat for a sail. She took bread and cheese wrapped securely in an oilcloth out to him for the trip.

"Goin' across now to pick up a boarder, Hannah. Young man, name o' Judd. Suppose' to take a coach from the rail stop to Babylon. Pickin' him up after I git supplies at Gillette's."

"How long will he stay?"

"Few days. Thinks he's a duck hunter. Take him out to the east marshes. Best huntin' there is around now."

From the kitchen window, she watched her husband test the wind, put up sail, then put out across the bay. Hannah turned, and caught sight of a crumpled letter left behind on the table. She smoothed out the paper, saying aloud, "Strange. He rarely hears from anyone by post…"

She read the letter. It was from his brother Andrew, brother so unlike brother. Warm were his words, sending greetings to her, never received. Andrew then asked Smith to take care of his young friend, Henry Judd, just graduating from law school, who wanted to visit the island for a break before he begins his new job. Then Andrew suggested that perhaps next month he would like to come out east for a short respite, too. To see the ocean and enjoy the shore. That would be welcome company, she thought, placing the letter away in the cupboard.

She busied herself preparing the guest room and the kitchen supplies. Men come home hungry from hunting, she knows.

20

Judd woke up in the Oaks' guestroom before dawn to the sound of ocean waves, but something more, an insistent scraping sound, repetitive and steady.

He got out of the bed and stretched his tall frame, feeling the humidity in the air, tasting the salt spray in his mouth. Ahhh, he thought as he stood before the open window. The wild Atlantic, … balm to the senses, and to the mind! The young man, eager to explore the shore pulled on yesterday's trousers, and went out to investigate the scraping sound, which against the roll of the waves and the cry of the gulls, sounded so out of place on the beach.

Ahead of him, in the growing dawn, he saw the long shadow of his host. There stood Smith Oaks on the back side of a dune, in a spot obscured from the house. He was peering down into a deep hole, just next to it a long handled shovel, now tossed aside carelessly on the sand. Spying the shovel, Judd thought, There! That's what made the sound I heard!

Oaks, deep in thought, stooped down, reaching both arms into the hole as if to lift something heavy.

Friendly in intention, Judd approached to help him with the burden. But Oaks, focused on the task, did not notice him.

"HEY! NEED A HAND WITH THAT?" Judd shouted, nearing his host.

Bent forward now and struggling with the weight, Oaks still did not hear. Judd continued his approach.

"HEY, SAY I! NEED SOME HELP?" Judd asked again, now nearly upon him.

Before Oaks reacted, Judd saw the sand fall away from a metal trunk, revealing a brass plate with the name engraven, "Captain Michael Baker" under another larger plate with the name "*LOUISA.*"

Now, Oaks turned, feeling eyes upon him. Sweat soaked shirt sticking to his muscled back: head, still facing down toward the trunk, he noticed the nameplates exposed. Instinctively, his body crouched, hovering over his possession, like a beast protecting its kill. Then, he turned his head toward Judd, his sun-burnt neck glistening with sweat, eyes squinting against the rising sun now, his upper lip curled into a sneer.

Just seeing him stopped Judd in his tracks. *Criminy, if he were a dog, he'd bite me!* he thought.

Judd waited.

"Never sneak up on a man like that, son," growled Oaks, rising to stand now between Judd and the trunk. "Whaddaya doin' here?"

"I heard the noise. Came out to investigate. Saw you, and thought I could help, that's all."

Smith spat into the sand then said, "Don' need no help, thank ye."

He stood, sweat glistening on his face, sandy hands firmly planted on his hips, challenging.

"Don' need no snoopin' round here, neither," he continued, standing his ground.

Judd felt the unspoken threat, and remained speechless.

Then Oaks pointed toward the house, and said, "Go an' git some food now. Be leavin' soon. Git us some huntin' done today."

21

In the kitchen, Hannah had thick chunks of bread with butter and newly made blackberry jam on the kitchen table, hot coffee on the hearth ready for the men.

"Out on the beach so early?" Hannah asked Judd when he returned from the dune.

"Yes," he said, as he accepted the steamy mug from her. "I have never seen such a beautiful shore." He added, looking out of the kitchen window at Oaks returning from the dune, "Both beautiful and dangerous at the same time, no?"

He turned his back on the window and sat at the rough wooden table, musing aloud. "Do I recall this beach being in the paper a while back? Shipwreck, I think."

Hannah kept her back to the new boarder, distractedly busy with chores, hoping he would drop the subject.

Judd slathered a thick slab of bread with butter in silence. Then a bite, chewing thoughtfully. Then, suddenly, "Yes," he recalled aloud… "A few years ago…a brig, it was, I think… I can't recall…What was her name?"

"The *Louisa*," replied Hannah, mechanically.

22

In an instant, all the fears of the Marshal's investigation returned to her, with the cold realization of all she has become since she married Smith Oaks.

She bears the daily heaviness. An overwhelming sadness and helplessness. Her mind preoccupied with that day of decision, to become wife to Smith Oaks. She has become resigned to his control of her life, that he has overtaken her very being; and she tries to imagine how her life would have been different had she not married him.

Truth be told, she willingly gave up all to him.

Alone in that shore town remote, no love or help for pain, no future to behold. Her tenderest care could not prevent death from taking all that she had loved.

So alone was she in that farmhouse decaying. Desolate in her being, afraid she would never get another chance for a home of her own. Or to have a child. To know some small happiness.

She remembers well. Hannah had noticed a man in the village. The ladies she sewed for knew about him, too.

She asked them. He was a loner from the shore across the bay, said they. A sportsman's guide, she was told. Seen about town sometimes, or picking up guests at Roe's. Other than that, always alone, as was she.

He was seen to wear a fancy brooch on a Sunday. He was known to pay in cash for all he took home with him on errand day.

Hannah had known poverty and want since her father died, and no prospects she, except what she could get from tending the garden in summer, and keeping the chicken coop. She sewed and mended when called.

This man, Smith Oaks, one day said to Hannah, "I am alone."

"As am I," she replied.

"I cannot keep a house."

"I can keep one for thee."

"You must come across the bay to live on the island."

"I will. But we must marry first," said she.

Security. A warm soul to talk to betimes. More than a crust of bread. The promise of a family, of a life, of belonging.

"You must be an obedient wife," said he.

"The bible tells us so," said she.

Now, the years spun out, Hannah knows him, and what he does. She lives with what they do that God does not like. She, obedient, has taken in with him, silent about his crimes and his schemes.

Hannah's mind revolves always with her guilt. It submerges the joys in her day, dominates her sleep at night. I am guilty, she thinks as she hangs the wash on a beautiful dry day. I am weak and cannot stand up for what I know is wrongdoing, she thinks as she watches her daughter Marietta play in the sunshine. I fear what happens to those who oppose, she thinks as she puts her head on the pillow at night.

But she also knows that Marietta needs her. I must take care of her and raise her in God's ways, she reasons. She weeps as she prays for release, so she may confess her soul. Daily, she makes small penances, feeling trapped between God's judgment and Smith Oaks' wrath.

No help for me, she knows.

23

Fire Island
August 1847

Though still summer, late August brings a change in the light. A slight slant of the sun causes the shadows to lengthen just a bit; the sun's gleam on the water now has a sharpness to it. An edge. A warning to get in all you can of the garden and the sea; soon to set the stores for the winter kitchen.

Hannah sat in her parlor absorbed in her sewing. Her reputation for fine needlework and dressmaking kept her busy all seasons with requests from the ladies from the towns across the bay. Monthly were her visits to bring her completed handiwork, and to pick up new orders. The income was especially helpful in the winter months, when Smith's business was at a lull.

A sudden noise outside the house caused her to gasp: needle paused in mid air, she turned to look toward the door. There, a familiar figure.

"Brother Andrew! I did not see you dropped off!" Hannah rose from her chair in surprise, her sewing spilling all onto the floor.

"I did not mean to startle you, Hannah," said Andrew as he stepped inside the open door.

She welcomed him to join her and sit in the parlor. She carefully folded the bodice of the dress she embroidered. She smiled at Andrew, welcoming him.

"Who sailed you across?" she asked.

"An islander coming for his own place, name o' Dominy. Says he has an inn near the lighthouse."

"Yes. Felix. A fine man. Family. Has a son same age as my Marietta. They play together on the beach."

"Where is she? When will I get to meet my niece?"

"Sleeping now. Tired from the heat and gardening the patch with me. She will wake soon. Have you eaten?"

"Not hungry now, thanks. I'll wait for Smith. Where is he?"

"Took a party eeling the bay this morning. Should be back soon. Meanwhile put your things away and rest up a bit. First room to the right."

Andrew picked up his canvas bag.

Hannah resumed her work; colorful embroidery thread and needle ready to embellish the plain dress.

Thank ye Hannah," as he started away. He stopped still in recall, then Andrew asked, "That the one used for boarders? That the one where young Judd stayed?"

"Yes." Hannah's working hands froze, needle and thread motionless, she became paralyzed by the memory.

"Such a terrible accident. Gun just went off by itself," she murmured quietly.

Andrew stopped still.

Her face paled as she continued, "Blew off his jaw and part of his skull."

The tears that filled Hannah's eyes obstructed her vision. Her needle stopped, looking south toward the ocean, out of the open window, air unnaturally still. "We pray every day for his soul," she said, barely above a whisper.

"I feel partly responsible," said Andrew. "I was the one who encouraged him to come out here for some rest. Thought the ocean air would do him some good." Andrew paused with thoughts of the young man. "He was so eager to start his new job. Had a young lady ready to marry him. Was to start a life. But it all just ended."

"Tragic, terrible accident. Nothing here's been the same since," replied Hannah, looking at Andrew full in the face, eyes wide and wounded.

In the guest room, Andrew surveyed his surroundings as he pulled his rumpled clothing from his travel bag. Rough floorboards that creaked. One window, opened bayside. A bed and a four-drawer dresser. That's all that's needed here, he thought, as he noticed the sky becoming heavy, darkening with afternoon clouds rolling in.

A breeze blew in from the north, pushing the bay water into small whitecaps, ruffling the white curtain. Andrew re-folded his clothing carefully to put away into the dresser. Pulling on the handle of the top draw only caused it to jam halfway open. Probably warped in the humidity, he thought. I can fix this for them while I'm here. He forced the drawer on one side to straighten it out, when he heard a ripping sound, coming from the side support. Probably something stuck, too, he muttered aloud.

He stood to the side and searched the drawer slide carefully now, and noticed a torn triangle of paper partly revealed. Aha! There's the culprit! He drew it out the rest of the way slowly, so as not to tear it further.

Without another thought, he opened the scrap of paper to read it. What he saw froze his very blood. He gasped, took a step backward to steady himself. He stared at the familiar writing – that of his friend, young Judd.

When his mind cleared he sat on the bed to read what was left of the torn letter. Broken phrases, but enough to make known what happened here a month since; *...to see booty had been buried....of the Captain of the wreck LOUISA... Trunk reported stolen by newspapers... As a lawyer, I am sworn to report...*

Oh, no, Smith, thought Andrew. Oh no, no, no...

*****

By the end of that week, illness struck the house. "Andrew's cold upon the chest seems to have gotten worse," remarked Hannah to her husband. "He's taken to his bed now, today, a fever setting in."

"Wa'al he shouldn't a gone swimming at dusk like he did and stayed out on the dunes. Caught his own chill he did. His own fault. Shoulda' known better," complained Oaks.

"Go in and see him. You've been gone these two days with the hunting party, and he's been asking for you. Go on now. He's your only brother."

"I know who he is, Hannah."

Oaks delayed seeing him until he packed away all his hunting gear and cleaned his guns properly. He shouldn't a' said nothin', Oaks muttered to himself over and over as he applied oil to the barrel. He's all'as made his own problems, that un. He's all's spoke when he shouldn' a'.

That angry run-in with Andrew before he left for hunting weighed heavily on Smith's mind during the whole trip. Confrontation caused the brothers' old rivalries and angers to arise instantly. First a push. Who first? Then as naturally as breathing, they came to blows, Smith, defensive.

Who the *hell* is he t' question me?... In my own place?... Come out here to tell *me* what's right? Smith had thoroughly convinced himself that concerning Judd, there had been no wrongdoing on his part. A man gits to hold and keep 'is territory, no matter what... no matter what.

I sure told him good, thought Smith, the argument revolving in his mind over and over.

Been waitin' all these three years since the wreck of the *Louisa*. All that booty's worth a fortune. Gold rings, diamond brooches. Shawls woven with real silver thread. Statute o' limitations' all's clear now. Nob'dy kin' say it ain't mine. Now's the time to unload and make some money. After all these three years, now, I hold onto it all….and, my luck, here comes trouble snoopin' around my bus'ness.

Don't know when I'd get another hit like that one.

Gettin' too old for this life, anyways. Gotta move to the main island someday.

Man's gotta make a livin' that's all. Man's gotta make a livin' by what ya' can out here, that's all. If the sea brings you treasure, brings it right to your very door, it's for you to take and say thank ye.

Fishin' and duck huntin ain't gonna get ya' too far, that's fer sure. Oaks' thoughts in repeated arguments justified his actions in his own mind.

"Stupid, stupid boy that Judd," concluded Smith to Andrew that night of their argument. "Brought it on hisself, he did. Shoulda' kept his mouth shut, 'at's all."

Andrew wept in horrified shock as to what his brother had become. This was way past his lies and thievery, he thought. And he defends his actions, and vindicates himself! Nearly in a stupor, though early evening, Andrew went to the sea to swim and to think of what to do.

24

Hannah reported to Oaks next evening, "Cold sponging isn't helping. Fever's getting worse."

Oaks just stared straight ahead. No reply. She had become used to his non-response when she spoke to him, so Hannah continued, "Started with laudanum today. Just brewed out the poppy seeds myself. Made it strong. Mixed it with sage leaves and wine. A drachm morning and evening, that's all, no more or it becomes dangerous."

Hannah placed the laudanum on the kitchen shelf, high, so Marietta couldn't get to it. "I'll keep him on the medicine schedule. Should bring down that fever."

"That's the way Hannah," said Oaks, finally. His eyes held a strange light. "Yep. Laudanum. That'll do the trick."

"Poor Andrew seems upset about something. But with the fever, he barely makes sense. His eyes keep drillin' into mine, as if to say something important."

"Oh yeah? What's *he* got to say?"

"Don't know. Fever's got him confused, I suppose." She opened the back door, "Got to empty the washbasin out back. Get him some fresh."

Oaks turned to Hannah as she stepped over the threshold, "By the way, anyone come by lookin' fer me t'day?"

"Lightkeeper needed you. Selah Strong sent a man. Think he wanted some help movin' a surfboat. Told him Andrew's sick, and you were clamming on the bay."

"Good," replied Oaks.

25

Fall approaches quickly on a barrier island. Cool nights make quick work of any vegetation left in the summer garden. "Best to clear this out on a sunny day, right Marietta? Help Mama, and we can get this finished before long."

Hannah loved the work. Using her long fingers and her strong grip, the spent plantings yielded their place in the ground easily. In her mind, she was already planning next year's garden as she worked; perhaps I'll try to grow beans instead; or move the lettuce to the back of the garden, away from the ocean breezes, and put the hardy cucumber vines up front instead…

Just then, her hand felt something foreign in the soil. Not vegetation, but something smooth and cold. Grasping, she pulled a half buried vial from the soil.

What's this… she wondered aloud, sweeping away the dirt with her fingers. Then surprised, she made out her apothecary bottle that she used for laudanum, the only one she owned, which had gone missing right around the time of Andrew's illness. What on earth… she said aloud, in puzzlement… How could this have ended up here? Her heart leapt to her throat with the unthinkable.

"How could *what* end up here?" asked Marietta.

Just then, a familiar figure was seen approaching. "It's Mrs. Dominy, Mama," said Marietta, her arms full of dead stalks.

Caught now in her confusion, she slipped the dirt-crusted bottle into her apron pocket to face her friend.

"Hello neighbors! We've come to visit so the children can play with Marietta," said Phebe to Hannah and Marietta in the garden. Marietta's eyes, in puzzlement, searched for her friends.

"Such an angel, she is," said Phebe when she saw Marietta's face brighten as she spotted the others on the shore. "Go to the beach to play, dear."

"Oh yes!" She turned, "May I, Mother?"

"Of course!" Phebe answered for Hannah. "And the Strongs are there, too. Mary and Antionetta from the lighthouse; and Conrad and Bradish Johnson, who are staying at the inn, too. Go run on now, dear."

Hannah gave Marietta a forced smile and a nod to go ahead. Hannah then straightened, turned and faced Phebe.

"How nice of you to come," said Hannah, taking her arm in friendship.

"A good day to take the children for a long walk" replied Phebe. "We are not busy at the inn today, so I took along Susan's two eldest. And Helen Johnson is spending the day to enjoy the ocean, so her two came along too. We've had quite a romp today!" she said. "Anyway, its good for the children to all play together while the weather is fine."

The two women strolled slowly toward the house. Phebe began, "I really came to check in on you, dear. Felix and I are so worried about you! You look so thin and pale of late. Two tragedies to bear this summer! First young Judd; then Andrew, too?"

Without waiting for a reply, Phebe continued, "And to think, my Felix sailed Andrew to the island, just days before! Such a pleasant man he said he was, and the picture of health, too!"

"Yes, poor Andrew. A severe cold upon the chest after swimming. Then, a complication of disorders that led to an affectation of the heart," recited Hannah woodenly.

"We all read that in the papers, dear. That is exactly what was said," remarked Phebe with worry. "But, how do *you* hold up?"

"Prayer and fasting is the way to the Lord," said Hannah.

"Yes, of course, dear. But look at you! And we worry about Marietta, too! And you, here so remote, with no company other than…"

Just then, Oaks was seen striding toward the house from the bay. Even from a distance, his form, unmistakable.

Hannah watched him. Long, lean, strong. Something menacing in his posture when he moves. Something menacing about him always, even in rest, she knew.

Oaks stopped short when he saw his nearest neighbor. "You a'gin, Phebe? Whats'a matter? Dominy don' keep you busy enough? Not enough for ye t' do at the inn, so you comin' 'round here a'gin?"

Phebe, ignoring his glare, retorted, "You should be happy to see me, Smith. I have news for Hannah that her reputation as a seamstress has spread to the home of Mrs. John D. Johnson of Islip, one of the wealthiest families on the south shore. She's here at the inn for the day… and she asked after Hannah. Want's to know if Hannah will sew for her."

Phebe turned toward Hannah. "Will you dear? She's a lovely woman." Then she turned back to Smith, adding, "And that'll bring *you* in a pretty penny, too, sir! More than the mending and embroidery paid for by the village ladies!"

Hannah's eyes dropped, absently fingering the crusted bottle in her apron pocket. She knew how much Smith hated anyone knowing his business. Phebe was only digging herself more deeply into his distrust the more she spoke.

"Marietta's playing with the other children, Smith," interrupted Hannah, pointing toward the shore.

"Yes. A fine day for that!" exclaimed Phebe. "Meanwhile, I was hoping to entice Hannah to offer me some tea. She could use some too, I reckon. She's looking mighty thin these days."

"Of course Phebe," said Hannah, ignoring Oaks' look of displeasure. "It's kind of you to take time to see us for the afternoon. I have fresh jam and biscuits today."

26

"How bad was it for poor Andrew?" asked Phebe as soon as the kettle boiled and they were settled in the kitchen.

"Convulsions at first. Went from fever to cold clammy skin in a night. The worst was the look in his eye. He kept at me directly, though he couldn't talk sense. He kept drilling those eyes into mine. Like he wanted to say something." Hannah got quiet suddenly. Her mind drifted away with the memory.

Laudanum bottle went missing, she thought. Now it's in the garden. No one else in the house but...

"Dear...? Dear!" Phebe spoke, touching Hannah's arm. " Hannah, you aren't paying attention... You were saying?"

"Oh," Hannah continued. "We had to ship his body back to Brooklyn for the burial. Smith will be going in a few days to close up his business."

"You needn't be alone here, Hannah, handling all this sadness on your own. Come to the inn for a while with Marietta. We've plenty of room."

PART IV

27

Margaret in Rome
October 1847

Her new situation in Rome was on the Via Del Corso, near the Piazza del Popolo and across from the entrance to the Borghese Gardens. Her building was large and baroque with tall imposing windows, from which she could see all that goes on in Rome. Her rooms were adequate and airy, and with a good hearth to ward off the cold in winter's dark months. Her landlady, Bernadetta, was eccentric but manageable. Each left the other to her privacy.

It was not long before Margaret realized the comings and goings at strange hours of a tall stately looking man. Judging from the erratic timing of his visits, Margaret surmised that this must be Bernadetta's consort. This left Margaret feeling secure about allowing Giovanni's liberal visits, their own relationship in its stage of newness and discovery.

Intimacy grew, their lives and desires intertwining, a sharing of a future to plan. Vivid heed had to be paid to all political events of Europe, as their future became intertwined with that of Italy's. Margaret filled Giovanni in on the progression of revolutions and protests on the continent, while Giovanni filled Margret in on the change in the political atmosphere in Rome while she was away.

"The Liberals boldly embrace Pope Pius as their leader. He opened up the strictures of the former papacy by offering some general representation in government by the people: they formed a *consulta*, a Council of State."

"It's no wonder he is so loved, then. He seems truly to make an effort to hear the voice of the people," replied Margaret.

"Yes," agreed Giovanni, "it would seem so among many; but the conservatives scream in protest of any increased freedoms, while the radical liberals claim that his "freedoms" are only half-measures. They want more, and they make that known with unruly demonstrations in the streets. Talk of revolution and tensions among factions increase daily."

Margaret and Giovanni found themselves deeply engrossed in the progress of the liberal movement. Giovanni believed strongly that this Pope would represent the needs of the people.

"And in order to ensure public safety with the increasing demonstrations, he instituted a *Guardia Civica,* a Civic Guard. A bold move, to allow a militia made up of ordinary citizens."

"Why is it considered bold?"

"To arm the *multitude?*" he returned.

Margaret reconsidered her question. "I see. Of course. From that perspective."

"However, that is not *my* perspective. I am very proud of my decision to volunteer."

"Giovanni!" she replied, surprised. "You are part of this? When? Why?"

"I joined while you traveled north. Margharita, I want to serve. I want to be a part of a force of citizens who can do some good. Not just stand by in idle talk."

"That is admirable," she acquiesced. Thinking further on the consequences, she asked, "But what of your family? Your brothers serve in the Vatican, do they not? They are members of the Pope's Noble Guard, aren't they? What do they say?"

"Ha!" replied Giovanni derisively. "The mere existence of the Civic Guard flies in their faces. They openly despise us. My brothers, among others of noble birth are blinded by self-interest. They are most threatened by giving power to the people."

A deep silence filled the room. He, visibly upset, recalling family confrontation on this matter.

After a moment, Giovanni continued: "Margharita, what my brothers say does not matter to me. We have been at odds over many years. This is merely one in a string of countless disagreements."

Margaret took this in, her expression revealing concern.

He explained, "This is the time to act. Now. Mere discussion of a democratic ideal yields nothing."

Margaret conceded, thinking of America's own history, its yearning for independence. The heroism of those who took action yielded the great democracy of *America*.

Giovanni continued, impassioned, "Our beloved Pope has granted us reforms. This is the momentum we need to make a change! He has even allowed our political exiles to return home after Pope Gregory had banished them. With amnesty, they are home with their families again."

"Yes, Giovanni. His liberalism is well known," replied Margaret. "But aren't those returnees the same men who cry for a Revolution?"

"Yes, there are several who have made their way into the *Consulta*. Like Angelo Brunetti, especially. They call him *Ciceruacchio*, 'The Big Boy,' …with affection, of course."

Margaret looked puzzled.

Giovanni laughed, explaining, "He is a large man with a loud voice and a big personality; a *popolano* who made money in horse dealing and wine distribution."

"Oh, I see," she smiled at the joke. "But with that background, he's a man who could probably convince anyone of anything," remarked Margaret dryly.

"This is true, Giovanni mused, "He is one of the most influential supporters of a liberal papacy. His was the voice for the people that got the Civic Guard started last July. And now, since Pius relaxed the censorship of the press, his voice spreads widely to the people."

"Pius' liberal changes have caused him much dismay," admitted Margaret. "There were rumors that the ecclesiastical conservatives were guilty of a failed coup last July."

"Yes. Hearsay is that the purpose of the plot was to show the Austrians that Pius is unable to keep order in his own territory. The conservatives were hoping to incite the Austrian occupation of Rome. But the Civic Guard was called out and handled the crisis admirably. Arrests and interrogations were made quickly, and order was restored. The slogan, *Let us show Europe that we suffice unto ourselves* rang out among all citizens of Rome."

"And still, the conservatives see the Civic Guard as a threat?"

"Of course!" Giovanni then added, "The conservatives are wary. They feel that the Civic Guard could potentially end up serving the powerful clubs, like the *Circulo Romano* led by the dangerous radicals; that is the risk of having 'the people in arms.'

But we are committed. Our sworn purpose is to Pope Pius, that of an armed force to prevent violence by the crowd and to protect property. We believe that Pius will lead us to freedom and independence from the Austrian oppressor."

"But, are the conservatives right? Is there a chance that the clubs become so powerful that the Civic Guard passes out of the control of the Papal government?"

"There is a chance of anything happening if it comes to a revolution," he replied. "Look at what is happening! The Austrians have sent 70,000 troops to Lombardy, Venetia and Ferrara. It is said that the Austrian Emperor is fearful of the political unrest here, and he is determined not to lose 'his' Italian territories."

"The people are fed up, Margharita. Tired of being overlooked! We, as a people, are nothing to him! He wrote in an open letter to the

European kings, saying that 'Italy is merely a *geographic expression.'* To them, we, as a people, do not even exist."

Giovanni rose, and then approached Margaret, adding, "It is time for a united Italy, ruled by Italians."

"Together, Giovanni, you and I will work for a free and independent Italy," replied Margaret, her voice resonant with emotion.

"I know of your passion. You understand what we as a people yearn for. It is what you in America have earned through your revolution against the English. And with your talents and public fame, Margharita, you can express our hopes to the world. Your respected reputation lends power to our cause," urged Giovanni.

"Of course! I have a loyal readership at home in a national newspaper. I can explain the righteousness of the cause. My exhortation of the purity of the Young Italy movement will sway the American people to see the honor in it. The United States must officially recognize that Italy's movement for independence is justified. America leads. And when it does, that influence will be felt by others."

Early evening approached. Their early supper ended, Giovanni stoked the fire while Margaret closed the windows against the damp fall chill.

"I must leave you now, Margharita. My father needs me. He is very weak in his old age."

"Will you come tomorrow?" asked Margaret.

"After duty at my post, of course I will."

"The brewing of revolution stirs the souls of us all," said Margaret to her young companion as he took her into his arms.

"Yes," he murmured, his lips finding hers, "our chance meeting a few months ago seems not so much chance as it is destiny, now, *Mia Cara.*"

Here, in this place and in this endeavor, and with this man pure and fervent, Margaret had found her new home.

28

Rome
November 1847

Margaret's concerns for Giovanni's political split with his family were insightful. Revolutionary leanings were anathema in his family. Italy as a Republic was unthinkable; more than that, a blasphemy in an aristocratic family. The noble name of Ossoli, as an entity, has existed through generations and in the same houses on the same properties and with the same convictions for centuries.

Arriving home, early twilight, his sister, Angela greeted him.

"Late again, eh, Giovanni?" He answered only with a shy smile. She continued, "Father has been asking for you. Bring up his supper while you see him, will you? He is too weak to come down to the table. He will enjoy your company…maybe you can encourage him to eat more… distract him with talk, the news of the day."

Angela finished setting up the tray with a light supper and a small vase with a single flower. She handed it over to Giovanni saying, "Go to him. He waits. And don't forget….be *cheerful*."

Giovanni knocked and entered the darkened bedroom. "Papa, I am here," he said, settling the tray on a nearby table.

"Ahhh, Giovanni, my son." The old man's voice was weak and hoarse, his body wasting, thin and haggard. Giovanni kissed him on the forehead, then helped him from the bed to a comfortable chair.

"There. You look so much better sitting up, Papa." He placed a lap blanket neatly on his legs to keep the chill away. "I will draw the drapes to let in what's left of the light. There will be a colorful sunset tonight."

The aroma of the supper now permeated the room and piqued his father's appetite. A bit of wine relaxed them both, and oiled the conversation. "I see you are in your uniform, Giovanni. *Guardia Civica*. Hmmm."

Giovanni did not reply.

"Your sentiments are such that the *Guardia Nobile* does not suit you?"

"Papa. We have been through this before," Giovanni answered. Only his love and respect for his father helped him to keep exasperation out of his voice. "You know that I feel I can serve better in the *Civic Guard*. Here I serve the *people* of Rome," he said, patting the insignia on his chest.

What Giovanni left unsaid was his hope that Pius IX will not remain embedded with the European monarchies of France and Spain and Austria. His desire was to support and protect the people while Pius leads Italy to freedom from European rule.

Understanding the silence, his father placed his fork on the table quietly. He said, simply, "As you wish, Giovanni."

Sitting back to lean his tired frame on the chair, his father continued, "You know your brothers do not approve of your politics. The family is divided, which troubles me. And, according to tradition, the eldest is the estate's executor when I am gone."

Giovanni listened respectfully.

His father paused in thought, gazing out of the window for a moment to consider his next words carefully, "I know there is an *Americana* with you in your life now."

Giovanni kept silent, surprised that in his condition his family would have told him. Giovanni marveled at his brother's greed.

Giovanni then said, "Yes, Papa. Her name is Margharita."

"Yes. A writer, I understand."

"Yes, Papa."

"*Donna Protestante?*"

"Yes."

The old man let out a small sigh, then waited, deep in thought. He then said, "You must govern your life for yourself, Giovanni. If you love her, then she is yours. You have chosen."

The old man's hands, fingers intertwined, moved slowly to rest in his lap. He continued, "My wishes are for you to be treated fairly when I am gone, with all rights to the Ossoli name and lineage for your children. But your brothers are strong minded, and have a great deal of influence in the Vatican."

His voice now began to sound strained, becoming raspy, and he became winded with the effort to speak. He waited a moment, then cleared his throat and continued, "You realize the law in Rome is not above ecclesiastical influence. Your politics and your choice of a *Protestante Americana* will not stand well with your brothers. If they decide to protest my will in court, their influence will serve them well. And I won't be here to defend your rights, my son."

"Papa. Do not worry about such things. I can take care of myself with them."

Giovanni rose and began to clear the dishes from the table, food only half eaten. "For now, just concentrate on getting your rest. Winter is coming, and you will need your strength."

Then, to brighten up the conversation, Giovanni added, "I want you to come outdoors in the springtime to see the walking path I made for you there. It leads to a nice sunny spot for you sit to enjoy the gardens."

But seeing how quickly his father tired, he hoped his father would make it to the spring. He rang for the nurse to ready his father for bed.

"Good night, Papa," Giovanni said, kissing his father on the cheek. "May the angels grant you restful sleep." He left his father's room, the heavy door closing solidly behind him.

*****

Now, with a quiet evening before him, Giovanni's mind remained restless. He knows his father's concerns are well founded. He knows clearly his brother's disapproval and their power.

One brother, Giuseppe, is older than Giovanni by twenty-one years. The gap in age had always lent to his air of authority over his youngest brother. Giuseppe is highest placed among the Ossoli in the Vatican, serving as the Secretary to the Pope's Privy Council. The other two, Ottovino and Allesasandro serve as *Guardia Nobilia*. All three frown on Giovanni's relationship with Margaret, and feel that her influence is the cause of Giovanni's liberal stance. It is clear that they will not brook any threat to their ultra conservative stronghold in the political power structure.

In the end, they are destined to be the benefactors of the family's standing. They watch their cousin Pietro carefully, he the next Marchese Ossoli. Only his demise would insure the title's shift to Giuseppe as next in line.

But Giovanni has had enough of it all. He has heard with disgust about titles and inheritance for his entire life. He had witnessed the avarice of his brothers, the sacred title bandied about the family as an elusive prize. And the elder brothers taunted Giovanni that for him, as youngest by decades, the prize would likely remain just out of reach.

The best legacy Giovanni can hope for now is his portion of his father's estate and property as a modest annual stipend, and a place in the family tree for his offspring. And now, with his and Margaret's liberalism, his brothers would have an excuse, whether from spite, or from greed, or from family loyalty, to influence a court decision for distribution of property and titular rights if their father's will goes to probate.

It is no surprise, then that Giovanni's politics are liberal. He identifies with the many, the *popolo*, the ordinary citizens who labor, yet have no say in their existence and their fate. I feel for the people of Italy, he thinks, embittered, because I feel *like* them. I know their frustration. I will fight for the voice of the people so that all may have a say in their governance and in their lives.

His brothers' have held their "familial rights" over him like a dark shadow over his life. But now, he is tired of them, and is tired of hearing about their positions of power. What they don't realize yet, Giovanni reflected, is that they are part of an archaic system whose days are numbered. They will soon see. The rise of the *popolo* will level the playing field...for us all!

This, the source of his quiet fury, fuels his revolutionary fervor. This is the necessary change for which the liberal Pope Pius will break the bonds of the families royal of Austria, France and of Spain, who rule over a land that does not belong to them, and who strangle and dominate the lives of the many.

Now is the changing of the tide for Rome, for Giovanni, and for the Italian people. A new world order will emerge.

29

This day, Giovanni was awakened before dawn to an insistent banging on the door of the family villa. He sprang from his bed to answer before his sister and brother-in-law were awakened.

At the front door was a messenger with an official communiqué from the office of Colonel Tittoni, Commanding Officer of the First Battalion, Civic Guard. A special set of duty orders, to report, instead of to his post, to headquarters on that day. Puzzled and curious, he dismissed the courier and dressed hurriedly.

There, in Colonel Tittoni's outer office sat a committee of officers, and save Giovanni's immediate commander, none did he recognize. He stood at attention after his salute, waiting.

Colonel Tittoni began: "We are here to congratulate you, Sergeant Giovanni Ossoli, on your tenure of duty excellently performed. And we, the officers of the Command wish to congratulate you on your consideration for promotion to the rank of Sergeant Major. You will be assigned a unit in the Fourth Battalion, and with it, a special duty."

"Sir!" He accepted with a sharp salute. He stood at attention until Colonel Tittoni said, "At ease, and join the officers at the table, Sergeant Major. We have some business to discuss."

"Now, as you know," Tittoni continued, "our duty is to protect the citizens of Rome and to provide safety.

With the latest developments, we find ourselves in a delicate situation. The people we are sworn to protect are in danger. Reports of brutality at the hands of the European Monarchies have gone unanswered by Papal authority.

The Austrian army murdered unarmed civilians in the Milan riots, then just days later they killed ten student protesters at the University in Padua. And now people of Palermo are being killed in their protests against the Bourbon King Ferdinand.

There is fighting on many fronts, north and south. Our own people are unsafe on their own soil and in their own homes and towns. Foreign governments invade with impunity, and Pope Pius makes no move to defend his people."

All at the table looked grave, eyes steady. Not one made a gesture. Tittoni registered the somber looks of the men, and continued, "The anger among the Italian people is mounting, and the power of the revolutionary clubs is growing, particularly the *Circolo Romano.* More and more civilians join in their secret meetings. They feel they need protection, and that the conservative Vatican government is failing them. They are afraid. And the revolutionaries who are among those representatives who serve in the Pope's lay councils become more powerful daily. It is thought they will soon control the vote."

All at the table realized the gravity, not only for the safety of the people, but that the power structure was shifting under their feet. And what of the Civic Guard? Is it our duty remain loyal to a Pope who does not seem to protect his own people?

Giovanni surveyed the men at the table. He wondered how he figured in on all of this. He, the lowest rank among the group. Why was he chosen to be at this meeting?

Tittoni continued, "We have some intelligence that there are spies among us in the Civic Guard. They pretend to be loyal to the Pope, but are instead revolutionaries who want chaos and disorder spread in order to overthrow the government Pius is trying to create. They believe he is weak, and will lead us into disorder and chaos.

And the Vatican has its spies, too. They attend the meetings of the revolutionary clubs and carry all the news and information straight to the Vatican's Privy Council."

Giovanni's mind raced as he began to see his role.

"These spies are the hotbed of the conservative movement," continued Tittoni. "This is the very Council who is trying to destroy the Civic Guard. They continue to lobby for our dissolution, and see us as a potential threat to Papal power."

Tittoni took a breath. "Gentleman, our very existence is being threatened from within. And Pius' weakness against the foreign monarchs fuels his enemies."

Giovanni tensed, now thinking of his eldest brother, Giuseppe. He is in the Pope's Privy Council. He must be receiving all of this intelligence from the Vatican spies. Does Tittoni know how high up the Ossoli are established in the Papal government? Should he reveal the extent of his brother's ties to Pope Pius? But Giovanni stayed silent, listening.

"As for you, Sergeant Major," Tittoni turned to face him directly, "Now with your new rank, you will be placed in one of the most visible assignments. We are hoping you will be contacted by those inside the Vatican to become one of their Civic Guard spies. If that happens, we want you to reveal the contacts to us immediately. We need to know who can be trusted."

"Yes sir." Giovanni assented.

"Oh, and one more thing. One of the men assigned to your unit is Luigi Brunetti, youngest son of *Ciceruacchio*. Keep an eye on him for us, won't you?"

*****

Giovanni reported to his duty assignment that morning, troubled. What had seemed to Ossoli a clear commitment to the citizens now seemed cloudy. Factions, spies, counterspies; infighting and dissention. To Giovanni, the cause was clear and simple. But after this meeting, it seemed that confusion reigned.

And, ultimately, there would be no release from the significance of his family name, it seemed, not even in the Civic Guard, where he thought he could strike out on his own, and be a force for right and freedom.

No, it was all too much. The spot promotion. The setup to be approached as a spy. The son of the most powerful radical placed in his unit. He mused, Tittoni has to know that my brother Giuseppe is in the Privy Council... And suddenly, the young Brunetti in my command? I am right in the center of the brewing conflict, a hub for opposing forces. I must tread carefully.

30

January 1848

Margaret found herself beset by illness, barely leaving her rooms in the cold dampness of January. Blinding headaches kept her abed, and waves of nausea engulfed her for days on end.

Giovanni insisted that a doctor be called.

"No, no. I am used to the headaches. I have had them since childhood," said Margaret. Giovanni, exasperated, answered with an imploring look.

"You must eat, then, if only a taste," exhorted Giovanni.

"Yes, my dear. I will as I can. Food only seems to upset my stomach now. I enjoy the broths Bernadetta brings to me. She has been so helpful and kind."

"It's these ceaseless rains and damp cold, returned Giovanni. "Our winters here are very disagreeable."

"In such a wet atmosphere, and deprived of exercise, I find myself without strength and without appetite."

"You know the solution, Margharita," he gazed at her lovingly. "Marry me so we can be together always. I will take care of you and nurture all of your needs."

"Oh, Giovanni, she returned softly and with care, "We've considered that carefully so many times. You know I love you fully and completely.

But as to marriage? What does it offer to us? We already have our love and commitment to each other. And what additional pain could it cause to you and your family?"

They could see that the same family politics that caused Giovanni's yearning to serve in the Civic Guard also complicated their personal lives. Liberal leanings. Freedoms. Margaret the republican, correspondent of Mazzini, the radical, could never be acceptable to his family. She stood for everything that wanted to dismantle the ancient power structure in which the Ossoli were embedded.

No, there was too much to lose.

Margaret knew that a marriage to her would forever put him at odds with his family. And even though he was already estranged from his brothers, this marriage could cause a rift in the family's structure into perpetuity.

Giovanni knew clearly what was at risk. Despite this, he said, "Marry me, Margharita, or I shall be miserable."

"For now, let us make our relationship as deep and as meaningful without entering into a partnership of daily life."

Giovanni, once again, accepted the impasse.

With as much brevity as he could manage, he told Margaret of the troubling events of the day, starting with the pre-dawn messenger at the door of the family villa and the spot promotion. He expressed his concern for the precarious situation he found himself in. Despite her illness, she listened with her usual concentration and concern.

At Giovanni's conclusion, he looked to her for her perspective.

"Where does he stand, Giovanni? Tittoni. Is he reliable?"

"He is the Commanding Officer of the Civic Guard. Sworn to the Pope and the protection of public order. Politically, he is loyal to Pius. But, I am sure that he knows that the noble name of Ossoli is connected to the Vatican. I am sure he wants to use that tie against the conservative spies."

"But the Civic Guard was formed by the Pope's *Consulta* and championed by Ciceruacchio, no?"

"Yes, Margharita. There's the confusion. Pius invited both the radicals and the conservative factions into the *Consulta* so all feel they have a say, but instead, affiliations and loyalties have become muddled, and are only getting worse. conservatives, radicals, revolutionaries… Dissention increases daily, and alliances change with the wind."

"And of course, Tittoni has no idea that you are all but estranged from your brother. Where does he think that *your* sympathies lie, Giovanni?"

"Good question. I wish I knew the answer."

Giovanni's face was clouded in thought. He saw only trouble lying ahead.

"The only solution then is to behave in line with your own conscience," said Margaret thoughtfully. "Always keep in mind why you enlisted, and act accordingly."

31

Unrest in Rome
January 1848

Milan is being torn asunder!
   Yes, tearing asunder to build anew!
   Away with the tyranny of the Austrian Empire!

These are the cries on the street, in the marketplace and it seems in every household.

And in Rome, a march to the University Church by the members of the Civic Guard to pray for the souls of their fallen brethren, and of all those killed by Austrian troops in the Milan uprising, and those University student protesters, murdered by their troops in Padua.

Sergeant Major Giovanni Ossoli accompanied his men in silent reverence there.

As they marched toward the church, the streets became thick with all who wished to attend. The crowd that surrounded the stone edifice was immense. Giovanni and his men could barely squeeze inside…the huge church was filled to the brink. All the studious youths, the noble and illustrious citizens of Rome attired in deep mourning wearing cypress branches in their coats. Despite its numbers, the crowd maintained a devout and profound silence, the church echoing only with solemn chants in reply to the prayers of the priests.

Then suddenly, a scuffle and raucous movement of men began among the otherwise orderly crowd. "Look there, Sergeant Major, said Private Trentanove, "Could be trouble starting… Shall we intervene?"

Trentanove was one of his sharpest young soldiers. He was smart, dedicated, and willing to use calm and logic before action. Ossoli considered him as potential officer material. But Trentanove was always in the shadow of his closest ally, the hot-headed Luigi Brunetti, who doesn't let an opportunity go by to proclaim that his father is the famous *Ciceruacchio*. And like his father, the young Brunetti was always willing to use violence at the slightest provocation.

Giovanni watched the crowd before deciding whether to order any action. After a moment, he replied to Trentanove, "No need. It is Father Gavazzi among us. He has been recognized. They seek him."

A devout leader of the movement for independence, Father Gavazzi was spotted among the crowd praying. Well known as a powerful speaker for a United Italy, he had been censured by Pope Pius, who too late realized the fervor that his liberal policies had unleashed among the people. Pius, however, did not want to support a radical a position against the monarchies of Europe. So, much to the disappointment of the people, he condemned Gavazzi to public silence.

On this day however, Gavazzi was recognized in the church, and word quickly spread among the youths, radical and strong of purpose. They called for him to disregard the Papal order and to ascend the pulpit.

He dutifully refused the request, but they were not taking "no" for an answer. The crowd, no longer in silent reverence, demanded to hear him. He was approached by the young and strong, picked up bodily and carried thither.

At the pulpit, he acquiesced. He rose to his full height, commanding and proud. Then, in a voice that started with deep mourning, sounding almost pathetic and broken, he spoke of the honor of sacrifice for a just cause. As he continued, gaining momentum and power, the force of his voice deepened, then raised to a mighty pitch, arousing all within to unite, to sacrifice, to fight to the death, for only that will result in the creation of a nation: an undivided, self-governed Italy!

"It is right and just! As all of Europe burns with desire for independence, Berlin, Vienna, Budapest! All citizens of Europe rise up against their monarchs. Venice declares independence from Austria while Milan still seethes and mourns its dead, the heroes who faced the Austrian oppressor!"

Gavazzi could see the effect of his words upon the crowd. He saw upturned faces transported, mesmerized. Young men's eyes aglaze with the fight, anger and righteousness prevailing. Other faces, aghast with tragic memories of battles in the streets, streaming with tears. Gavazzi continued, the feverish pitch of his voice rising yet more.

The crowd roused beyond control, now roared their approval. Some sang hymns of praise to a just God. Some cried for their loss of loved ones in the battle. Some shouted against the Austrians who wrongly occupy Italian soil.

Then a hush when Gavazzi continued, as he condemned the monarchies for their atrocities against the Italian people. "To fight and win against centuries of power! Il popolo! The power lies with us! God supports right! God supports the people!" He enumerated the savagery perpetrated upon the innocents, utterance intense, and when at its utmost, cried, "Out! Out with the barbarians!"

The youth of Rome transfixed by Gavazzi's severe and inspired voice, joined in a repeated, frenzied chorus, *Out! Out with the barbarians!*

Now all, all spilled out of the church, and into the streets. *Out! Out with the barbarians!* The rallying call gained power with the momentum of the masses.

Giovanni was pushed out of the church with the crowd, as it dispersed into groups who stood now, shouts increasing in strength, arms waving, emotions escalating, watching for Gavazzi to emerge from the ancient doorway.

Ossoli, with his men, made their way to a position where they could observe, ready for action, but hoping for a peaceful demonstration.

"Rome is alive with the fever for revolution," he said to his men. Then, "Steady. Steady, all. The streets seethe with fury."

He stood rapt with attention to the crowd with Trentanove and the young Brunetti and the rest of his men, young and willing.

PART V

32

Fire Island, New York
1847

The single sail caught the stiff wind, and he felt like he was flying. A swift sail on the bay, thought Smith Oaks. So much better than living in Brooklyn. There it was crowded, houses jammed together in rows. Not like here. The sky is open and blue, sunshine, high and dry. Not much trouble to close out Andrew's business, he recalled. Not much trouble at all. I should make it home in no time, his stomach rumbling hungrily, eagerly anticipating supper on the table.

From his dock, he could sense the emptiness of the house. No wash hanging on a dry day like today? he thought. No Marietta playing outside? No smoke from the chimney?

He tied up quickly, and approached the kitchen door. Shut tight, Smith unlatched it and swung it open, hard, banging it against the wall adjacent. He was not a man who liked the unexpected. He scanned the room quickly.

Inside, the hearth swept clean looking like it has been cold for days. Bedrooms left neat and tidy, but empty. Gone, he thought. Right from the time I left for Brooklyn, prob'ly.

He spun on his heel for the dock immediately, grumbling all the way. Man's wife should be home a'waitin' fer 'im. Mus' be that nosy Phebe a'gin. Puttin' ideas in 'er head. Should mind 'er own damn bus'ness.

The catboat swung out over the bay quickly for the sail west to Dominy's Inn.

33

A pleasant place built up and enlarged over time, the inn had met with great success. The owner, Felix Dominy snagged a lot of business as sportsman's guide, while Phebe ran the inn, cooking up the catch and keeping rooms neat and clean for the guests.

Of course, Felix had an advantage to grow his business. He was a local insider. Dominy's antecedents left New England for Long Island in the 1600's, and quickly became well known as clockmakers and craftsmen.

Generations later, Felix himself had been the lighthouse keeper on Fire Island; until he got caught allowing paying guests to stay there overnight to do some ocean fishing. The U.S. government didn't take kindly to his using Federal land for personal profit, and asked him to leave his post.

It was the best thing that ever happened to him. He went a mile east, bought some land and built a thriving business, doing what he loves.

Oaks soon arrived and tied up his boat at Dominy's dock. He was, by now, seething muttering and swearing as he headed for the inn from the dock.

And there's the scoundrel himself, said Smith Oaks aloud, catching sight of Dominy.

Felix was digging to repair his garden fence. He saw Oaks, stopped his work, stood tall, shovel in hand beside him, waiting. He greeted Smith, "Sorry 'bout Andrew," he said.

"Thank ye," replied Oaks absently as squinted into the sun. He spat into the sand.

Oaks surveyed the property, then turned toward the inn. "My wife and young'n here? Yr keepin' 'em inside?" he spoke, more of a statement than a question.

"They're inside. But Hannah isn't a prisoner. We're not *keepin'* her. She came of her own accord," replied Dominy, meeting Oaks' challenging attitude square on.

"Go on inside the parlor. Phebe's there." Dominy turned away from Oaks, dismissively. He dug his shovel into the sandy soil.

Oaks strode purposefully toward the door.

Sure'd like to use this shovel on him someday, Felix muttered aloud, vexed.

34

Oaks was furious, and he had no intention of hiding it. On Dominy's dock, he angrily threw Hannah's bags into the catboat, shouting at her, "What'r ye doin' stayin' here, anyways? Wife's suppos'd t' be home. *Home*, Hannah!"

"Please! Not in front of Marietta!" Hannah protectively stepped in front of the child. Marietta, however, stood sill, nonplussed, quite used to his outbursts.

"Don' care 'bout her and *what* she hears," he snapped. "And DON' tell me what to do! Now git in the boat, the both o' ya'."

Hannah stood. She stood, for the first time against him.

Oaks glared in disbelief.

"That damned Phebe git to ye? Now yer *defyin'* me, right here in the open?" His voice was at a pitch now, his face red and veins popping as if to burst. His body twisted, raised arm toward her, his open hand slapping Hannah hard across her face.

Caught off guard, the force caused her to lose her balance. She tottered, nearly off the dock and into the bay. Tears sprang to her eyes, but she would not let them fall. She would not let him see that he'd hurt her. She regained her balance and faced him. She hissed into his face, "I don't care *who* hears and *what* they think anymore, Smith! *This* has gone far enough. *You* have gone far enough!" Her voice spoke against him for the first time.

Now, Oaks' right hand balled into a fist. Muscles and veins bulging, he instinctively drew his powerful arm back before he even realized it.

But this time, Hannah stood, ready.

"Go ahead, Smith. Do it. Do it right in front of the inn. They'll all have a pretty story to tell."

Oaks came to, and used all his strength for an outward show of calm.

"Alright. Git in," he acquiesced, seething, dropping his fist.

Hannah and Marietta huddled together in the prow as Oaks guided the boat along the shoreline eastward.

The sail home was swift and tense.

35

"How was it in here this afternoon with Oaks and Hannah?" Felix asked Phebe during supper that evening.

"She quietly took her things, held Marietta's hand, thanked me and left with him."

"Well, they had some shouting match on the dock, that's fer sure," replied Felix. "Couldn't hear what they were sayin' but it was sure loud."

"I don't know how she tolerates that man," said Phebe. "Didn't talk much the days she was here. She was surely upset about something." Phebe looked sadly at her husband. "Those two deaths happening right under her nose, I guess. But you could tell she was relieved, too, just to be here. I think, just to be away from him, and in a normal household."

Felix pushed his plate away from him, sated. He said, "Talk is he's got a string of 'mishaps and suspicions' following him since the Ohio days. Can't just seem to pin him down to any of it, though."

"Everyone seems to know that but Hannah. Why does she tolerate him? She's afraid of him for sure; but why? And why does she stay?"

"It's a marriage, Phebe. Can't interfere much. Best we can do is keep an eye on him, and to let Hannah know she's all'ays got us if needs be."

36

After a fire had been lit in the hearth, Marietta was put to bed. Oaks was at the kitchen table alone, staring into the fire.

Hannah approached, hand in her apron pocket. He looked tired, dirty, and dangerous, a look that would normally have sent her into a mode of quiet camouflage, trying to blend into the surroundings to go unnoticed.

But all that was to change. Hannah decided that this was the moment, come what may. Wordlessly, she placed the dirt-crusted laudanum bottle in front of Oaks at the table.

She stood above him now, arms folded over her chest. He looked at it, then her, and then looked away in silence.

"Did you think I would never find this?" she asked finally.

She waited.

At length, he stood, scraping the chair backward on the wooden floor. He pushed past her as he crossed the room, and got the bottle of whisky off the kitchen shelf. He stood, and drank a long draught from it. In time, he looked at Hannah and said finally, "Don' have to explain nothin' to *nobody*."

Hannah persisted, "*Did* you, Smith?"

Her legs suddenly felt weak. She sat now at the crude table. "Your own brother?" she asked. Now emotion overcame her. Tears welled in her eyes, "And that *boy*?"

Smith saw her strength against him falter. He maintained his stance. "Got nothin' to say to ye Hannah." He strode across the floor toward her. He stood above her as she sat helplessly in the chair. He drank again from the bottle, capped it and slammed it hard on the table before her. Hannah flinched.

He stood over her, menacingly. She saw his dirty fingernails as he placed both hands on the table; then he slowly and deliberately bent toward her. She trembled. She could smell his sweat on his grimy clothes, and his foul breath as he drawled slowly, taking her in with his eyes: "You ain't nothin' but a *wife*, Hannah. Don' try bein' nothin' else."

Then, straightening, he took the laudanum bottle in his calloused hand.

He added, "Take care of the house and young'un, Hannah. That's yourn bus'ness."

He crossed the room, and spoke with his back to her. "*This* business," he said holding the apothecary bottle in the air, "this here bus'ness 's *mine.*"

He turned toward her as he opened the door, "Man's got a *right* in 'is home and property," he declared as he left the house.

37

Fire Island

It was as if she'd never left here for Phebe's. Her stomach returned to its familiar twist. Again, Hannah could hardly eat. Fatigue, her constant. Her breathing, shallow, as if ready for flight. It was a fear that she came to accept as part of her life. Deep inside, she knew she needed to break the bonds that held her. For her soul; a restitution. For Marietta's sake... and for hers.

Some respite now, Oaks gone with a hunting party for a few days. Some calm and freedom. These were the nights of deep sleep. And dreams.

Hannah, alone in her bed, the covers in a tangle, her hair loose and free. From the open window, her skin brushed gently by the breeze, steady from the shore. She awoke in a start from the dream, no longer feeling frightened. The familiar setting in the dreamscape, the familiar confusion in her mind, she accepts as a part of her now. She accepts it into her wakening and brings it into her day.

The dream comes in two parts. It speaks of the death of her baby. Or of herself. One and the same, she has come to realize.

There's a knock on the door first. The knock belongs to the sheriff. The girl had turned in the book – something about the erased words on the pages incriminating me.

Or did the girl write over the erasures on the page to make me look guilty?

Then the girl with the book becomes me; and they want to arrest me. In confusion I comply. In confusion I ask; am I the murdered? Or the murderess?

Hannah, now alone in the kitchen started her daily chores. The hearth began to blaze, the kettle to a simmer. Some breakfast for Marietta when she awakens. The dream revolved in her mind. She was consumed by guilt. Her mind conflates the infant and herself. A punishment awaits. She wondered aloud as she worked, can I ever make it right? Can I ever be forgiven? Is my baby still with me? Does he forgive me? Does he watch me from heaven? Is he in heaven? When he died, I buried him unbaptized.

I have Marietta, who is my treasure now. But my lost one was a boy child. Will God grant me another boy child to make it right?

That afternoon, Hannah walked the beach, Marietta playing in and out of the waves, collecting shells, happy. Hannah saw her hair tousled, hem of her skirt wet and caked with sand, free in the glorious surroundings, golden and glittery. Be strong Marietta, thought Hannah. Grow up strong. My hopes are in you.

To Hannah's mind came thoughts of the baby she lost. My boy child lies dead, in an unmarked grave. No one knows but me. A part of me buried, solitary, swallowed up by the earth.

His conception was violent, the rape. Her childhood and innocence taken from her. The baby's death, an accident. She, only a young girl herself, did not carry him to term. Out, alone searching for wild raspberries, she slipped and fell in the mud of the stream. She got up, gathered her things, but then the cramping started, violent shudders ran through her. Frightened and alone, she bent in pain, panting. Then the blood. She sank to the muddy bank on her knees. The baby slipped out of her, blood and mucus all. He blue and tangled.

She, in shock, mechanically her hands worked to free the cord herself. Held him to her chest, afraid. To the stream to wash, the baby limp and blue, hoping to revive him. But no breath. No movement. No life.

Crudely, she dug a hole near her mother's grave. Watch him for me, Mamma, she said aloud. She wept. She sat with him at her mother's grave until the sun began to set. She washed again in the stream.

No one at home to tell.

"Why'r you late, Hannah? Why'r you all wet?"

"Fell in the mud, Papa. Near the creek. Went in to wash."

"Yr' lookin' a might pale. Go git dry. Git to bed. You'll catch yr death o' cold."

There she remained in her room for days; no one thought anything else of it. The dreams started then, and return regularly.

And on this beautiful afternoon, Marietta splashing at the shore, Hannah's mind returns to last night's dream, the rest of it. She narrates it to herself in her mind, as if a tale that is told and repeated.

I killed someone, an accident. Had to bury the body. I washed and washed. The people I lived with did not know I did it. They looked and looked. They called the sheriff, who looked and looked, but they could not find where I buried him. Time went by, and all seemed normal, but I realized that the people I lived with still were not satisfied.

There was a blue light where he was buried. A crack showed the light. I thought, how will I hide that before they see it? I was ready to confess. I almost slipped a few times. ... Searching, someone kept calling aloud. The name they called became mine.

Sooner or later someone would find out. The sheriff kept coming back. They were all going to find out that I buried him.

I fear this "murderer." But the dream makes the child me. In the dream, I murdered me.

The sun now beginning to set, she called to Marietta to come in for supper. Watching her child run toward her on the shoreline, splashing the sea foam, her footprints disappearing after her nearly as quickly as they are made. Hannah resolves now to let go of the haunting dream. For now, a fire is needed in the hearth, supper to make, a child to put to bed.

In our lives, chores and the needs of daily living take precedence over memory. The clock moves and it seems that time passes. For Hannah, all that came before seems so long ago. But really, in the innermost mind, time does not pass at all. There, events are timeless. All that has happened, was, is now, and is forever.

*****

Late, the evening embers glowing, Hannah's hand toiled busily on a sketch. Working the charcoal, she caught the grasses' swaying movement on the dunes. Caught the late afternoon's shadows just so. The distant bay peeking between. Gulls careening on the air currents, searching for supper.

But this time, she adds a figure. A woman. Herself, she thought as she worked. The movement of the dress in the breeze. The shawl, gripped tightly closed. Knuckles prominent. Atop the highest dune, standing, her head erect, gaze straight ahead, looking, eyes wide; what do I see, wondered Hannah, staring out at the horizon? Hannah viewed the figure in the sketch, as if staring into a mirror.

She paused and put down her work to close the window. On the shore, the air has changed, warm breezes diminished by the evening chill. The water shimmers with the light of the moon. The promise of a new tomorrow.

The fire still lit, hearth warm. I will save this sketch, she thought. It seems to have some merit.

38

Fire Island Inlet - 1848

A watery twist of tide and weather, the inlet was its own place, where the laws of physics seemed suspended, yielding to forces there unlike anywhere else. Where the waters of the bay and the mighty Atlantic either come to blows, or blend in harmony. Where conditions, mild or wild, change without detectable cause. In an instant, beauty becomes horror, or danger calms to peace.

This was where the island's other year-round resident family lived. Over three miles distance from Hannah, the lightkeeper and his family thrived on the inlet, the westernmost tip of Fire Island. There, Selah and Susan Strong and their children dwelled on the wild shore.

On this day, an unexpected squall blew in from the ocean.

"When will Papa be back?" asked their youngest.

"He left early this morning to fetch supplies," Susan replied. "Don't worry. Papa's not coming back till later. This squall will be passed long before that."

But in the ocean, about a mile past the inlet, tossing in a sloop without aim, a young man's face rested sidewise, almost at slumber, dreamlike, floating, adrift as if in a fantasy. Then, out of this half-consciousness, sharp pain at the crown of his head. And cold, stinging cold, like pin-pricks. Richard tried to see, but could only open one eye-painfully, partially-toward the light. He watched helplessly from his one good eye as the clouds above disappeared, obscured by the whitewater that curled above, that came crashing down upon him. Gasping, the involuntary intake of water choking him, gurgling, salt stinging his lungs. Now, awake fully, struggling against line tight around his torso. Suddenly, in a burst, memory of the disaster returned.

Heading north by northeast returning to the inlet for the safety of the bay, wind gusting, a wind-wave hit the small craft. Main boom ninety degrees to port dragging in the water. Quick thinking Henry, his mate, having tied a life-line about his middle on deck, tried desperately to retrieve the boom.

The small sloop faced the wind increasing, gusting; she began pitching out of control. The last Richard remembered was a loud crack, the keel snapped, the small craft now sidewise, the sloop capsized, then, for Richard, all went dark.

His head, now just above water, torso lashed to what was left of the mast of the capsized vessel. He tried to turn his head, bolts of pain shot up from his spine, around to the crown of his head, across his forehead. He cried out in desperation for his friend. "*Henry!*"

A reply almost immediately, there his mate clinging to the tip of the hull peeking just above water.

"I say! Richard! Awake now?"

"You okay?"

"Better than you. The boom got you in your head when she fell."

"Where are we?"

"Big one from the east got us comin' in over the bar," Henry shouted. "We're about a mile south west of the light."

"They'll see us. They'll hear us if we shout. They'll send help. Hang on, Richard."

*****

All had been serene before, in the dawn light, Henry and Richard loading the sloop for a routine run.

"That's the last of it Henry," said his brother-in-law. Poor Richard panting, sat on the dock to catch his breath.

"We're only half full, though. Thought there was more." Henry was disappointed in their take. He wondered for a moment if it would be worth the sail to New York to sell only a half load of scrap metal.

"Was supposed to be more, but Havens didn't come through. Said we could have his old kettles but he's still waitin' on the new ones to be delivered. Said with the new ones, he'd be set to increase his fish oil business by half."

Henry wasn't listening. He was more concerned about their cargo than Haven's fish-oil business.

Richard asked, "So what do you think, Henry? Go anyway?"

"Why not?" Henry decided. "We did all this work loadin' and I could use the money, with Anna pregnant and due soon."

"Yep. My sister always said she wanted a big family."

"Yep, she has. And another babe on the way makes four."

*****

They left the dock in the small village of Babylon, the early dawn's sun just giving way to clouds from the south.

"Wind's beginning to pick up, Henry."

"We've sailed in worse. Let's go, so we can be back by supper."

"This scrap will be weighed out in no time. Pays in cash on the spot."

"Aye," agreed Richard. "Could sure use a few extra dollars in my sad, empty purse!"

They set off in their small sloop, wending their way through the bay toward the Fire Island inlet that opens to the sea. It's a sail that they've done since they were boys. First, sail south out of the bay, over the sandbar, into deeper waters, then set course west toward New York Harbor, following the coastline of Long Island all the way in.

But the first heavy gust of wind over the bar took them by surprise. The day turned dark in an instant, thick grey clouds impenetrable seemed to blend with the murky horizon; the sea suddenly vexed.

"Not worth it, Henry. Turn back over the bar," Richard shouted above the rushing wind.

"I'll take her out a bit, then tack sharp starboard," Henry assented. "Back to the inlet."

He watched, and knew in this sea it would be a test of split-second timing to get the boat about safely.

*****

Henry had always been surprised at her strength for such a little girl. Katie's bony arms wrapped around his knees, pressing him to her tiny chest, insisting that he stay.

"Don't go tomorrow, Papa! I want you home with me!"

Henry had difficulty releasing her fingers, not wanting to hurt them, wound so tightly together at the backs of his knees.

"Nooo. Nooo! Papa! Don't *do* that!" Then seeing all her strength couldn't match his, she gave in weeping. He lifted her to hold her to him. She held him tight around his neck, as he gently kissed her.

"You get to sleep now, Katie. I'll be leaving in the early morning. When you get up, you and Mama bake me some cinnamon biscuits. Ok? I'll be home for supper..." he crooned to her reassuringly. "And help Mamma as much as you can. She's tired these days, but will soon bring us a new little one to love."

*****

Katie's sad little face seemed before him as Henry struggled to control the sails in sharp tack. The little sloop, always responsive, instead skimmed freely along the top of the sea, seemingly on its own course.

The boat easily rode a roller from behind that lifted her up facing her high, then just as suddenly, dropped her. But she's sturdy. She stood for it.

"You've got her!" shouted Richard, elated, proud of Henry's seamanship.

But then, sidewise, coming from the east, another swell approached so high that it engulfed the sloop from the starboard side. They heard the shift of their cargo in the hold; metal all tumbling as the small craft took a roll, unrecoverable.

*****

Shivering now, the men were weakened from exposure. They had been in the sea for hours, they could tell by the light that began to wane in the afternoon sky. They could tell by the hoarseness of their throats from hours of shouting that proved worthless. No help had come.

"Kick, Richard. Kick your feet to stay warm," encouraged Henry.

But Richard's injuries prevented much movement. He told himself to kick, but he felt nothing from his torso down; were his legs even moving at all?

"The surfboat. Why hasn't it come? They have one at the lighthouse. Selah Strong is there. He'll come, I know it. He's as good a man there is."

"Don't give up, Richard. They'll be here. I know it. Keep calling out."

But both knew that Henry gave false hope.

The men, exhausted, had no voice left to give. They waited silently as the sea continued to punish the half-submerged hull. They knew by then no one was coming.

*****

Susan Strong's eyes were swollen by late afternoon while she waited on the dock, bayside, for her husband to arrive home in the catboat from his business on the main island across the bay.

"Why are ye out here this late?" Selah asked her as he jumped from the boat onto the dock. In the dimming light of dusk, he saw Susan's eyes. "What's wrong?" he asked. "Are the children...?"

"No, Selah. They are fine. I am fine..."

He held her in his arms a moment, almost impatiently now, knowing that the last light would wane and the supplies must be unloaded before dark.

"It's the men," she stammered..." They are still out there..."

"Men? Who? What men? Where?" He held her now at arm's length, looking directly into her face. "Susan," he demanded, "make some sense!"

*****

Just before sunset next evening Selah Strong ended the search for the missing men. All that was left was to wait; perhaps the sea would relinquish their bodies to the shore, small comfort for grieving families.

His visit from Felix Dominy was a welcome one. He understood best the frustrations of the job.

"No, Felix, there *is* no Lifesaving Station if there's no one to man it!" Selah unnecessarily raised his voice to his friendly interlocutor. His letters to the Life Saving Benevolent Association, the agency that put up rescue huts for the U.S. Treasury Department, have gone unheeded for months, and now two deaths can be attributed to the faulty "rescue" system the government has set up. His frustration got the better of him.

"Both these young men left wives and children alone now, and destitute. And in perfect view of the lighthouse, in midday. Sure, the surfboat was in the rescue hut, but it needs seven men to launch! There aren't seven men on this entire barrier island in the winter months! It's a system set to fail, it is."

He and Felix left the small keeper's cottage where Selah and Susan lived with their children. They passed through the gate that supported a neat fence, which surrounded their vegetable garden that grew in the summer months.

The men walked the grounds of the lighthouse together. There sat the new rescue hut next to the octagonal lighthouse tower, Connecticut bluestone, proudly standing watch at eighty feet high. Its position on the western tip of the barrier island was key to all the seagoing vessels heading to and from New York Harbor. An essential beacon, crucial for the safety of the ever-increasing commerce of a growing nation.

Selah continued, "They came and built a rescue hut here. Then dumped equipment in it! How am I to tend to that, too? I have my hands full already as the light keeper here. This here so-called Lifesaving System needs an overhaul… the huts need to be manned of their own accord."

"All that's true," said Felix.

"Those men *died*!" continued Selah. "And on *my* watch!" His voice cracked with emotion, thinking of their widows and fatherless children.

He then thought of his own family. Susan, unable to sleep at night, dark circles under her eyes, and under the eyes of his children. Sadness prevailed in his household, all his family haunted by the memory. Selah explained, "Those men's cries were heard for hours by my wife and children, and my one assistant keeper. Helpless and desperate they were. What were they to do? Were *they* to launch a thousand pound lifeboat?"

Selah and Felix stopped in front of the lifesaving hut's locked door. He continued, sadly, "So there it sat and went unused while two young men drowned."

Felix Dominy had heard this all before. He'd lived it. The frustration of a system in its infancy. He was well aware of the growing pains the Lifesaving System was experiencing.

"It's money, Selah. There's no money for supplies *and* to pay men's salaries both."

"There's money for the things they *want* to pay for, there is!" replied Selah, frustrated.

"Look. Everyone's upset now. It's all the talk on the main island. Thank the Lord that the widows and children have the community to lean on. Everyone's pitching in for them."

Selah continued, "But here, Susan and my little ones had to bear the brunt of it, helpless."

"Yep. Life on this island's only for the strong, it is," remarked Felix sadly.

"Look, I'll have the inn open on the beach in a month, soon as winter breaks. Then Susan and the kids will have my Phebe and our kids to keep company," replied Felix. "Things will be calmer then."

He continued, "Business was good last season. Lots of men looking for sportsman's guides these days. So there'll be men around just a mile away at the inn to help launch a surfboat if needed. It's just these winter months…"

"Yes. But it's the winter when we see most of our storms. And that's when this island's most desolate. All that's here year round besides us is Smith Oaks' place more than three miles east. And he's a loner. Not much for neighborliness. Not sure if he'd help launch a surfboat even if asked."

Then, sadness took over Selah's anger. His shoulders drooped and his eyes lowered. "I'm at a loss, Felix."

"Don't blame yourself," he replied, his hand resting on Selah's shoulder now. "All's we can do is what we can do with the circumstances we are given."

*****

Winter's cold began to give way, the days getting longer. Hannah's fingers had been busy mending. Any clothes that Marietta outgrew that needed a stitch or two, any household linens that could be spared were called for the use of the two young widows and their families.

All must be made ready, for Phebe and Felix were coming to the island to start the preliminary cleaning and repairs to the inn to make ready for the upcoming season. Hannah packed several baskets, and with the clothing, included some jars of preserves and wrapped loaves and cakes.

Hannah packed the pony cart and drove with Marietta to Phebe's.

The sands of the beach looked like a fantastic landscape, dunes sculpted anew, cut away in jagged shapes, contoured by the wind and high seas of brutal winter storms. Despite the coming spring thaw, in some places, crests made by wind erosion featured frost and old snow crusted atop, glittering in the early afternoon sunshine.

She arrived at the inn to see boxes and trunks piled on the front porch. She saw Phebe busy, arms pointing and sweeping, directing their passage or removal. Hearing the clatter of Hannah's cart, she turned with a welcoming smile.

"So happy to see you!" she cried. Then, directing her gaze to the child said, "And Marietta! My! How you have grown!"

Marietta beamed. Then, delighted, she spotted her friend Arthur. He was busy at work, cleaning up the front garden from the winter's debris. She ran to see.

Phebe called after her, "Enough cleaning, Arthur! Go into the kitchen with Marietta for some cider and cakes!"

Hannah embraced her friend. "I am happy to see you. It has been a long winter here." She added, "You look hale and hearty, though."

"Yes, a bit too hearty, I'm, afraid," said Phebe laughing, patting her ample hips.

"How are those poor families?" asked Hannah, unloading the cart.

"Oh, it's a terrible loss. They're beside themselves. But there are many helping hands, you know."

With the last basket unloaded, Phebe said, "That's the way. Just leave these lovely baskets right here. I'll get Felix to take your horse and cart to the shed, and to load these baskets along with mine. Susan should be here soon with hers, too."

She appraised Hannah's pale skin and thin frame with one quick glance. "What about a cup of hot tea? That'll take the March chill right out of your bones. Come… we'll go inside."

Hannah felt grateful for the offer and followed her friend.

After they settled inside at the hearth, Susan arrived with her bundles of donations and her children in tow. The young ones squealed with delight to see their mates again after so long a lonely winter.

The room was soon filled with warmth and companionship.

"Selah is still furious at the tragedy," said Susan. "His frustration at the illogic of this system is taking its toll on him," said Susan.

Phebe added, "Felix says that there were two souls that did not have to be lost. An unmanned lifesaving system does not save lives, says he."

"And the vast distance! Ten miles between stations!" cried Susan.

"It's the lack of funding," said Phebe, repeating Felix's words.

"Hannah, what does Smith say? What does he hear about any of this? Are they talking about it in any of the towns east?"

Hannah stayed silent. It would be embarrassing to report Smith's heartless comments on the matter. *Stupid two shouldn't a gone out.* His disdain for Hannah's efforts to help. *Let 'em be, Hannah. An' don' git involved with those busybodies sayin' thy want t' help. All's they want is to know eve'ybodys business.*

All her sewing and preparing had to be hidden from Smith's eyes, along with the extra preserves and baking. Even today's visit, she told Smith, was just for the children to play. The supplies had to be loaded in secret.

"I feel for those families," said Hannah to the ladies, averting her eyes and avoiding the question. "We must help as we can."

PART VI

39

Rome
February 1848

"My Dearest Margherita, my heart breaks of sadness," whispered Giovanni as he lay in Margaret's embrace.

"There was nothing more that you could do, my love," she replied softly.

Despite his tenderest care, Giovanni's father was interred in the family chapel in the church of Santa Maria Maddalena, near their family villa in Rome.

"Seeing Papa laid to rest in the dim light of the church, around the ornate cask," he let go of a deep sigh, "those four marble columns of green seem as cold arms to surround his remains."

Giovanni's emotion overwhelmed him. Margaret understood. She knew first hand the emptiness of a father's death. The helplessness one feels after caring for a loved one in a final illness, that feeling of a failing, owning the death as if it could have been prevented by further action, more care.

However, Giovanni took great comfort in his religion and his ancestry. He referred to the painting of St. Nicholas in their family chapel, "Papa is now under the watch of Jesus Christ and the Virgin Mary who, eternally appear in glory to our patron, St. Nicholas. Papa will rest in the peace of eternity now, under the azure, silver and gold Ossoli coat of arms."

"Yes," agreed Margaret. After a moment, she asked, "How did your brothers…?"

Giovanni responded before she could finish, "Giuseppe was there with the other members of the Pope's Privy Council. Of course he provided for the burial ceremony all the honors of the Vatican. Ottovino and Allesandro wore the uniform of the ancient order of the *Guardia Nobile*. And there was I, in my uniform of the Civic Guard, looked down upon by my brothers. I could sense their sneers, even at this tragic time. And with Giuseppe now it's worse. He hates me even more now. He knows of our commitment to the cause of the revolution, and now he sees me not as a brother, but as his enemy."

Margaret held him close, hoping to ease his pain. "But no matter," continued Giovanni, "my brothers are mere sheep. Unthinking and blind. He rose from the settee to peer out of the window. After a moment, his long frame turned back toward Margaret as he continued, "As for me, I am sorry Papa will not see a united Italy; this country self-governed and strong in purpose."

He reached for her hand to steady her as she awkwardly rose. "My dear Margherita, you grow strong in purpose, too." He placed his hands lovingly on her thickening waist. "This is what our love has produced. Our child will be born in a free Italy, to grow in liberty and flourish with all of its people."

"Yes. Our child, Giovanni. And I, a mother, my desire, my love. An embodiment of our commitment to each other and to our cause."

"*Mia cara*, Margharita, we give birth to freedom," he spoke fervently. "We give birth to the first generation of Free Italy. To prosper and thrive in a vigorous country, ruled by its own and for the good of its own people." Then, eyes filling with tears, he dropped to his knees before her, and crooned to her belly, "*Viva l'Italia. Viva il mio bambino.*"

He looked up to see Margaret's full blossomed beauty, her complexion never so bright, her eyes so warm, her hair loosened and tumbling toward him, as she cradled his head, pressing him into her warm body. "You, who have a child for me in your womb. *Mia Cara.* Our passion, our love you have made incarnate. Now I live to feel our baby in my arms. To love and protect our little family… I am padre, *protettore.* "

She gazed down at him with the fullness of love. "I grow now in might, Margharita. I stand guard, and I wait. And when necessary, will fight now even more fiercely. My blows in battle vicious, my bullets fly sharp and keen to pierce any enemy of this new Roman Republic. I will make a safe place for our child to grow."

Rising now to his full height, tall and splendid in his uniform, he stepped back from Margaret, and, looking upward with liquid eyes, added, "And now, *mi Papa…* Fatherless, I become a father."

40

March 1848
The Colosseum

At first, Pope Pius had garnered a loving constituency with his attempt at a liberal papacy, one that seemed to reach out to all. He could not be seen in public without the cry of *Vivo Pio!* on the lips of all who passed. A good man, kind and gentle, he had warm intentions to embrace his people.

In early March, he granted a Constitutional Monarchy, a measure that would allow him to retain his power, but also grant some representation in the government by the people. But no matter his good intentions, his move devolved into chaos. All factions registered disagreement with the compromise. The conservatives were furious with him for allowing any representation at all. The liberals were disappointed, hoping instead for total freedom of rule. But the radicals wanted more, nothing short of a revolution against the European Monarchs, with Pope Pius as their figurehead.

The January assault by the Austrians on Milan was now eclipsed by their latest attack in March. Demands were being made upon the Pope to answer this act of Austrian aggression with a declaration of war against the Empire.

But Pius flatly refused to order war against another Catholic nation.

Furious now, the Italian people took matters into their own hands. Here, at Rome's ancient Colosseum, a great demonstration was organized; a rally to call for recruits who would be sent to protect Italy from foreign aggression, to protect the borders.

Called to duty today to keep order at the great demonstration forming there, Ossoli and his men marched to their posts.

There, the shadows of the ancient ruins of Rome whispered of the days of Roman glory, of victory and power and world dominion. History belongs to these people, in the Roman blood which courses through their veins. So on this day of fine blue sky, a clarity of purpose overtook the crowd. A furious flame fanned their passions. In front of the Colosseum the crowd chanted, *We fight against the Monarchies! Il popolo!* Their mission today was beyond doubt; inspired.

The throng parted as a tall figure approached the makeshift stage. Chatter hushed into silence, as Father Gavazzi was recognized in the dark robes of the Order of St. Barnabas. His stature was made greater by the voluminous fabric of the dark garment. His arms, opened wide, expanded the cape's folds that filled with the gentle breeze. Gavazzi looked as if he could encompass all the souls who watched.

He began, "The horror of the January assault of the Austrian Empire on Milan is now outdone by their outrageous attack in March! But, this time the people prevailed! The most powerful army of the Empire was repulsed by the Milanese people.... in five days! *Five* glorious days of heroism."

A roar from the multitude. He continued, "In *five* days…five days of battle fierce in the streets and in the houses all! Men fought like *lions*; women and children made weapons from their kitchens, knives, burning oil; and from their barns, pitchforks, shovels…all that could be used were wrought against the oppressor…and the rebels, the Italian *people*, victorious over the might of the Austrian Empire! *Il popolo!*"

The crowd returned the chant, *Il popolo! The power lies with us! God supports right! God supports the people!*

Father Gavazzi, relentless, roused all.

Then, the sturdy wine merchant and horse dealer, Angelo Brunetti, famous now and loved by the masses, approached the podium.

Brunetti had all the presence of a performer. He used his great height and girth to fill the space to the fullest. His arms both upraised greeted the crowd as he heard his nickname being chanted, *Ciceruacchio! Ciceruacchio!* The familiar name, adopted by the many, and embraced by him as a sign of affection.

He swayed the crowd with ease, altering his good-natured affection with passionate fiery speeches. He encouraged all to enlist, to defend the homeland, to support the formation of the Republic of Rome.

"I go!" he shouted, his massive fist over his heart. "Follow me! *I* will march to the northern border with the troops to defend our land from the oppressor! Will you come with me?" he cried.

The crowd roared its support.

But suddenly the cries of "No! No, *Ciceruacchio!*" hushed the frenzy. One by one, people quieted. A wave of silence crossed the piazza. Each head turned from side to side to see who dared to dissent.

One clear voice then rang out, "No, *Ciceruacchio! You* must not go! You are needed here in Rome. You are our voice in the *Consulta!*"

Murmurs of assent began to circulate, and one by one, the wave of silence turned into a wave of sound murmured at first, then which increased to shouts of "Stay! Stay! Stay!"

Brunetti heard the crowd, and waited. He theatrically turned his head sidewise, to the sky. Then he raised one huge hand, a bear-like paw, to cover his forehead in thought. The last gesture brought an expectant whisper that traveled across the multitude like a rock skillfully thrown skips across a pond.

Finally he raised both arms while his great head lowered in acquiescence. He started in a somber, humble, tone, "I have my duty to you here, and I will not abandon that post."

Murmurs of approval spread among the crowd.

He continued, "BUT, in my stead, Brunetti continued theatrically, "I offer to this cause of a United Italy, my able son, my first son, Italy's son of the Civic Guard, Luigi Brunetti!"

Ossoli turned abruptly to see Luigi among the soldiers of his platoon, his face all emotion, tears streaming. He raised a fist high to assent. The men surrounding him lifted him upon their shoulders for all to see. Father and son, their eyes locked across a sea of people, glistening in the ancient sunshine, united in their single cause.

Under the spell of Brunetti and Gavazzi, the crowds choking pressed toward the enlistment booths, which, within twenty-four hours had to be closed, they were so overwhelmed with the volume of volunteers. An army was raised of some 17,000 men, a forceful presence that could not be denied.

The next day, Father Gavazzi asked Pope Pius in a private audience to acknowledge the troops and bless them. How could he refuse? But, also, how could he remain leader of all Catholic nations? He reached a compromise position.

In a ceremony formal, among the people, Gavazzi was appointed military chaplain, to march with the men some 300 miles to assemble at Bologna. The crowd roared its approval. Then, Pope Pius blessed the force of volunteers. However, he added strict instruction *not* to cross the border of the Papal States into Austria. Their only job would be to protect Italy *inside* its border. Pius' measure on that day seemed pleasing to all.

The march out of the city was a scene of passion. Men and women and children embracing, praying, crying and laughing with excitement as they made their goodbyes. Promises to write at every chance, to come home safely, to protect the country, children clung to their father's legs, wives to their husbands, parting.

Finally the columns were formed, filled with men of every type: dukes and commoners, citizens rich and poor, all of whom were united in singing verses addressed to the glory of Rome.

And in the streets, all say, *The men march!*

And Gavazzi marches now! He will march with them!
It is a Crusade! A Crusade from Rome!
The force will be unstoppable!

Ossoli and his men stood careful watch, knowing they were on the edge. Life as they knew it was over, and the shape of their new world was forming before their very eyes.

41

The frequency of Margaret's articles to the *New York Daily Tribune* suffered over the winter as her health had suffered. But now in the Roman sunshine of spring and under the blue sky, the headaches and nausea left her, and she was able to get out of her rooms for her daily walks. She strode down Via del Corso, the city awakening to spring blossoms in the gardens, and in trees reaching toward the sky offering their season's new foliage to the sunlight. She felt energized, her blood coursing through her veins, a new beginning in this bountiful spring, with new life strong in her womb.

Her professional duty now was to update her readers on the many political developments of the revolutionary movements in Europe and in Italy. King Ferdinand acquiesced to a constitutional monarchy demanded by resistance fighters in Sicily, Louis Philippe of France was dethroned by his people, and the resistance movements in Venice, Milan, Parma and Modena succeeded against their Austrian rulers. News of these victories all reached the streets of Rome, where there was dancing in the streets, and where men and women wept with joy.

For Margaret, the political and social merged with the personal; her life here, directly intertwined with the revolutionary movement. She reported to the *Tribune* of all political developments, she privy to Ossoli's first hand accounts of the Roman military strategies and movements.

News of the Vatican's politics and the battles and skirmishes on the borders was readily on the lips of all in the marketplace.

What's more, Margaret and Giovanni frequented the cafes of the radical clubs. There they would sit for the afternoon over coffee, newspapers in hand skimming them with their eyes, while attentively listening to the hubbub around them.

Many were there to see, or to be seen. Some came to exchange news and gossip. For others, meetings were arranged, confidences exchanged with a note passed in secret, or a nod, or a wink. Spies of every faction passed through.

Margaret had ample and varied viewpoints from which to write and record the progress of the revolution. Enough, also, to write a thorough history. Her life now dedicated to the cause, to Giovanni and their coming child, and to writing a history of the formation of the new Republic of Rome. All was movement and excitement, thrilling and terrifying all at once.

And in her quiet moments, in her favorite chair in the dusky light of evening, she would hold her hands gently on her thickening middle to feel any movement, contact with their child. Bambino, she would whisper, child of our love, you will be proud of your parents, who helped your country in this great cause.

Then, memories of her childhood would flood in of Father, who taught her well the lesson of "Public duty before private good." He the example, having left the family for extended months to serve in Congress.

And like Father, she thought, in Rome, I too could use my talents to influence the formation of *this* great nation. Father would be proud, she thought.

But for Margaret, oh, she remembered her pain even now as she missed him so. She remembered his absences as a great gap in her very being. As if the best part of her were torn asunder; she, crippled with longing for his return.

My lessons. I must complete my lessons, she would think. This will please father when he returns. I must know my lessons. His letter to Mama said that he would love me more if I can read when he returns. I must, so he will love me.

Childhood memories floated to the surface of her consciousness as she dozed, hands on her belly, in the warmth of spring.

42

Villa Ossoli; Rome

"Giuseppe comes for supper tonight," announced Angela to Giovanni when he arrived home that evening.

"Really? Why? He has not been here for months." Giovanni knew that his brother has been swamped at the Papal offices, sleeping there most nights, barely seeing his own family and home.

"He has some business with Father's estate. You should know so you can decide whether you want to be here or not."

"What business? Doesn't he know that domestic cases are not being addressed by the courts now with all the civil unrest?"

"Giovanni. He is looking for Father's records and documents. I cannot stop him," replied Angela. "Besides, it would be good for you to see him." After a moment's hesitation, Angela added, "Our family has been divided for too long."

Giovanni and Angela stood, facing each other, knowing that this would be a contentious visit. About the will, they knew they were helpless. Giuseppe held all the power.

"Good," said Giovanni at last. "I will wait for my brother."

43

The stones and mortar of the Palazzo Ossoli spoke of time and history. Baldassare Peruzzi's architectural design in 1525 presented to the street a stone archway that held proudly carved doors, heavy with lock and hinges huge, forged then and still in use now. Opening them into the courtyard announced any visitor, as time and decay hung heavily upon the iron hinges.

Guisseppe, familiar, entered the courtyard and strode upon the uneven stones that paved the way toward the house. He greeted his sister, and waited for Giovanni in the family parlor where ponderous brocades hung and volumes of histories dusty, stood nobly on the shelves. Lining the walls to ceiling height, were trophies of glories past, shields and armor, weapons of war dark and menacing. This aristocratic history remained foremost in the Ossoli family, and in this palazzo where they and their family identity reside.

No greeting by Giuseppe for his brother as Giovanni as entered the room. Giuseppe saw him and started abruptly.

"I know about you and the *Americana*." He stood square and stocky, his hair greying and the lines of worry apparent on his face. His voice, condescending, as usual, his age, a badge of authority over Giovanni.

"Her name is *Margharita*," replied Giovanni, standing youthful and tall in opposition, slender and dark, his vigor shining and his voice strong.

166

"I know that," Giuseppe continued. " I know about you and your visits to her on the Via Del Corso...."

On the defensive, Giovanni stood, arms crossed over his chest. He bore his eyes straight into his brothers. He would not flinch, or show surprise or weakness.

"... I know your movements and all the movement of the Civic Guard. I also know about your so-called promotion."

Giovanni erect, resolute.

Giuseppe was the one to break the stand-off. He turned slowly away from Giovanni's stare to look out of the window. "I am under strict security for what I know as Papal Secretary. But you, my little brother, are in grave danger. That promotion puts you in a most vulnerable position."

"I am not afraid to fight for what is right for our country," replied Giovanni. "Do not think you can use your intimidation tactics on me anymore, Giuseppe. I am a man, as you are a man. I choose the Revolution. I..."

"Have you asked yourself *why* you were put there?" interrupted Giuseppe. "Do they know who you are? Do they know about me? Do they trust you? Think before you answer. Carefully weigh all the pieces, Giovanni."

"They are my family, now," he replied. My brothers in arms. I will not let you interfere with my commitment. These will be the new leaders of a united Italy."

"Nonsense!" spat Giuseppe suddenly his voice quaking with anger. "You are of *noble* birth. These rabble are *nothing* like us!" He continued, his voice rose powerful and fierce, "How *could* you, Giovanni? How could you get involved with those people? Those, those *thugs*!"

The brothers, eldest and youngest, now turned and faced each other, inches apart. Giuseppe's rage caused him to go further than he should have. "Is it your so-called *Margharita*?" He added derisively, "has she made you her *hero*? Her young, stupid, Italian hero?

So she can write about you in her newspaper in America? Wake up, Giovanni! Pope Pius will not be dissuaded. He will not be displaced. Papal power has ruled here for centuries, and it will continue for centuries more."

Giovanni's eyes glowered as he leaned forward menacingly, forcing his brother back. "You will *never* say her name again in my presence, Giuseppe. You will never speak of her again," he seethed, glaring eye to eye with his brother, dominating.

Satisfied, Giovanni stepped away to leave the room. He then stopped momentarily, turned and shot back, "And you are wrong, Giuseppe… the power is now in the hands of the people. Il *popolo*, Giuseppe!"

By then, Giuseppe had recovered his composure. He answered, "Ha! You *fool!*" He reached for his leather folio.

Giovanni continued across the threshold. "Wait!" his brother shouted after him.

Giovanni turned. He saw his brother pull out a packet of papers, neatly wrapped. He paused as Giuseppe approached him, hand outstretched with the documents.

"Here," said Giuseppe, offering them to Giovanni. "Give this to your Colonel Tittoni. And tell him that we laugh and mock him and his band of misfits."

"What *is* this?" his hand automatically accepting the bundle.

"A transcript of a 'secret' revolutionary meeting held at just a few days ago about the Civic Guard. We know all that is going on; and I know all about you too, Giovanni. There is nothing going on that the Vatican does not know about."

Giuseppe continued, "I will see to Father's business now, but my visit here was also to see you. To warn you, as my *familia*. Those thugs are not your brothers, Giovanni. They use you. They think you can get to me."

It all made sense to Giovanni now.

Giuseppe continued, "Abandon your post. You are not safe."

Giovanni heard, then turned his back on his brother to leave the room.

Giuseppe glowered. His voice resonated, strong and deep with insult, "Giovanni, you young fool; there will never *be* a united Italy."

44

May 1848

Though he stood strong against his brother, Giovanni felt shaken as he entered Margaret's rooms that evening. But here, the tension did not last long. He felt a calm and peace in her presence that he felt nowhere else. He put his hands gently on her pregnant belly.

"*Mia Cara*, our bambino grows," remarked Giovanni with pride.

"Yes. I feel movement in my womb growing stronger each day. Our child is healthy and strong."

Margaret rose awkwardly from the settee. "I fear I won't be able to conceal my condition any longer, my love."

He told her of Giuseppe's visit. "He knows about us. But he said nothing about your condition. This must be held a secret from him for as long as possible. We must ensure, first, that our child's name is properly listed on the record of noble births."

"Besides," Giovanni continued, "The streets are becoming increasingly dangerous since the Pope's allocution. There is too much instability in Rome now. We should consider a safer location for you for a while."

Margaret could see that Giovanni was unnerved. She agreed. "And now would be the time for a move, my love. My health is good, as our baby grows daily. If I waited much longer, the travel in a coach over those rutted roads will become even more difficult for me. But where?" she asked.

"The mountains south of Rome. There are small towns around Pietraforte, where my family name is still known. There are small villages there where you will be safe."

"Do you know of any of the families there now?"

"I will ask my cousin Pietro. He has closer ties in the towns. He will write and find a safe home where we can rent some rooms."

"Yes, she agreed. She gazed around at her books and papers; all will have to be organized into trunks for the journey. "I will write my family that I am moving for some rest into the country. They do not know of my condition, and I prefer it that way for now."

"Begin to pack your things, and we can travel as soon as I get word. The sooner we can get you out of here and settled, the better."

"And you?" Margaret asked.

"I must remain here at my post."

Seeing Margaret's look of disappointment, he continued, "We will write daily. I will visit at every opportunity. You and our child must be away from the unrest brewing here. And from the prying eyes of my brothers."

45

September 1848
Margaret in Rieti

Margaret felt safe in the small village of Rieti. A walled city from the time of the Romans, its red and brown roofed dwellings and churches were built on a rich plain encircled by lush green mountains. The Velino River made nearly a full a circuit around its ancient walls. Margaret felt she had found a secure home there to have her child.

She occupied the top floor of a small villa that belonged to a family who has lived in the town for generations. They suggested a trusted mid-wife to help with the birth, and she found for Margaret and the baby a reliable nurse to help care for the infant.

Her days in the country were spent in seclusion with her beautiful baby. And the nurse, Chiara was there to help with the day to day, since Giovanni left for Rome. She, a strong and healthy young mother herself, became Margaret's source of comfort and aide.

"Why does he sleep so little at night?" Margaret asked her, utterly exhausted.

Chiara took Angelino from her with a knowing smile. "It is not unusual, Signora. Infants sometimes confuse night and day when they are first born." She swaddled the child and sat with him, rocking and humming a lullaby.

"How long does that last?"

"Not too long. But it is important for you to sleep when they sleep. If Angelino naps, you do too. Until his schedule is regular."

Margaret looked out the window to see her landlord and his wife bending over their small garden with a wicker basket, gathering the last of the season's vegetables. Almost distractedly, she asked Chiara, "What do you know about Paolo and Maria?"

"The landlords?"

"Yes."

"It seems their families have always lived in Rieti. They own land at the base of the hills for farming. They turn a nice profit from their labors."

"I see," replied Margaret. "But I sometimes feel uncomfortable around them, though they seem to be willing and helpful. They eye me with much curiosity."

"Signora, they are naturally suspicious people. And you are a foreigner. An *Americana*, with a baby here in this small village. Even at the marketplace, it is whispered that visits from the baby's father are becoming less and less frequent."

"A small town. I see. Everyone watches everyone."

"Paolo is probably concerned that you will not keep up the rent. His concern is not for you. He is only worried that his purse is full."

"There," said Chiara satisfied. "Angelino is sleeping deeply now, and I must get home to my husband. He does not like me to be away for too long."

She gathered her shawl and started for the door. Looking back toward Margaret, she added, "Why not get some sleep now? Have some rest while Angelino is quiet." She held out her hand to Margaret. "And do not look so worried, Signora. All will be fine. For now, you must regain your strength."

Margaret agreed. She had been already exhausted in the last months of pregnancy with the burdens of moving from Rome and settling in to new lodgings.

She gazed at beautiful Angelino, sleeping peacefully now. She became absorbed in wonderment at the mere existence of the child, his beautiful and perfect form. She understood now the power that desire and passion could create new... *life*. A new *soul*; a new existence on this earth.

But worries intervened with her joy. She felt fully the responsibility of motherhood, felt inadequate to protect such a helpless being alone. She worried constantly for the child, for Giovanni's safety, and for their future together. His new duty post on the Vatican wall was most dangerous, and tensions in Rome increased daily.

This strange combination of wonderment and fear increased Margaret's fatigue. Her few hours of sleep were disturbed by deep dreams; partial memories reimagined from her youth in Boston. Now, falling into exhausted sleep midday while the child napped in the soft September afternoon.

A blending of the warm breeze from the window opened wide, and with the sound of her rhythmic breathing in the moments of nether consciousness, a memory of the death of a young woman in Boston emerged from her past, as awareness faded softly into sleep.

Coming from the deathwatch of a poor town girl, once so fair and young. She who gave her life all for once yielding to desire, the crime of sexual pleasure, outside of holy matrimony.

On my breast her head heavy lay until she breathed no more. Her death, the price of love.

Prayers and sorrow only remained for her on my long walk home. And I in exhaustion from the watch entered my house, mercifully empty. The quiet disquieting, not even the ticking of the clock, which, post haste to leave for my duty to comfort the poor girl, had forgot to wind, now, its time attesting to the past.

....And so, into my house cold and silent, exhausted and saddened by the young girl's death, thus entranced, I entered Father's room, and on his empty bed went I to rest, as if drawn there by the occasion.

His room, now tomblike. The place in which I settled his notes of law, and papers all, even those from his young life, at his father's home, Puritan minister severe. His letters, his Harvard papers, the notes that formed the education he passed on to me. This, his legacy, for otherwise he died insolvent. And now, I, once the child consumed by the mighty figure father fierce, ordered his life past. It would be I who feed and nourish his legacy, his children; so that he lives on. The debt of Roman Charity.

The line of poetry learned long ago, "Lie silent in your graves, ye dead!" echoed in my aching head, as I dozed there on his empty bed. And in the dream's half dream I knew again the poem of the solitary doe, who comes to the grave, gliding in from the wood soft and silent: "Harbors she a sense of sorrow, or of reverence?"

For me, I harbor both, was the thought that struck suddenly, strident and cogent and cold.

As if receiving a cold slap, Margaret woke from her memory-dream with a start, bedclothes tangled, head aching, a ritual pain. Memories of her childhood in her mind, her powerful father, always ending sharply. Unresolved and haunting. She turned onto her side, still, resting.

The years of her father all swim in, half reverie, and in her drowsiness, feelings exposed; the mixing of desire and the release of death. Her memories focus on the puzzle of strain and tension and fear of not pleasing her demanding father, all stimulated in her too young by too late nights, too long lessons; then only to be awakened by him from the deep slumber of her bed in the dark of night with kisses on her lips as if to show approval, to reward her, to express a love he could not express in the daylight.

No respite, thought Margaret, even in her sleep. Can I ever divide from this choking father-love?

And now, untangling from the twisted bedclothes, she rose and moved across the room toward her only joy.

My own child. *Mio bambino*, crooned Margaret to little Angelino dozing peacefully still in the warm afternoon. She tenderly moved the thin coverlet protectively to cover his bared chest. The breeze from the bedroom windows, open to the Sabine Hills on one side and vineyards on the other, permeated the apartment with a fragrant sweetness.

Her attention shifted to the scene below her windows. In the mountains, now is the season of the vintage, as donkeys pulled wagons loaded with white and purple clusters, parading from the vineyards daily. Margaret heard the bare-chested boys, skin brown from the sun, singing as they cut the fruit ripened now from the trees on which the vines are grown. The maids and matrons in their red corsets and white head scarves gathered the harvest into baskets while their babies and children played beside the vineyard on the grassy slope. Connection to the earth. Simplicity. Purity.

Turning again toward Angelino as the child stirred in his sleep, his every sweet breath, the scent of his skin, his clear blue eyes that when playful seek hers, filled Margaret with the wonder of creation. That this child is not her, but is *of* her. That he is his own force, a living power that is his own. Yet so much about him can resemble her brother Arthur, and so much of him carries her family traits. And his expression so often, his father's, yes, Giovanni's smile, or the furrowed brow, and now, the peaceful look while he sleeps.

The fullness of emotion for this child suffuses her days with a clarity of love she has never known.

She considered her distance from Rome, and the shift from city to the farming life here, so far away.

Perhaps, she thought, it is no surprise she finds herself in these rural surroundings, as she did in the family farm in Massachusetts. She remembered the isolation, the unhappy change for her when the family left the social and intellectual life of Cambridge.

But, her father loved the farm he bought in his retirement. Away from the business of Boston, the rural life he once idealized became a reality. He loved the work, physical and so different from his life that had been consumed by the cerebral. It was there, on this farm, while working to divert a stream as an irrigation source, not known by him to be contaminated, the cholera struck him wholly and completely.

His suffering was short and absolute. Afflicted suddenly, his body voided all, siphoning him, so that his bony frame protruded only; emptying him so that the skin of the man, once full and hearty, sagged like an empty sack, winkled and flaccid.

Deep brown eyes, arched strong brow, once holding her in thrall, once her lifeline, his windows into her soul. She saw those eyes change, and sink into a skull covered with skin dull, bluish, unearthly. She saw his skeletal hands resting aside and weak.

Margaret, remembering her fear, faithfully watching at Father's deathbed. The astonishment at his passing into the next world, and the astonishment that he had no words for her in his parting. He who had had for her in her young life *only* words; in the wisdom of the ages he imparted to her since a child of four.

Father, thought Margaret, my stern, demanding tutor. I, so young, unready, but duty-filled to please to him. For Father only were my precious first feelings, Margaret knew now.

"I will love you best only if you can read this," he declared, "or only that you can recite well."

Dido and Dante and Plutarch were set before her as conditions of his love. And only through her struggle to please him, only in this way, could she earn whatever meager affection he expressed for her.

Margaret considered his powerful influence on her life. He buried me under intellectual burdens beyond my years, she thought. His demands created a void that I could not fill. He emptied me of me, and fashioned my innermost self with himself. So overwhelmed was I, so that I could never be what I should have been on this earth. How could I be? I could not be.

Not even distance and the travels of his business dissipated his effect on me. He knew me all and saw all always, I thought, for his voice became my own inner voice. He became my very consciousness.

There were days and nights of labor at books, beginning at dawn and lasting well past supper and the candle. I worried still, have I studied enough? Will I pass his questioning examination when he arrives home? Will I be loved because I have learned well?

I did not exist other than the knowledge he instilled in me from across time and the world. How could I fill the shoes of those giants of mind? What had I to offer? To exist, I must depend on Father, and his knowledge of all the best of the minds of mankind. I felt as privileged to know of these things as I felt burdened by them.

I was made to know of the ancient gods and their foibles and all the troubles that humans caused. I was made to learn languages, mathematics and the sciences. It wasn't long before my body suffered, and took on the symptoms of what we study of our human ills. Sleeplessness, headaches, nightmares were my ritual pain.

And my very soul suffered with the sin of mankind, all the faults we are born into through the sin of Adam, and must be wary of always, even in our sleep, lest frailty take over and invite the devil into our human form.

And there, I saw him on his deathbed. Father. Once all-powerful to me, my whole world, now shrunken... small and empty in death. His life force drained, seeped from him, a hollow form, powerless. Yet still, powerful.

He lives on in me. And will he now in my son, my Angelino?

And now, she worried, my Giovanni daily exposed to danger. He, my one true love, selfless and kind, father to my child. If anything happens to him, I will be again, as I once acted for my brothers, both provider and father.

PART VII

46

Formation of a Republic
October 1848

Giovanni struggled daily, missing Margaret and his son, yet duty bound to lead his men in Rome. Margaret, faithful to her obligation, supported the cause using her strong voice to advocate for the righteousness of Italian independence in her *Tribune* articles sent by ship to New York. She must raise awareness and support for this burgeoning nation across the sea in America, and encourage the United States to recognize the new Roman Republic.

She petitioned Giovanni for news and information, who sent along with his letters the latest newspapers, pamphlets, leaflets and bulletins. But the mail was slow and unreliable. She realized that the demands of her work dictate that she must return to Rome. To stay abreast of the politics was too difficult from the remote countryside.

*****

In Rome, Giovanni threw together a canvas bag to make the journey to Rieti; his cousin Pietro, Giovanni's only friend and confidante with him, watching.

"I return now to see my beloved and my child, who every day grows and wails. He is loud! He makes himself known," Giovanni explained proudly.

"Yes, I am sure! But for how long will you be gone?" asked his cousin.

"Just two days leave. I have to see Margherita. You should see her, Pietro! She has never been more fulfilled than when holding and loving our child."

Pietro smiled, understanding his cousin's happiness. Then he asked, "And what is the favor you request of me, Giovanni. What can I do?"

"We need your help," Giovanni replied bluntly. "You know that Giuseppe controls my father's property and assets. My brothers do not know about Angelino, and they look down upon Margherita. She is to them merely an *Americana Protestante.* They will never accept her in the family. And with our political position firmly for the revolution... to them, we are traitors. You are the only one we can count on to help us secure our family ties for the child...the records of the Ossoli crest and title must include Angelino when the time comes."

Giovanni fastened the rough canvas bag closed for the journey, and sat now on the edge of the bed.

"In Rieti, Margharita and I will arrange a secret marriage and baptism with Father Trinchi so that the lineage of my son will be legitimized both by church and state mandates. It is my duty to assure that Angelino retain familial rights. Meanwhile, Margharita and Angelino must remain concealed until the will is properly accepted and filed."

Pietro understood. "With the confusion of the revolution, the courts are closed to family business. Your father's will cannot be probated now. But that works in your favor, Giovanni. If the liberals are victorious, you would stand a better chance of a fair hearing if the will goes under protest."

"Yes," agreed Giovanni. "And you, the rightful heir to the title of *Marchese,* would have most sway with the courts if necessary, in declaring Angelino's legitimacy. Margherita and I agree that you are the only family member that we can trust...trust with our secret, and trust to help secure Angelino's place in the family record."

He stood now, gathering his things, and waited for his reaction.

"Your brothers are hard ones," Pietro agreed. "They always have been. We grew up together with their condescending attitudes. They are still as selfish and cruel now as they were then. Their only concern is for themselves and the family land. They would stop at nothing to try to illegitimize your son."

"My cousin and my friend," said Giovanni warmly. "And further," now he asked Pietro, "Will you honor Margharita and me to be Angelino's godfather? Baptize the child in the faith. Be his guardian if disaster befalls? I know you will keep him safe and protect his familial rights."

"I will stand for him. Do not worry. It would be my privilege to do this for you."

Giovanni stepped forward to embrace him. He was Giovanni's closest ally, having endured years of family conflict together. There was no one better to choose to protect Angelino's interests.

Pietro continued, "But when? Why not now? Do not return from Rieti so soon. I can meet you there in two days if you would like."

"No, Pietro. This will be a quick visit, for I must return to my post. The city teems with fury and violence since the Pope appointed Pellegrino Rossi as his new Minister. Rumors are that Pius gave him free reign to clamp down on many of our new freedoms. To control the revolutionary clubs. To help regain power and political control."

"Yes. Rossi has made only enemies with his proposals and changes. Hatred for him ferments on both sides. He has taken away some of the conservative's ecclesiastical power, and at the same time he despises the liberals in the *Consulta*."

Giovanni added, "He outright refuses to acknowledge the democratic leaders. He keeps no terms with them, not even in appearance. He will stop at nothing to crush a free Italy."

"It becomes harder to keep order in the streets."

"The extremists are using disorder to try to overthrow the existing government, and the Vatican is watching all."

"I must leave now, to Margharita. Then return to Rome in haste to my post and to my men. All necessary requirements will be arranged with Father Trinchi early next month, in Rieti."

47

Rieti
November 1848

Pietro could not doze for more than a minute in the lurching carriage as it jolted along the rutted back roads toward Rieti, nestled in the hills just south of Rome. Suddenly, the sleepy village came into view, framed neatly in the morning haze through the carriage window.

He thanked the driver, took his bag, and walked the quiet village street to the pleasant and simple country house where Margaret and Giovanni set up home.

"Giovanni! Open the door! It's Pietro!" came his exclamation accompanied by insistent knocking.

Upon seeing Giovanni, Pietro's wide grin overtook his exhaustion from the journey. The two embraced in anticipation of the joy of the event to come, knowing that there will be time later for the heavy news that each carried inside.

Their greeting was interrupted by the infant Angelino's emphatic wails coming from the bedroom, loudly objecting to Margaret's last stages of bundling him in wools against November's morning chill for the walk to the church to meet Father Trinchi.

"He's got your voice," said Pietro to Giovanni with a grin.

"Pietro! We are so happy you have come!" said Margaret entering the room and immediately handing the baby, now happy, to his prospective godfather. "How was the journey? Any troubles?"

"We can save discussion of troubles for after church," said Giovanni. "For now, this is a day of great devotion for our family."

"Yes. That is true," acknowledged Margaret, handing Angelino off to Pietro. "Meet your godson, Pietro. His soul, as well as his earthly matters, could be in your hands one day."

Together, they began the walk to the town Church of San Nicola, originally a beloved shrine dedicated in 1442. Rebuilt several times over its four hundred years as a place of worship, it stands as the pride of the town.

Father Trinchi awaited, and greeted them warmly in the narthex, ushering them all inside. Approaching the altar, the masterpiece painting of St. Nicholas could be seen in the dim light.

Pietro held the child. Giovanni turned to face Margaret and thought he'd never seen her look so beautiful.

Father Trinchi began the ceremony, his words fading away from their hearing as they gazed into each other's eyes. Margaret embraced the fullness of love. Their love. Their child. To Giovanni, who has given her his all, she willingly gave this gift, their marriage.

Giovanni, understanding, trembled with emotion.

Father Trinchi completed the small ceremony with a blessing.

The couple exchanged a tender kiss.

They then turned to Pietro, who, balancing Angelino dozing in his arms, reached out to the couple to embrace and congratulate them. All were filled with quiet warmth and emotion and joy.

Then Father Trinchi began the baptismal ceremony with the traditional questions asked of godparents on behalf of the child:

"What do you ask of the Church of God?" the priest addressed Angelino.

"Faith," dutifully answered Pietro.

"And what does faith offer you?"

"Everlasting life…"

After the ceremony, Margaret rocked the child to sleep and placed him in his cradle in their bedroom while Giovanni and Pietro sat in the small parlor catching up on family matters.

"Thank you for doing this for us, Pietro," said Giovanni.

"Father Trinchi was more than helpful today. And I will make sure that the proper paperwork of the sacraments will be registered and recorded both here and in Rome," he replied.

Margaret entered the room at that point and embraced Pietro to add her thanks. Then she went to sit at her husband's side.

"Giovanni," she said, "I am packed to return to Rome with you. Chiara is ready to attend to Angelino here. He is in good hands. Angelino will be her only charge. She will treat him like her own."

"Good, Margharita. He will be safer here than in Rome. And our situation will have greater secrecy than if we brought him with us."

"I know. But my heart breaks to leave him. I am torn in two, Giovanni."

"The coach between Rome and Rieti is dependable. We shall see him often."

"Yes. And my work is to write of the revolution and to witness. It is best achieved there."

Her thoughts turned to her fears for Giovanni's safety. "It seems the number of militant factions in Rome grows daily. How long can order be maintained under these conditions?"

Both men looked grave. Pietro responded, "Margaret, you are right to ask. Pope Pius has lost a great deal of power in the Vatican. The agitators are winning more and more seats in the *Consulta* daily, and are becoming the power in the government. Their followers are causing civil unrest. They act more like mobs, really."

"There are rumors at the barracks," Giovanni added, "that they are plotting against the Pope, and against Rossi, who has taken control of the Finance, Transportation, Communication Ministries."

"Yes. In short, he has control of anything that matters," observed Margaret.

"Rossi is the scourge of Italian freedom. He will not rest until the Revolution is crushed," Pietro added.

"Speculations and rumors are not worth repeating," said Giovanni. "But it is said that Garibaldi arrives with his troops soon to defend the northern border."

And blessed Father Gavazzi is on the march with the volunteers from the rally at the Colosseum. Garibaldi and Gavazzi will meet in Bologna. We will wait and see what orders Rossi gives then."

Margaret understood the dangers that lie ahead. The whole country, and all of Europe, a tinderbox of revolution.

48

The Vatican
November 1848

Pellegrino Rossi was faced with immense toil, and a great number of enemies.

Rossi's reforms left no group untouched. The radicals hated him because he was against a constitutional government; those who mistrusted priestly government hated him because he supported Pius; revolutionaries and officers of the Civic Guard hated him because he wanted power kept away from the people: they were joined by small shopkeepers, loafers and informants, and the youths who hated all authority. He was hated by the magistrates who were used to making money from a faulty system; and the underground mob movement hated him because his power thwarted theirs.

Conspiracies against Rossi were preached openly in the streets, in the neighborhoods and in the taverns. He openly foiled the hopes of the people, who eagerly awaited the meeting of Gavazzi and the army of volunteers with Garibaldi and his men. But Rossi sent orders not to allow Garibaldi into the Papal States at Bologna.

Outraged, Father Gavazzi stepped up in a great theatrical show to escort Garibaldi himself over the border. For this act of defiance, Gavazzi was later dragged from his home in the middle of the night, arrested by Rossi's orders.

To have set himself against Father Gavazzi, most loved by the people, was a message that was loud and clear to the people of Rome.

His power firmly established, his immediate objective now was to deliver a clear policy statement during Parliament's opening session. The stakes were high; if his policies were accepted and he received support of Parliament and the Chamber of Deputies, his way would be paved for clear steps to save the power of the papacy.

Among opponents, the importance of Rossi's opening speech was fully realized. His new policy statement could carry a majority in the Chamber if it got a fair hearing. Council members *Ciceruacchio*, Sterbini and their revolutionary followers, who were about to reap the fruit of their many years' labor, were desperate to stop Rossi's rise to power.

49

Ossoli in Rome
November 14, 1848

"Come! Come with us! We will meet and have drinks after duty tonight. You should let off some steam. So serious always!" Private Trentenove repeated the offer to come along for a drink.

Giovanni had been hounded by him for weeks to join with some of his younger men in a bit of after-hours carousing. He always refused, thinking first of Margaret, and thinking always of his son, away in Rieti.

But even he grew weary. A few hours of relief may do me some good tonight, he thought.

"Yes. Perhaps I will join you this time," he assented. "Where will you be?"

"At the Ripetta. Brunetti and Neri will be there. They are always good for inside information. Brunetti lets loose after a few draughts of wine. And for some laughs, after Neri drinks, he does his imitations, you know," Trentanove smiling, recalling Neri's antics. "Good! There will be others, too!"

"Fine." Giovanni smiled, thinking he could enjoy some of their boyish humor. "I will meet you there later."

The Ripetta was a known meeting place for the revolutionaries. Rumors and news flew in and out of the tavern. It was a place to hear and be overheard. To be seen by those active in the movement, and by spies for all factions.

This night, Ossoli's young men went there direct from guard duty still in their uniforms, now disarrayed and untidy. There they sat, rowdy and roaring with laughter, their youth apparent and unguarded.

They were perfect targets for the agitator, who entered the smoke-filled room, seeking out some innocents to recruit for his dirty work, desperately, for the time for action was upon him. He scanned the tavern, and saw the five, laughing loudly and drinking, having an uproarious time. He approached their table, and he pounced.

"You sloppy, good-for-nothing *pigs!*" shouted the man of medium height, wide and broad, stocky and strong, dressed in black, his face weathered and stern. He stood at their table, looking down upon them, berating them so everyone could hear.

Their hilarity stopped instantly when they saw who he was. Pietro Sterbini, the most powerful leader of the revolutionary clubs.

Eyes downcast, immediately the five young men put down their glasses on the sticky table, wet with spilled drink and looked at the floor, at nothing.

"In your uniforms, stained with wine, open at the collar," he shouted, eyes wide with rage, he grabbed Neri by his open shirt, lurching him to his feet. "A disgrace to the Civic Guard uniform...and to our cause." He spat upon the young man's shoes, and pushed him roughly back to his seat.

"And you, the biggest disappointment," he said to Luigi Brunetti, who sat humiliated. "Your father, our great leader, *Ciceruacchio*, would be shamed to see you here like this! Loafing and drinking when there is so much at stake."

All the room quieted, each voice in the tavern died down in turn, the clinking of glasses slowly silenced, the onlookers watched and stared.

"You all sit and do *nothing* when our cause is at a threshold..."

"Sir…" Luigi Brunetti was the one with enough nerve to remark, but his voice was almost inaudible. "We have been on duty for ten days straight, and…"

"Enough!" Sterbini shouted. "Thousands of men have sacrificed their *lives*!" And what have you given? Now here, drunk, carousing… and when confronted, whining like women! When our revolution now faces its utmost crisis."

Seeing now that he had damaged their pride, he knew they would do anything to gain it back in their own eyes, and in the eyes of all those who watched. Sterbini knew their vulnerability. He slowly circled the table, looking at each young man in his face as he passed by, studying one after another. In the tavern, once rowdy and loud, now only Sterbini's footfall could be heard in the room.

Seeing he had control of the young men at the table, he broke the silence, speaking quietly now, almost gently, asking, "Which one of you would do a deed of great bravery?" He took a few more steps in silence, staging his request. "Which of you would perform a deed so daring that it that could guarantee our victory, a free Italy?" Another calculated pause, then, "Which of you has the courage to act like a man?"

"I," said Luigi Brunetti first. He pushed out the chair from the table, scraping the wooden floor, the sound reverberating in the quiet tavern.

Sterbini turned to look, maintaining his stern demeanor to hide his pleasure. So easy to manipulate when they are young, he thought, as he watched the boy rise from his chair. Brunetti stood now, full height, to face Sterbini. Their eyes locked in challenge.

Now, the room was filled with the sound of the creaking of each of the boys' chairs, wood scraping the floor audibly as the five young men stood in turn, soberly echoing each other's words with "I will," "And I," and, "I too," standing, assenting.

"Good." said Sterbini, satisfied with the results of his effort. Then, scanning the tavern with a look that suggested that all the onlookers all go back to their drink and conversation, he said to the five, "Come with me outside. I have a plan…"

Just then, Ossoli crossed the Piazza del Popolo, approaching the Ripetta to join his men. He barely caught sight of them as they left as a group, heads down in serious contemplation, following their brawny leader, Sterbini, clearly in control.

Thinking they would return soon, Giovanni took a table in the tavern to wait. He sat alone, perplexed. Why was Sterbini here? And with my men? As his wine was being poured in the noisy tavern, he noticed three men at a table nearby who pointed in his direction. They shifted their gaze away when he turned toward them. Eventually, one approached.

"Well, Sergeant Major," noting the bars on his uniform, "I see you are alone tonight."

Giovanni's gaze took in a lanky, tousled young man, his aspect bold and daring, and not a little drunk.

"What is it to you?" Giovanni asked, nonplussed.

"I see your friends left without you. Important business, no?" The man boldly moved the empty chair with his foot away from the table so there was only open space between them.

Giovanni pretended not to notice and drank his wine casually. But his free hand moved to his weapon in readiness.

"I don't know what you are talking about. Go back to your friends. You're drunk," Giovanni replied quietly.

Just then, two voices spoke from across the room. "Hey! Come back here! You won't get anywhere with him! Not here, anyway."

Giovanni's questioner looked toward his compatriots as if to concede, and then slowly turned back to him. He stepped nearer to Giovanni and bent close to be heard distinctively. He smelled of sweat and wine. He hissed, "I know you…And I will watch. Your men left with Sterbini. They did not wait for you."

50

Rome
November 15, 1848

"Palazzo Cancelleria will be our duty today men," Ossoli delivered the orders to his troops after roll call.

Brunetti, Trentanove and Neri had not reported for duty that morning. The last he saw of them was their backs as they left the Ripetta Taverna last night. Noting this with concern, he continued to address his men.

"Today is the opening of the new Parliament, and Prime Minister Rossi will address the Council of Deputies. Trouble is anticipated. Rumors are flying. Many factions will be in the courtyard awaiting his arrival. Utmost caution is urged. We are there as peacekeepers in case protests become violent."

Ossoli and his men arrived, wending their way through groups tightly bound in animated conversation, passing through the gates that featured columns of cherubs swirling in bound ecstasy, frozen for centuries in relief on the grand entrance of Rome's Palazzo Cancelleria. Just past the portal to the fifteenth century church, built atop an ancient pagan sanctuary, the bone colored travertine marble gives way to a spacious plaza, lined with majestic arched entryways.

The crowd gathered inside and outside the ancient walls of the Cancelleria. Inside the walls in the square there was a composite battalion hundreds of soldiers of the Civic Guard. Giovanni and his men approached their assigned station and waited, anxious and tense.

They watched the crowd gathering, men and women of every type, nobles, citizens, shopkeepers and poor. Undercover police agents were strolling and watching. People of various demeanors assembled in constituent groupings in the Piazza. Among them were merchants and university students; clerics, off duty soldiers, and politicians; the merely curious, the hostile, and the angry.

A sudden sound of raised voices and shouts in the square, and the crowd merged together like a swarm to see. Then, the crowd parted to allow a carriage through, and cheers were heard as Sterbini dismounted the carriage, and strode with purpose to the Chamber entrance.

Inside the Cancelleria, in the Chamber of Deputies, the assembly was gathered, awaiting their leader. The Council, influenced by Sterbini, was prepared to register dissent of Rossi's new policies. They gathered on the opposition benches, ready to repudiate Rossi's address to the opening session, to obstruct any plan that would strengthen papal authority.

Outside in the piazza, the crowd became thick. The people talked among themselves in rapid and excited tones as they awaited the coming of Rossi's carriage, their outrage evident after his show of power against Garibaldi and Gavazzi.

"The anger here is palpable," said Colonel Tittoni to Ossoli after reviewing his troops.

"Yes sir," he replied. "Rossi's orders to stop Garibaldi's entrance to Bologna made the people furious. Then, Father Gavazzi's arrest destroyed any faith in Pius and his administration."

"Such insults to two of their most beloved leaders," Tittoni added, "Rossi makes such mistakes. He does not care if the people are behind him or not."

Their eyes continued to search the crowd uneasily as they spoke.

Ossoli responded, "Rossi was warned that this last public offense could cause retaliation."

But no warning could deter Rossi from appearing today. Revolution was spreading like contagion throughout the monarchies of Europe. He had had enough as he watched as European crowned heads flee into exile, were killed, or capitulated to the demands by the people for self-government.

Yet here, in Rome, he felt he could do his part to stabilize and preserve the old order. Here, he felt he could exercise his influence in the Chamber of Deputies on behalf of Papal authority in this assembly on this day of November 15, 1848.

"Your unit is in order, Sergeant Major," said Tittoni with a sharp salute, as he left to review the other stations.

Ossoli stood on guard now among his men.

"There! I see them, Sir!" A private in the battalion caught sight of Trentanove, Brunetti and Neri among the crowd.

"Where? Are they in uniform?" asked Giovanni.

"No Sir, they are not. And they stand together near the entrance to the Chamber. They are in a small crowd of men who they came in with. They are not in uniform and stand with them."

Just then, Rossi's carriage made its way inside the gates, slowly, as the crowd became silent and only reluctantly made way. Each onlooker pressed forward to catch sight of the powerful man. The clattering of hooves on the paving stones announced the carriage as it made way toward the entrance closest to the Chamber of Deputies. The horses were reined in sharply to allow a quick descent from the carriage for Count Pellegrino Rossi, whose countenance still held his proud sneer shown to the multitudes that had lined the streets of Rome, a crowd whose faces showed a mix of mere curiosity, abject fear, and outright anger. There were those who hissed and heckled his approach.

Count Rossi's close-cropped curly hair crowned his head with a youthful look; but that impression was quickly dissipated by his deeply dark-ringed, heavily lidded eyes, which betrayed worry and trouble. His straight, falcon-like nose led to shapely lips permanently checked from smiling. His grim, sarcastic demeanor greeted the crowd as he gathered his overcoat around him preparing to descend the carriage: high collar stiff and straight, ample shoulder cape triple layered, sleeves deeply cuffed, tailored in the latest French fashion.

Rossi was to alight on the left hand side of the carriage. As if on cue, some fifty or sixty men silently formed two long lines on either side, which led the way from the carriage door to the foot of the stairs.

Rossi refused the aid of the driver as he descended from the carriage, proud frame upright. He was followed by Cavaliere Pietro Righeti and a footservant.

There was an eerie hush from the crowd. Only the crunch of gravel on the ancient stone could be heard as Rossi and his men started toward the travertine entranceway through which the Chamber of Deputies could be easily gained.

Then, in the still and brilliant sunshine of the afternoon, a silent signal was made. As Rossi ascended the first step of the small stairway, the three were suddenly surrounded by a ready crowd of rough men, who skillfully jostled and hustled them apart, separating Rossi from his two compatriots.

In the midst the of sudden confusion and motion, one swift blow to Rossi's left ribcage caused him to turn his head instinctively toward his attacker, exposing his neck opposite from the folds of the stiff collar. A sudden bright flash of a knife blade gleamed in the afternoon sun; the assassin's hand, expert and sure; bright blood spurted with each jab of swift steel.

Stunned, stopped and still, no sound came from his gaping mouth. Rossi's heart, pumping wildly from the shock and tumult, only hastened his death, blood flowing from his neck before his fixed eyes. Slowly, he swooned, then tried to step forward, but his legs sank as if from exhaustion as his form melted to the ground; tight grip releasing all that he held, papers of his speech so carefully prepared, falling, scattering, then lifting momentarily in a gentle breeze only to drop carelessly, one by one, across the piazza.

While the assassin escaped, the accomplices stood shoulder to shoulder, using their bodies as a human wall to surround Rossi, shielding him from onlookers who might call for aid. They watched, guarding, as his lifeblood darkened the ancient stone.

51

Rome

The day after the assassination of Minister Rossi, the Papal government faltered with the desertion of most of the cabinet ministers. The Pope fortified himself in his palace, the Quirinal, with the few men of his staff who stood by him.

The Civic Guard marched in full force to the Piazza del Popolo to organize their march to the Quirinal.

After reviewing the troops, Colonel Tittioni addressed them.

"This is the day, men. The Pope's government is in disarray. His ministers have deserted him. He hides now in his palace, trying to hold desperately to any power he might have. Today, our leaders, those of the *Circulo Romano* elected to the Chamber of Deputies will address the Pope and demand a change of Ministry and of governmental measures."

The men raised shouts of joy in a wave of sound that filled the air. Whoops and cries of jubilation and relief took over the piazza. Tittoni raised his voice over the cacophony of sound, shouting,

"Together we march to the Quirinal as a show of power of the people!" The troops roared their approval. Then Tittoni ended with a cry of words that would echo in the ears of the men, "There we will keep peace; there we will witness history, there will be the formation of the Roman Republic, a nation, made by all of us!"

The trumpets sounded, and all marched with great purpose toward the Pope's palace. The men, made proud and bold by the powerful words of the Colonel, now marched to their assigned posts within the Quirinal walls.

Neri, Trentanove and Brunetti were still missing. Ossoli's heart sank. His suspicions seemed confirmed that they must have been involved with yesterday's terrible deed.

After the assassination, confusion in the streets of Rome was rampant. Armed gangs roved everywhere, shouting support for Rossi's murderers. Some marched to the widow Rossi's home and chanted with glee under her windows in support for the death of her husband. Spy networks were buzzing, appearing then disappearing like apparitions in the night. Chatter and gossip flew, careening around corners, into homes, shops and offices. People appeared. People disappeared. An undercurrent of suspense and danger was everywhere.

Where were his men, wondered Giovanni? How far were they involved in the plot? Where are they now? Are they safe? In hiding? Giovanni worried for them, for their safety, for their fates.

Meanwhile, groups of civilians had gathered in the piazza of the Quirinal awaiting any news. All now on the palace grounds, word was received that the formal request for a change in Ministries and in the workings of the Papal government, made by members of the Chamber of Deputies, received a peremptory negative from the Pope's aides.

Unsatisfied, the Ministers insisted on seeing the Pope himself, but to no avail. Pius blatantly disregarded the request. The doors of the Quirinal would not open for them. Word of this refusal spread among the crowd. Whispers turned to shouts, and shouts turned to cries of indignation.

The atmosphere on the Quirinal grounds tensed. Tempers escalated. The crowd demanded the Pope show himself. Chants and outrage filled the air. The Civic Guard slowly pressed forward. Tensions flared. An attempt at entry was made when a door of the Palace was set ablaze.

The Pope's Swiss Guard, so few in number against the dissenters, now in a panic, fired on the crowd. At once, the Civic Guard returned fire. A lone and stray bullet found the Pope's secretary, who stood at a second floor open window to watch the scene below.

Now, panic spread, the scene devolving into chaos. Movement of men, all against purposes, colliding, changing course, pushing on again. Allies found one another, shouted instructions, then dispersed, making their way for the safety of the ancient alleyways.

Among the tumult of sight and sound, sharp voices shouting, "There! There!" stood out to Giovanni's ears. He turned to see that it was he who was being singled out. The men cried and pointed Giovanni out to others, "There's the man! The one who was at the Ripetta that night, looking for them! The ones who stabbed Rossi. That's the man who looked for them!"

The men forced their way forward into the crowd, but too late. For Giovanni, too, pushed his way into the mad scene and became part of the sea of confusion. Faces, uniforms, civilians, shouts, all a blur of color, sound and motion.

Giovanni ran, dodged, ducked his way out of sight. He stopped, leaning on the damp stone in an abandoned alleyway, panting. Who were those men? They're not the drunken ones from the Ripetta. They must have reported me to others. Am I being followed? He wondered. Am I betrayed? Accused? Set up as involved in the plot? But by whom? For the first time, fear showed in Giovanni's eyes.

52

The Siege
Margaret

I try to sleep, alone in my rooms. But sleep does not come easily now. I pray for Giovanni. I worry for Angelino. But the situation here moves too quickly to be with my baby in the country. This is my public duty, my little Angelino. I am here to witness and to report.

After Rossi's assassination and the chaos at the Quirinal, Pope Pius, in fear for his life, fled the Vatican in the dark of night dressed as a common priest. He made his way out of Rome south, to Gaeta outside of Naples, to the protection of the Bourbon King Ferdinand.

Rome was now deserted by its leader. The radical ministers of the Chamber of Deputies wasted no time. Rome was declared a Republic. A constitution was ratified and a ruling triumvirate was formed, Giuseppe Mazzini elected as First Triumvir.

He soon entered the city for the first time since his exile and was made a Roman Citizen. Crowds lined the streets when he arrived, greeting him with cheers. They felt that Mazzini, the statesman, would be their leader.

Not long after his arrival, Mazzini sent me a note, asking that he might visit. With joy, I received him in my parlor for tea. Although in constant correspondence, not since France have I seen him. He now appeared thin and haggard, the strain showing in his face and frame. We spoke of the future of the Republic. We spoke at length.

He beseeched me to continue the dispatches to the American people of our cause. To try to influence the American government to officially recognize our young Republic.

He knew that the challenge would be great. The foes are many, strong and subtle. He prayed that heaven would help.

Since declaring independence, I have witnessed the fervor of the people. I have witnessed the flag of the Roman Republic placed in the hands of the statue of Emperor Marcus Aurelius. The opening of the Constituent Assembly and the fine procession; all the troops in Rome turned out in in uniforms red, robust and bold. I have observed the citizens of the new Republic in my walks from the Quirinal, to the Forum, to the Capitol. All is alive here with excitement and energy.

53

The news of all the activity in Rome reached Pope Pius, who, from his exile, called for the aid of all Catholic nations to rid Rome of the new government that had been declared in his absence. Which would be the first of those countries to restore the Pope to the Vatican? The monarchies of Europe all scrambled to be the first, to be most favored, to be the savior of the Catholic seat of power.

The Spanish made preparations to march upon Rome from the south. The Austrian army prepared to march from the north. And now, the arrival of French troops sent by Louis Napoleon to the port of Civitavecchia, just west of Rome, to answer the call.

Six thousand French troops and armaments arrived in Italy. French General Ouidinot set up his operation, then sent his aide to Rome to meet with Mazzini and the Triumvirs. It was explained that they sought to block the intervention of Austrian and Spanish troops. Then the aide expressed the desire of the French to promote accord between the Pope and the Roman people.

Mazzini listened patiently. At length, he asked, "And if the Roman people do not *wish* the Pope to be restored?"

"He will be restored, just the same," came the reply.

*****

When they heard the news, the Roman citizenry were incensed. "The French will not take Rome!" The air resounded with the cries of the people, "*Viva La Republica!*" Preparations began immediately. Men and women worked to barricade the streets; stockades were built in strategic positions. Provisions were stored, making ready for a siege.

Margaret went out to witness. The streets were alive with people on foot with arms full of bundles, all they could carry, rushing to and fro. Donkeys pulled carts filled to the brink. Horses pulled carriages. Households were being dismantled. Lumber and masonry on the move. Carts, carriages, horses and people scurried in every which direction, collisions, near-misses, danger at every turn, most movement at cross-purposes.

There were those who were fleeing the city, faces filled with fear, dragging crying children by their arms. There were those who served the cause, carrying bricks and stones to build barricades, shouting orders to others while they tramped heavily to their labors. There were those who, protecting their property, boarded up their windows and doors, the sound of hammers frantically rapping iron nails.

Among the confusion Margaret saw a cart filled with medical supplies for the wounded; antiseptic and bandages, and wood for splints, cots, blankets and linens.

"Where are you taking those?" she shouted to the man who did not stop his cart.

"The hospital, Signora…Fate Bene Fratelli," his answer nearly unheard as he moved among the streams of others, wheels clattering on the uneven stone street.

Margaret was passed by a group of women talking loudly about the review of the troops of the Civic Guard at Piazza Santa Apostali. She saw a crowd of people heading that way. She allowed herself to be swept along, among the citizens of Rome, to watch the review, hoping to catch a glimpse of Giovanni among them.

The piazza was filled with men, the volunteers, ten thousand strong, handsome in their uniforms, standing at attention in their battalions. The citizens who came to watch stood in a hushed awe.

She strained to find Giovanni, but he was lost in the faces of the many.

The troops stood tall, shining and fierce. There were some whose faces were smooth and fresh, eyes staring clear and straight ahead. Some faces were brown from labor in the sun, deep lines embedded, eyes misty and knowing. There were those whose professions stood out on their countenances, maybe physicians, accountants, clerks or scribes, their eyes surrounded with lines from study, their backs bowed slightly from years bent over book and desk. All were resolute. All were determined.

Satisfied with his review of the troops, Colonel Tittoni climbed the steps to the podium to address them. "Our Republic is being threatened!" he shouted. "You are the volunteer force. The *best citizens of Rome!*" he pounded his fist. "Will you defend our city?" His question rallied the troops.

To a man, they raised their voices. The air was filled with deep, intense huzzahs. Some raised their muskets and shouted, *"Si! Si!"* Others raised their hats and chanted, *"Roma o Morte!"* The piazza was alive with a fierce energy.

Now the battalions stood, ready.

Margaret was moved deeply by the commitment of the men in formation. She knew that she must do more for the cause in this hour of human need. She thought of the man on his way to the hospital with the supply cart. She left the piazza and made her way there directly. As she crossed the old Roman bridge to the small island in the middle of the Tiber she saw the large stone structure, built by the monks in the middle ages. It was alive with people, scurrying to and fro, preparing wards that have not been in use for years. It was there that she knew she could be of some help.

She saw the Principessa Belgioioso, Directress of Hospitals, at the center of the hubbub. There, she shouted instructions, or handed out papers with orders. Others came to her to and fro with questions, or reports. Margaret approached her, asking, "What can I do? Do you need any assistance?"

Margaret was assigned immediately to organize and prepare for the opening of the old west wing wards for the wounded that will soon be sure to come.

*****

The next morning, Giovanni surveyed the countryside below him. He and the men of the Second Battalion stood guard on the Aurelian wall of the Vatican gardens, a wall that has withstood many attacks over the centuries. Made of thick Roman brick, there were inner chambers for catapults, where now cannons stood ready. There were ample walkways that once offered access for aim of the bow and arrow, now for musket fire.

"How long do you think these old stones could withstand our modern armaments?" Giovanni asked his Captain who patrolled among the men.

"It's impossible to tell," came the reply. "But good reason to dispatch the enemy quickly so we don't find out!" he added dryly.

It was just past dawn, and an eerie mist still hovered above the ground. All was quiet. The men were nervous, knowing that their position was most vulnerable to attack from the French, who will approach from the southeast.

"Sir," one of his soldiers addressed him. "Where do Garibaldi's men stand?"

"There. Just south of us. Janiculum Hill. They guard the Porta San Pancrazio, in case the enemy attacks the city's main gate. Or they may come here first, toward us from Civitavecchia. If they attack these walls they could gain direct access into the Vatican."

The young soldier's eyes traced the surrounding countryside. He tried to imagine enemy soldiers in a landscape he had known all his life. All that had once been familiar seemed suddenly strange to him.

"Are you ready to fight?" the soldier's voice quavered.

Giovanni looked into his eyes, and could see he was not much more than a boy.

"Is anyone ever ready?" he replied.

Giovanni thought of the makeup of his patrol. That the defense of Rome depended mostly on the inexperienced like himself, or shopkeepers, or farmers, or this young boy, probably a university student.

"Have you ever fought in a war?" asked the young man.

"No. I have not," he said. "But I will put down my life for the safety of the Roman Republic," came Giovanni's honest reply. But in his mind he beheld his beloved Margarita and his infant son, Angelino.

Fear registered on the face of the young man. Giovanni softened toward him.

"What is your name, son?"

"Enzo Proscio, sir."

"We stick together now, no?"

"Yes sir," the boy replied with a weak smile.

The Roman defense was a hodgepodge force of volunteers and seasoned troops. The Papal Regular troops, eager to fight, having always been called second rate to the Pope's Suisse Guard. There was a brigade of Bersigliari, the light infantry sharpshooters of the Royal Italian Army; and last, there were the rough and ready guerilla forces of Garibaldi.

No one was sure how they would all hold up against the storied French battalions, disciplined and trained. Nonetheless, Giovanni stood lookout on the wall, resolute and firm, awaiting the attack.

*****

Near Civitavecchia, General Ouidinot finished preparations for his troops to approach Rome. He had a notion that Italians are not predisposed to fight, so he expected no more than a token resistance. He sent his men without siege guns or scaling ladders. The forward scouts, even, were perfunctory, as they marched only a short way in front of the troops, who were more interested in making an impression, marching in precision ranks, in their straight columns and their splendid uniforms.

From the Vatican's westernmost wall, Ossoli's Second Battalion was first to spot the enemy's approach. On the Captain's command, they sprang into action, barraging them with heavy artillery and musket fire from the walls. French troops were caught by surprise at the ferocity of the assault. They broke ranks and scurried for cover behind the trees and in the dykes that cut across the valley beneath Vatican Hill.

Taking advantage of the enemy's confusion, the Captain ordered a charge. Ossoli was ready. His was the first detail on ground offensive. Private Proscio and the men readied their muskets and followed him double-time out through the Vatican gardens.

They proceeded relentlessly forward, eyes straining to see through billows of smoke from cannon fire. All senses sharp with fear, yet the surroundings soft, hazy, subdued. Through the ghostly gardens, passing fountains and statues forms indistinct, only their footfall on the soft earth seemed real. The sudden snap of a twig. The enemy around them, unseen. Deafening cannon fire from the height of the wall above, a distant and different reality, they alone in a hazy underworld.

When they reached the gate of the ancient wall, Ossoli's eyes flashing, grimace firm, holding bayonet forward, shouted, *"Charge!"* boldly leading his men. All dashed recklessly forward, firing their muskets, brandishing their bayonets and pushing into the brush to flush out the French attackers.

They saw not their faces. They saw them not as men, but as enemy. They splashed the grass with blood, a savage desire overtaking them all.

54

Margaret

I work at the hospital until I feel my legs will give out. Until I can no more. The city's cab drivers in a constant stream, rush in with the wounded, brought down from the hills in wheelbarrows, bleeding and moaning, or limp and unconscious, or white with death. From the wide entranceway, I direct the stretchers toward the ward, toward surgery, or toward the morgue.

I am sometimes overcome with grief for these men; nonetheless I encourage and hearten each soldier. I search the faces as they arrive, in fear that it might be Giovanni's that I would see.

I work among the dying, the wounded, the amputees. Men in every form of pain and horror; yet I never shrink from them. I pray that if Giovanni were in such a position, there would be a kind soul there to help him in my place.

I check the men in the wards to see that they are receiving the attention they need. I sit with them and listen to their fears, their stories. I offer comfort. I write letters to their loved ones, dictated in weak and fading voices.

Alone in the evenings in my rooms, I write my dispatches with urgent appeal to America to recognize this young Republic. I write. I must impress on the American people the importance, nay, the *duty* of

America to recognize Italy as a sovereign nation, with its elected government, and an approved constitution. I urge my readers to cry out for the souls that have perished in its creation, and for those who now stand guard. I say, "America! Declare Italy's legitimacy among nations! Send a talisman to your ambassadors, that they may aid with their words this just cause!" I pray that I am heard.

In the dark hours, alone in my room, I hear the wail of a child in my ears, although there are no children here. Families have long since evacuated this area of Rome.

In the light of the day, among the noise of war, reports of cannon, and musket, I hear the wail of a child.

I remember when I was a child. Father would leave me at home while he served. I, bereft.

Papa, please come home. When will you be home? I will study and recite for you.

"Here is a letter from Papa, Margaret," said mother.

"I don't want a letter. I want Papa."

"You know, Margaret, he serves our country. He must be away from us to serve."

How cruel, now, to know now first hand, the pain of separation, for both parent and child.

I whisper to my little one, so far away. Duty, my little Angelino. My heart is torn in two. I yearn for you, to hold you in my arms.

But, duty first, little Angelino. Your Papa and I are helping to form a nation. One that will be free, so you can live wholly and fully here. Public duty before personal needs.

Duty, mio bambino. Then I will return to you.

55

After days of battle, the combined forces of the Roman Republic routed the army of the French attackers, despite the foreigner's superior armaments and training.

Citizen volunteers defended the wall with fervor. Then, Garibaldi and his legions surrounded the enemy forces outside the walls of the city, the French no match for the guerillas' relentless ferocity. Now the enemy lay helpless and broken.

Every citizen of Rome knew the details of the battle. They were elated. Overcome with joy. All rushed to the piazzas and streets to celebrate. But Garibaldi knew the job wasn't finished. He immediately petitioned Mazzini to continue their strike, to vanquish the enemy while in disarray. "They were caught unprepared!" he said. "Now is the time!"

But Mazzini and the Triumvirate disagreed. They had already been approached by the French to negotiate. As a statesman, Mazzini's desire was for Italy to be recognized as free and independent, a nation among nations. He convinced the Triumvirate to agree to talks in good faith.

A truce was called. Weeks were spent in negotiations, which Louis Napoleon never intended to honor. He was merely toying with the vanity of the Republic. The talks, merely a delay tactic while reinforcements of men and armaments made their way from France by ship to Civitavecchia.

*****

The time of the truce made for a strange lull in the city. French soldiers were nursed back to health in Italian hospitals and sent back to Civitavecchia.

Citizens tried to return to normal, but, what was normal now? A mix of fear and uncertainty. There was a great victory. Or was there a victory? The city still on guard, barricaded. Lives suspended. The city still with the enemy's camp nearby. Rumors of the negotiations flew around the city's cafes and among its citizens. Is the fighting over? Will it resume?

A month went by in this way, in false negotiations; the neophyte government misled, until the enemy's reinforcements arrived. Then, for the French, all was ready.

Louis Napoleon now declared war against Rome. Mazzini was devastated by the betrayal. General Ouidinot gave notice to the citizens of Rome that the city will be under attack on Monday, he warned. He gave three days for residents to leave if they wish. Again, the exhausted citizens made ready for a siege.

But instead, more deception. Sunday morning's dawn was greeted by cannon fire, a full-scale assault launched on the sleeping city, its defenders fast asleep in their bivouacs.

Rome was in turmoil. All over the city the church bells rang, drums sounded, crowds collected in the piazzas. Soldiers ran shouting through the streets to their posts, horses and carts drove full tilt through the narrow streets with the wounded who were being carried down from Janiculum Hill. Smoke blinded their path. Cannon shot deafened their ears.

The French occupied the four-storied Villa Corsini on the hill just outside the city's wall and Rome's western gate. Their sharpshooters crouched behind the villa's low stone enclosure and covered the entire western slope with musket fire. In front of the villa, large earthenware pots filled with lemon trees provided cover for the French soldiers. High box hedges lined the narrow stone drive that meandered from the front door to the garden wall offering further camouflage.

Time and again attempts were made to take the Villa, but every attempt failed. Soldiers and volunteers shouting, "*Viva Roma!*" charged the wall, only to fall dead or wounded. Men struck down on every side, pierced by musket balls and scraps of flying metal; yet rather than turn back, the wounded stayed and breathed their last, firing one last time upon the enemy.

The Roman defenses pounded the Villa with cannon fire. The assault continued for hours, until finally, the Villa Corsini began to collapse into ruins. The soldiers could see the walls give way and the French defenders left clinging to the shattered floor beams.

Then the Roman infantry was sent in, and captured the ruined villa and drove the French out of its grounds. Word spread immediately to civilians gathered in the city's piazzas. Overcome with excitement, they poured out of the city gate, and up the hill toward the sight of the victory.

But the French, ready for the tenacity of the Roman fighters this time, had a counterattack prepared, and fought relentlessly until by evening they again took the villa and many more Italians fell to join the wounded and dead.

Day and night, French batteries ceaselessly pounded Roman defenses, ensuring the troops could never rest. Barricaded Rome suffered: the city, under siege now for a second time. Revolutionary troops, already exhausted and depleted, were no match for the French army, replete with fresh battalions and armaments

Giovanni was stationed this time on Rome's Pincian Hill, the highest point in the city, overlooking the Vatican. Given a field promotion for bravery during his first battle on the Vatican wall, he now was Captain of his own battalion. His men cried out, "*Roma o Morte! Long live the Republic!*" with the news of the loss of Villa Corsini, but their verve was lacking, their exhaustion was evident.

For nearly a month, the guns in the batteries maintained a regular fire. Food supplies were getting low, and the enemy had sundered the aqueducts that supplied Rome with fresh water. With little sleep, hungry and weakening, the men maintained control of the hill. They rushed out with muskets and bayonets whenever the French launched an attack on an exposed part of the line. All men worked bravely under fire to repair battlements and dig new defenses.

The night attacks allowed no one rest or respite. French cannonade bombarded the streets of Rome. Gore stained the ancient walls, the grounds watered in Republican blood. Volley after volley destroyed homes and families, ancient monuments, the history of ages past obliterated in one terrific blow after another. Slaughter of Romans and of Rome.

Then, on this one night of cannonade, commencing as usual around midnight, suddenly the intensity of the attack increased a hundred fold. The French focused, attacking the wall at the main gate, San Pancrazio, their intended point of entry.

The noise, the smoke, the reverberations of the cannon blasts, seeming endless, were nearly unbearable. Until, a sudden silence ensued. The silence, its own horror; more horrible than the explosions. A breach, the ancient wall had given way. The French entered the city.

The citizens took to the streets. *Roma o' Morte!* Bloody battles, hand-to-hand, street to street, among ancient walls and monuments already destroyed by cannonade and bombs. So many men lost and maimed in the name of freedom.

Garibaldi saw his army being destroyed, his best officers slaughtered. He went to Mazzini and the Assembly. He reported that further resistance is futile. The French will occupy Rome.

By dawn Rome was controlled by French patrols. Their heavy artillery situated upon Janiculum Hill ensured peace.

The French had crushed the Republic of Rome.

56

July 1849

The Roman Republic failed like the glare of a fine rocket that shines brilliant, but brief.

By mid-day the streets were a scene of chaos. Again, carts, wagons, and carriages clogged the city. All was hastily gathered by any who wished to flee. Hurried goodbyes, shouts, embraces and tears, lodgings abandoned, doors left ajar to empty homes and larders. Those with horses and carriages careened down the city's thoroughfares, barely missing pedestrians. Others pushed what was left of their households in hand carts, the tops covered with canvas. Yet others walked, and the wounded were pushed in wheelbarrows. All who were part of the revolutionary forces ran for their lives.

Giovanni immediately collected Margaret for the journey to Angelino in Rieti. "We must fetch him quickly, then leave the Papal States. The French will begin the roundup of traitors. Retributions will be merciless. We cannot linger, *Mia Cara*," said Giovanni as they jostled in the lurching carriage on the rutted road to Rieti.

The sun was just beginning to set on what otherwise would have been a day of beauty. Margaret thought of the fate of those left in the hospitals. She thought of her friends. She told Giovanni, "Just before you arrived, Mazzini sent a letter by messenger asking my help for procuring passports for Brunetti and his son. They must leave now, or they will never get out."

"What of Mazzini?" asked Giovanni.

"I procured a passport for him too, from the American Consulate. He leaves on safe passage tonight on a steamer from Livorno."

Margaret saw the strain of the war on Giovanni's face. He was pale and thin, haggard and tired. His frame, now bent, seemed much aged. Margaret took his hand in sadness. Then she said, "And you? You are in danger, too. You were recognized after that night at the Ripetta. You can be associated too, with the assassination of Rossi. What of us, Giovanni? Where will we go?"

"For now, north. North of Rome. Florence. It is large enough to hide us while we plan our future. We must lose no time, *Mia Cara*. We must away with Angelino to Florence."

*****

But their plans for a quick escape were thwarted when they arrived in Rieti to find their Angelino in the home of the landlords, Paolo and Maria.

Margaret beheld her child, once robust and healthy, now withered and weak. The landlord, Paolo was nowhere to be found. The landlady, looking desperate and afraid upon seeing Giovanni's rage, explained.

"The bambino is sick. There was no milk for him. Chiara and her family left the town during the siege. The rumors here of the destruction of the city frightened many away."

"And Angelino?"

"I took pity on him. I took care as best I could," Maria explained. "He would only take watered wine." Maria tried to look sad. "The child languishes."

Margaret held her weakened child to her breast. He barely moved. Tears streamed down her cheeks.

"They took pity on him," said Margaret to Giovanni in English, "but not enough to pay for milk. He is half starved."

They rented a small room in town. Margaret found a wet-nurse nearby to feed Angelino.

"We cannot travel with him in this condition," said Margaret after they'd settled in. "We must stay until he strengthens," she declared cradling Angelino, the babe still too weak to cry.

"Yes. It's a danger, but we must stay," said Giovanni, tears in his eyes as he beheld his son. "Our care will have him well. We must never trust him to others again, Margharita. Our family, united remains."

While Margaret nursed Angelino back to health, Giovanni calculated their funds for travel and lodging in Florence. Margaret's payment for her dispatches to America had never arrived during the war, and the family suffered in their poverty.

"I must appeal to my family," declared Giovanni with resolve. "The Ossoli property of Pietraforte is not far from here. Perhaps a small stipend against its value could be arranged for our support."

"But Giovanni, travel for you is dangerous! It is too short a time since we left Rome. They still hunt for escaped revolutionaries. Neighbor turns in neighbor for rewards. No. It's too dangerous. Perhaps my payment from the newspaper will find its way here," declared Margaret, afraid of separation again.

"That's not likely," declared Giovanni. "Margharita, Angelino already flourishes under your care. And it's becoming dangerous for us to remain here. The locals are talking. They know we do not belong. Have faith. I will be gone but a day."

But one day turned into two, then several days passed with no word from Giovanni.

Margaret became sick with worry. She could sense the stares directed her way in the market place. This *Americana* with her babe, alone in this rural town. Were they spies? Would she be reported to authorities as a revolutionary? She knew that her safety and that of Angelino was at risk. What if they'd captured Giovanni, and now look for me? What will become of Angelino? He cannot be left to the care of others again.

She began to pack and arrange a carriage to Florence. Giovanni will know where to find us. He will seek us there, waiting for him in safety, she reasoned.

"I leave tonight with the child," Margaret told her landlord. She handed him a letter for Giovanni. "Here. Please give this to my husband when he arrives."

The man took the envelope with doubt in his eyes. He asked no questions, but he readily accepted some coins from Margaret for his troubles.

The coach rumbled down the dirt road with Margaret, Angelino and their few bags on that dark night. The babe, content and warm in the arms of his mother, slept peacefully.

But Margaret's mind was in a whirl of doubt and fear. She kept her eyes trained on the road, hoping that Giovanni was yet on his way back to them.

A few miles from town, a man alone, tousled in appearance, his gait uneven and unsteady, was seen approaching the carriage from its direction opposite.

Margaret gasped in hope. Could it be?

"Driver, stop for that man!" she cried out.

"I will not Signora," came the reply. "These are dangerous times. No one is to be trusted on the road."

She considered the safety of the child. Perhaps. Perhaps he was right.

She held her breath as the carriage slowly lurched its way toward the figure. Her heart took pity, for the traveller was in evident pain.

"No, driver. You must. The man is hurt."

"That is a common ruse, Signora, to arouse pity. It is not safe to stop."

As the carriage approached, a glimmer of moonlight emerged from behind a cloud. Margaret could make out his profile, unmistakable, though his gaze was cast down upon the rocky terrain of the road. And behold. It was!

"Giovanni!" a tearful Margaret called out in the darkness to him.

*****

His story was that of treachery and danger. On the road to Pietraforte, he was approached by men on horseback, arrested, and thrown into jail.

He was a stranger in a provincial town, and had to await interrogation by an official. He protested. He argued. He anguished, knowing Margaret would worry until his return.

"Guard. Guard! Release me! I am of the family Ossoli, of Pietraforte."

"Ha! You look like a vagabond more than a noble. You stay," replied the guard through teeth that clenched a stinking smoldering cigar. He turned on his heel and started for his chair in the adjoining room.

"No. Wait! Please!" cried Giovanni. "Sir! How did I come to be arrested? he asked. "I've done nothing wrong!"

He heard the desperation in Giovanni's voice and thought some talk might prove entertaining. "You were seen by others when you passed though the last village," the guard deigned to explain. "They said you were involved in the assassination plot of Rossi." His stubbled face broke into a grin, delighted to deliver the news.

Giovanni forced his look to remain impassive.

Getting no reaction from the prisoner, the guard continued, "We haven't seen any action out here in the country for a long time. Everyone will come from near and far to see if you will be hanged here, or taken to Rome for the privilege." He smiled a wide yellow-toothed grin, replaced his cigar between his teeth, and strode away.

Giovanni searched his mind's eye for the faces he'd seen on his journey. Did a stranger stare at him too long? Did he notice anyone point and whisper? Are these the men from the Ripetta? Or the ones who pursued him at the Quirinal? Were these retributions for all of the members of the Civic Guard?

His fate awaited him. His anguish was not for himself but for his family who depended upon him. For Margharita and Angelino, so newly reunited. Who waited for him in Rieti.

He sat awake in his cell overnight. Water, but no food was given him at dawn. As the morning wore on, the sounds of horses approaching both revived and terrified him.

This will be the turning of my fate, he realized.

Rough faced men approached the cell, kicking up dust from the dirt floor. They seemed weary and dirty themselves, the strain of the road upon them.

"So this is the man?" the one in charge asked of the keeper.

"It's what they say," he replied.

"Get him out of there, but keep him in chains."

Giovanni stepped from the cell, stood his full height and looked at the interrogator straight in the eyes. "I am Giovanni Ossoli, of the Castle Pietraforte in the Sabine Hills. I am on family business," he started.

He fell forward as a blow landed on the back of his head, given by an unseen hand for his impertinence. His vision cleared, still lying on the dirt floor of the prison. Hands still shackled behind, he dared not move. A wave of nausea overtook him. Then, rough hands pulled him up to standing. Balance unsteady, he waited.

The interrogator looked him up and down. "Arrogance will not help you here," he said.

He gave a nod to the guard, then Giovanni was pushed down onto a rough stool, chains rattling behind him.

The interrogator looked down upon him and continued, "We are told by witnesses that you helped plan the assassination of Minister Rossi. Your trial will be local and quick."

"No!" Giovanni reacted immediately. "I had no part in that!"

"Why should we believe you? You look destitute. Desperate. Like a refugee, maybe from Rome? Like one who fled quickly? What have you got to hide?"

The interrogator eyed him with suspicion, eagerly anticipating his reward for turning in a traitor.

"Why do you travel alone? Have you proof of who you say you are? Identification?" He nodded toward the guard to approach Giovanni.

The guard twisted his shackles from behind. Giovanni stayed motionless, still and quiet while the investigators roughed him up to search his pockets. He felt relieved that he had had thought to destroy his Civic Guard identification papers before leaving Rome. He allowed the men to seize him. He knew better than to resist.

Just then, a rough hand felt the edge of an envelope in Giovanni's breast pocket. He pulled it out, held it high for the lead investigator to see.

"A letter," declared the guard.

"Yes," stated Giovanni with relief. "It is from my sister. It is to help me conduct family business at Pietraforte. It explains the intention of my father's will for rights to the property."

The interrogator slowly and carefully read the letter, and verified its recent post date. He knew of the family Ossoli and of the trusted high positions they have held for generations in the Vatican.

His whole demeanor changed as he considered his options. He paused, holding the letter. It would not go well for him to risk offending a ranking family.

Deftly, he motioned for the jailer to unlock Giovanni's chains.

*****

"That is what saved me, Margharita. Angela's letter. They would not have released me otherwise." A deep sigh concluded Giovanni's story in the carriage on their way to Florence.

He looked lovingly at Angelino, peacefully asleep with the rocking of the carriage along the dirt road. "It's only a matter of time, Margharita, before they realize that despite my family name, I fought for the Revolution. And the men who saw me at the Ripetta will witness that I was part of Rossi's assassination plan."

"I thank God you are safe. We must never be parted again, Giovanni." She held his hand, cold and shaking, in hers. She saw fear in his eyes as he nervously scanned the road, forward and behind, and the trees and fields beside them.

"Our movements from here on must be furtive. We must protect Angelino," she said.

"Yes." He added, "*Mia Cara*, our stay in Florence must be brief. We are not safe anywhere."

"We shall," agreed Margaret, "arrange for passage to America. We must leave as soon as possible."

PART VIII

57

Homeward Bound
May, 1850
Voyage

And now, tossed in the churning sea, I can see Father's face before me. Benevolent. Loving, he smiles as he sees me approaching. I feel a deep, deep swell gather from the ocean's depths. His eyes light as my body floats toward him, his arms opening wide for me. I know a gentle peace now. Father... My loving, dearest Father.

Giovanni and I engaged the *Elizabeth,* a fine sailing vessel; an American ship registered in Philadelphia and barely five years old. Seth Hasty, its hale and hearty Captain from a worthy New England seafaring family, with his virtuous wife on board, offered a sound ship and able crew for passage across the sea.

Our small family made ready for the journey to New York from Livorno, Italy, feeling fortunate and with confidence for a swift passage, spirits high with hopes for the future.

Mother's letter welcomes us most warmly. We will have a safe harbor with her who will have us happily for as long as we need. I miss her so. Much have I suffered without the solace of a mother's arms about me.

With joy I will present her with Angelino, her first grandchild. She is most excited to hold and to love him.

As to my prospects for work, I have maintained a strong readership that has followed my articles in the *Tribune*, and my reputation is still quite strong. My last book having been received quite well, gives me high hopes of publishing the history I have written, *The History of the Roman Republic*.

Giovanni's English has improved, and he continues to study. He learns quickly and will find work in America. And once my family sees how good and kind he is, I know they will love and embrace him as I do.

But this, our enthusiasm for our new life in America was doomed to be short lived. Tragedy struck the *Elizabeth* soon after we embarked.

The pox, exposed to Captain Hasty on shore, revealed itself onboard ship, and took untimely, the good Captain. Not long after anchors aweigh, suffering from headaches then high fever, he took himself abed, Mrs. Hasty his constant aide. Then, the blisters appeared about the mouth, and spread about his face and body, developing into pustules, the all too familiar odor of the open sores making the diagnosis unmistakable.

Mrs. Hasty was immune, once affected long ago, a survivor of the disease. She stayed with him unfailingly. To the crew and passengers outside the cabin, the sound of his advancing cough in the day, and in the evening his restlessness and raving delirium in the quiet of the moon bespoke the advance of the disease. Then finally, his pulse weakening, he lapsed into drowsiness, then unconsciousness. No physic could help now, only tears and prayers to speed the end of suffering. He died after much misery, here on shipboard, under sail, no doctor, no physic, no help for pain.

And now, at Gibraltar, our voyage across the sea barely begun, we wait this morning for burial rites to commence. Across the straits, enshrouded today in grey clouds, the Pillars of Hercules stand hazy in view through a fine mist, the darkness of the day reflecting our mourning.

To the ancients, this place was the earth's boundary. No sailors would venture past the two great pillars of rock that mark the straits and stand as gateway of the then known world. Its inscription of yore, *Nothing Further Beyond*, warned all travelers of the abyss that lies ahead. These warning words, in this place, never more fitting than today for the burial at sea for dear Captain Hasty.

The body prepared in his best dress uniform, and then wrapped in canvas sail, a length of chains weighted the feet. The sewing of the canvas carefully started there, and progressing toward the head, the last stitch taken through the nose, a step both traditional and practical, attaching the body to the canvas, and if no bleeding occurs, ensuring the body is indeed deceased.

Meanwhile, the sailors on deck perform their duties, adjusting sails so the ship remains motionless, the top-gallant yards set cock-a bill to speak of death and burial, a signal for all ships to see; the lift lines left out of trim to speak of grief. Then the entry port on the starboard gangway positioned to windward and left open.

Captain Hasty's body brought there by strong sailors on a wide plank; short procession. For those buried at sea, no slow winding progression through the town, past home and neighbors and farm and field. No prayers and song of walkers accompany them to the gravesite. Here, nothing solid will remain. A burial at sea provides no lasting memorial for closure, no sealing of a grave, no place to return and mourn and plant rue and rosemary.

A true burial it is not, then. Only a ceremonial commitment to the deep, fluid and unstable. At times ferocious, at times calm, but always in flux and movement, the sea ever changeable, made wild by winds and storm.

The old sailors knew, and did not trust the sea to keep the bodies of the dead. They knew her power, as she cast objects ashore far and wide that have been deposited into her depths. The old ones knew, sad and unsatisfied for this end for their dear Captain.

A ceremony formal, all hands on deck, sailors in their best coats, some with old lace at the wrist, some with broad bars showing, or sporting several bright buttons. The men were not ashamed to show their feelings, though at attention they stood, respectful, eyes filling with tears, some muted audible sobs.

The passengers all dressed in mourning black. The grieving widow was held about the waist, though she stood straight, her eyes never leaving the enshrouded form.

Short service concluding, words from scripture resounded, reassuring, *In the sure and certain hope of the Resurrection to eternal life, through Our Lord, Jesus Christ...* Innocent Angelino, only two years of age, yet still, sensing the sadness of the day, did not yet know that he will soon miss his favorite playmate.

The ceremony brief, all at attention, waves lapping gently against the bow, the ship barely rocking as if in sympathy. Then a soft breeze began to blow, the clouds beginning to lift, revealing a horizon bright and clear.

The words of the final prayer, *We commit his body to the deep...* a signal to the sailors at the gangway to tilt the plank at the head, sending the Captain sliding into the depths feet first, the unmistakable sound of the splash the only monument to his last journey.

The finality of the ceremony underscored by the crack of a volley fired, all looked aloft then instinctively, toward the heavens and there the mourners beheld a sea bird, wheeling away into the wind, all the sky ahead.

Afterward, the young first-mate, Henry Bangs, now Captain at the helm, promised us good passage.

58

The Crossing

The crew now operated under the orders of the inexperienced Captain. Grumbling was heard among the men as to his lack of skill. It wasn't long before the other senior members of the crew approached First Mate Charles Davis. The ship's carpenter, a big Swede, John Helstrom, led the way, followed by seaman Westerveldt, and Sanford, the ship's steward.

"His orders are allay's too late, and we have to scramble to tack after time's passed. We lose alotta time that way!"

"He don't see the stars right through the glass. Should know better. Don' record our position right."

"Jes' a bit heavier on the wheel t' starboard and we'd 'v been on course. Now we gotta sail t' correct the course!"

Davis was most trusted by the men, and the next in command. With little confidence in their new captain's skills, they depended upon Davis for leadership.

"These are mistakes of the inexperienced. But they pose no danger," Davis said. "Besides, it's mutiny to disobey Captain's order at sea," he added.

"But jes' point it out, Davis. Jes' say so. That ain't mutiny."

Davis watched Captain Bangs carefully to witness what the men were saying, and they were right. He miscalculated readings. He didn't seem to know the *Elizabeth* and how she handled. His orders to set course seemed impulsive and careless. Davis decided he would act at the next opportunity.

He approached Bangs one evening, under the stars, when he was taking a sight of Polaris to estimate latitude. The position line would be used on the navigation chart. Davis could see his error on the angle of the instrument and tactfully offered a correction.

"How *dare* you, sir… replied Bangs, immediately indignant, "…question *me*!" Bang's face was red with rage. *"I'm* the captain of the *Elizabeth* now, Davis," he spat angrily. Realizing his error with the sextant, he was too proud to admit. Aggressive anger replaced his embarrassment. "And I don't need no help from the likes o' you."

"But, Captain… Sir, with all due respe…"

"Another word, and you will be charged with insubordination," Bangs threatened. He turned toward Davis, eyes ablaze, *"You,* sir, are dismissed. Now *get off my deck!"*

No further attempts were made. The captain began to keep his distance from the men. He spent as much time as possible in his quarters.

The *Elizabeth* had the good fortune of a stretch of fine weather. Over weeks, the crew settled in. Everyone to his assigned tasks. Tensions eased outwardly. Among the crew, there was a tacit acceptance of the new Captain's ways, knowing that Davis always had an eye on things.

Nearly two months of sail ensued with no further incidents. Good wind and bright weather afforded attention to be paid to the ship, painting and maintenance done in the sea breeze and sunshine.

Angelino's boundless energy was a welcome entertainment to the sailors, and a good distraction for poor Mrs. Hasty, who deeply mourned her husband's passing.

Eager to improve his English, Giovanni was at his lessons with the American passenger, a young man from Massachusetts and he, the happy recipient of Italian lessons from Giovanni.

Margaret, as usual, was at her books and pen, editing her history of the Italian Revolution, preparing letters for its introduction to potential publishers and friends, anticipating her first article to be published on her return for the *Tribune*, and arranging documents for their new life in America.

They passed their time in this way for weeks, the *Elizabeth* tacking, crisscrossing the wide Atlantic, sails aloft against the blue sky, its bow slicing through the blue waters, swift and sure.

All was well, until nearing the coast of America. There the weather changed to fog and wind and high seas accompanying.

59

"*Mia Cara*, this storm is getting stronger," remarked Giovanni in their cabin as they organized and packed their trunks.

"Yes. But the Captain says that we should be in New York in the morning; our long journey nearly at an end. A new life in America to begin, Giovanni," a weary worried smile on Margaret's lips. She continued, "Our young Captain says that the stiff warm wind on our stern will deliver us home even more quickly than anticipated."

"I pray he is right. The wind grew to a gale overnight and Angelino turns pale and trembles with each rush and dip of this small ship. I pray for our safety."

"We shall be there by morning, my love," soothed Margaret.

But the night only proved the increased fierceness of the storm. They were tossed about, helpless in its madness.

The *Elizabeth* climbed up the back of each wave with the surge of it, then fell off, down, down, the feeling of endless falling as if from the earth into the abyss. Seconds would pass, the ship nearly still, unearthly and eerie. Then, another surge, and another climb would begin – only to face another wall of water that seemed to reach the sky. The rollers ahead rose up into tall, vertical walls of white that then exploded into thick spray, immense piles of foam that obscured all.

Below decks, the passengers' joy of a homecoming after many months at sea was tempered with fear. Trunks packed, they tried to rest. Any who could doze in their bunks were visited with fitful scattered dreams on that deep dark night of wind and rain.

Margaret and Giovanni held onto one another, Angelino between them. Prayers whispered to calm the sea, to deliver them safely.

All is enshrouded now. They cling only to hope.

60

Storm
July, 1850

The warm tailwind from the south that pushed the *Elizabeth* ahead was deemed a friend by Captain Bangs. With it came plenty of rain and wind, but Bangs' inexperience left him in ignorance that this was indeed a tropical storm, raging and gathering force as it chased and bore down upon the small ship.

Through his glass, he sighted a flashing beam from a lighthouse as harbinger, estimating that he was nearing Sandy Hook Bay, just south of New York harbor.

Satisfied, he took a final depth reading, and gave instructions to Davis to run before the wind on bare poles. "Should bring us in safe by dawn," said Bangs.

Davis was displeased with the order, and offered an objection. "Sir, with all due respect, we cannot outrun this storm. She's comin' at us from south westward. I think we'd be best to turn hard to starboard and reach due east to escape its path, then…"

Bangs again reacted with rage.

"*I* have given a direct order, sir!" shouted Bangs, "And your impudence is akin to mutiny!"

Davis kept silent.

"There is only one man who *thinks* aboard this ship." He added angrily, *"You, sir, are to carry out my orders!"*

"Aye Captain."

Bangs turned abruptly, satisfied, and left the deck for his stateroom to get some rest. Davis, deeply troubled, complied with the Captain's orders.

The crew expressed mixed fears and doubts about their course; between them years on the sea and many a storm.

"I seen this b'fore. That storm's comin right fer us," Helstrom remarked.

"She'll outrun us fer sure," added Sanford.

Davis said, "Captain don't want opinions. He gave his orders, men."

Still grumbling, the men carried them out.

The small ship flew northward into the thick night, gale force winds propelling them relentlessly ahead.

The young captain, in his bunk, was grateful this long journey was at its end. Exhausted from months of unexpected responsibility with Captain Hasty's death, he was one of the few who slept that night.

Not until he awoke did he learn that the beacon of light he thought was to herald the ship to New York harbor was mistaken for one nearly fifty miles to the east on the coast of a long, lonely barrier island.

The course he set for his ship was a course for disaster.

61

Fire Island
Ship Ashore!

The wind propelled the door open wide as Oaks entered the small kitchen. He came in with the two journeymen from Patchogue, Daniel Jones and Benaja Wood, two drifters that had settled in the busy shore town. Hannah was not surprised to see them. They have worked here on many an odd job. In with the men blew hot humid air and rain gusting from the shore.

"Almos' never seen this much rain before. The gale has the sea whipped up, breaching o'er to the bay a'reddy," said Oaks to Hannah.

The three deposited their wet work clothes on the hooks next to the door. Hannah took out some bread and jam, and put up the kettle for some hot tea for the men.

"G'd day, ma'am," said the men in turn, "And thank ye."

Oaks checked the storm from the bay side window. "Good thing I built this house up high or we might'n survive this 'un Hannah," he said, proud of his workmanship.

The men settled in at the rough table.

The three workmen, too large for the small kitchen, filled the room with their size and sweat and awkwardness.

Hannah cut the bread into large chunks. Wood took his first, saying, "Folks who got in yestiddy down at Dominy's says the papers tells it started two days ago off o' North Carolina."

"Yep." Busted up boats and houses alla'way up the coast," agreed Jones, slurping his tea.

Oaks added, "We got as far as we could today, boys, on the fence and shed. This storm's here t' stay a while. Got to finish up soon's the storm's blown over. Ain't no duck huntin' fer us t'morrow. Mays' well stay here fer the night, boys, keep outta the weather."

Later that evening, the two journeymen from across the bay were safely ensconced in the guest room, deep asleep after a day's labor on the outside repairs.

"Got t' turn in m'self," said Oaks to Hannah. "This storm's dangerous. Best fer' us t' sleep light an' keep a watch on things overnight."

But instead, that night, Hannah had slipped off, deep asleep in the chair beside Marietta's bed. A recent illness, fever, having reduced the night before, left a pale and weak child still to be watched over. Deprived for two nights prior, a heavy sleep came over both mother and child despite the storm that raged outside.

*****

The force of the waves hitting the shore vibrated the walls of the small house like a deep rumbling thunder. Smith Oaks' fitful sleep now broke completely before dawn as he remembered with a start the pile of lumber left near the house from the day's unfinished work. *Damn!* He hurriedly dressed in the dark. That lumber'll pick up in this wind an' come smashin' right through the house like rockets. Better pull the boat in off the bay, too, close t' the house, before I lose 'er altogether. No sleep t'night anyways, with this wind.

Over his clothes, he pulled on his oilskins and storm gear in the kitchen. Loosening the latch, the wind wrenched the kitchen door out of his hand, banging the wall behind with the force of the storm. Oaks made his way bay side first to check the boat. Too late, though, as he could just make out its form capsized, but still tied to the dock. He scowled, damage done a'ready, he thought, leaving it there to repair in the morning. He turned then, eastward, head down against the stinging rain, toward the garden, to secure the timber in time.

Should shore up whatevers' left o' the garden fence while I'm out here…Be first light soon anyways….

Then the unmistakable sound. First, the grating, grinding sound of a hull into a sandbar at speed. Then, the sound suddenly stopped, silent for a brief moment, followed by the report of violent cracking, the distinct report of splintering wood carried across the shore with the sharp wind.

Shipwreck! Just east! Oaks scrambled up the nearest dune to see what he could make out in the early morning gloom of the storm-swept coast. He could barely perceive the form of a small barque as it sat helpless, lying beam-to with the seas breaking over her, flopped on her side near capsize.

He stood, registering the scene in his mind, scanning the horizon. Then, the worst happened. The next wave unfastened the stern of the crippled ship from the sandbar, and threw her forward and onto her side, the sound echoing down the distance of the beach. Then the sharp snap, a monstrous shattering of beams and timber.

Christ! Cargo right through her hull prob'bly, muttered Oaks. He took a further moment to survey the beach. Not a soul on shore. The wind brought to his ears faint cries for help. Looking eastward toward the sound, he could now see the shape of the vessel, stranded, listing, and parallel to shore, each wave of the sea washing over her completely. He made his way back to the house to get some help, and get the wagon ready. He scrambled and slipped his way down the dune.

Eyes widened with anticipation, he could barely contain his joy. A garish smile grew, parting his chapped lips. Booty! he thought with glee. An' I git the pick of it! But I got t'hurry an' git there first!

Oaks burst into the sleeping household and barged into the guest room upon the two sleeping journeymen. "Git up! Git up an' come outside *now*!" he hissed into their faces, rolling them off the bed and spilling them onto the floor.

They were outside in a moment, to find Oaks hitching his horse to the wagon.

"Come on," he shouted against the wind, pointing to Jones, the younger and stronger of the two, "You, with me. We'll be first on the beach. First pick. Look for a captain's chest. Watch for locked trunks. Bring a hatchet to break 'em open. Usually the best stuff."

"What about me?" cried the other, anxiously.

"Here. Take this shovel," he said, thrusting the long handle toward Wood. "Go over the crest of that there dune and dig. We'll have to bury this stuff quick before word gets out. Keep it quiet till after the heat blows over…"

Wood nodded as he started for the dune. Oaks shouted after him, "Work fast and be ready for us when we git back. Won't be long before the others all come."

61

The *Elizabeth*: Offshore Fire Island

The *Elizabeth* lay exposed broadside to the power of the storm. Each wave seemed to come through all of time to slam this small ship with power primeval.

The sandbar off Long Island's south shore held the small barque tight in the wee hours of the morning. The first collision hit head on, wrenching the ship to a sudden halt in its swift flight northward. The shock of it. Then stillness, but only a moment - until the next mountainous wave slammed against her hull and shifted her sidewise, facing east, and dislodging the cargo - tons of Carrera marble - crashing it through her side. The seas poured over and through her, canting the helpless vessel onto her side.

All cabins flooded immediately; there were shouts and cries from the passengers as the seas gushed over them in their bunks. Panic as the ship listed. Scrambling, no, climbing upward on the slanted floorboards now vertical, the cabin door above. The seas continued to flood the cabins with each wave, all persons and belongings in motion, their world dislodged from gravity and logic. Passengers in their nightclothes, shivering and wet, cried out frantically for help as the cabin was filling with the cold salty sea.

Margaret and Giovanni were desperate to hold onto Angelino, all things around them in hectic motion. They wrapped him in a blanket, knotted tight to help grip him securely.

Their ears deafened with the cracking and splintering of beams, spar and plank, all sound competed with the thunderous roar of the wind and waves. The ship shuddered, its timbers, as if alive, groaned with the strain of it all, the *Elizabeth* wedged even more deeply into the sandbar.

The passengers soon heard rough and welcome shouts. It was Davis first, who slid his way down the deck as every wave washed over him. His soaking head appeared in the broken hatch, "Come, Come with me!" he shouted, grabbing for Margaret's hand.

"No!" she shouted back. "Giovanni has the baby! They first! Make way!"

Giovanni had Angelino wrapped fiercely now around his waist in bunting tight, and Davis helped him through the hole to the slanted deck. "To the forecastle," he pointed. "It's the only place that's above water now." The ship shuddered and Giovanni's feet slipped out from beneath him. His hands on the rail are all that kept him from washing out to sea. Angelino let out a wail that faded into the storm as they made their way to the front of the ship. The *Elizabeth* shuddered, seemed ready to give up her form, her timbers about to give way to the relentless sea.

Margaret, next, was guided by Davis out of the hole and into the dark and the storm. Out into the tempest, she gasped, lost her breath, surprised by the wild power surrounding her. Rain struck her skin like sharp pellets. Her white nightgown whipping outward, doused with each wave, she dragged herself forward by whatever solid object her hand could grasp, crawling; the slippery slanting deck made more perilous by rigging and sail that had been torn from the mast and lay now amidships. She slowly made her way toward Angelino. Toward Giovanni.

The strong arm of Davis now about her waist stood her upright on the slanted deck. He guided her safely the rest of the way to her family. She embraced husband and child, held them to her, gasping.

She turned to Davis. "Thank you," she shouted against the roar of the storm.

"Any valuables left behind?" he replied. "Quickly, while I can still get there."

"We have one life vest," said Giovanni. "In the black trunk. It's unlocked," he shouted to Davis.

Margaret added, "And in the desk, a purse with doubloons; and one with jewelry."

Davis obeyed. He soon returned safely, carrying what was needed, two woven purses with the valuables, for these would be helpful to pay for their passage to New York when they reach the shore, and a single cork life vest.

Eventually all passengers were gathered, shivering and wet, in the forecastle. It seemed impossible to gauge the shape of the shoreline against the sheets of rain and breaking waves, but the utter desolation of this beach was quite clear to all.

What would be their best chances of survival? Captain Bangs reported that the storm had broken away the ship's lifeboat, which contained all floatation devices. Margaret was in possession of the only life jacket on board the *Elizabeth*. It was she who would decide how it was to be used.

"The strongest swimmer," said she. "One who will be most likely to handle the dangers of the sea. He could be our only hope to survive: to get help to come to this deserted shore."

Ossoli agreed. All agreed. The Captain suggested the new sailor, willing and strong, James McNulty, fresh from the Irish coast.

"It is a great responsibility, Madam," the young sailor said breathlessly, as he fitted himself with the device.

"We will all pray for your safety," said Margaret.

He first turned toward the sea to face the storm, then turned his back on it and to face the coast. He whispered a prayer, eyes closed, head bowed. Ready, he approached the bow of the ship.

They watched with hope as he jumped into the stormy sea.

Resigned to this plan, the small family found a place to shelter and sat together, huddled for warmth and comfort. Giovanni soothed Angelino, who quieted now. Margaret took the child, holding him against on her skin, her body heat to warm him as best she could, all helplessly soaked with the sea and rain.

Giovanni reached for the woven purse that held two ancient rings, battered and worn, bearing the Ossoli crest. "Let us each wear one," he said, slipping the smaller of the two onto Margaret's wet finger, while he the other.

She felt comforted by this act of love and unity, their little family together for the moment, in a tightly knit cocoon against the storm.

Then it came to her at once. "My papers," she said to Giovanni. "My manuscript… the history, all my work," she said in dismay. Then in a moment, "But I cannot. I cannot ask Davis to return to the cabin again. It is too dangerous."

"Rest assured," *Mia Cara*, said Giovanni," It will remain dry and safe inside the iron trunk. We will collect it on the shore."

They all three sat quietly. Margaret, still and silent in her nightdress, her back to the bulwarks on the upper deck, her feet toward the foremast, each sea breaking over all.

A small contentment in the moment, they, together. Angelino did not cry.

62

On shore, Hannah awoke with a start, still in the bedside chair, neck and back aching, aware of the raging wind outside the window of the small house. She looked toward her sleeping child, and stood to touch her forehead and cheeks. She found Marietta was cool to the touch and her color had returned to normal during the night. She'd slept soundly, her breathing now deep and steady. Hannah's watch over the child proved unnecessary that night.

Feeling relieved, Hannah went to the window to peer north toward the bay. She could hardly see with the rain coming in torrents, the morning swept with wind and dark clouds, the whole world seeming to shriek with the sounds of the raging storm. There was no movement from the guests or her husband. She made her way to the small kitchen to start the morning's fire and saw wet sand and footmarks smeared across the floorboards. All out early, thought Hannah, and in this terrible storm.

She searched now toward the beach out of the kitchen window, to see Wood and Jones approaching the shed, sandy and soaked through, shovels in hand. They stopped to exchange a few words with Oaks, who stood with horse and wagon. Then the three men parted company, journeymen toward the house, while Oaks, shovels in hand, made his way with horse and wagon around back, toward the shed.

Dear God, she thought. Not this. Quickly throwing on her shawl and a bonnet, she stepped out of the house to make her way out across the yard toward her husband.

But the cries of despair, carried across the dunes with the unceasing wind, froze her very first step. She turned eastward toward the chilling sound.

Shipwreck! Survivors! she thought. How many this time? Hannah wondered. I will have to make ready.

She caught up with Oaks at the horse shed. "There are survivors! Can you not hear them?" her voice struggled against the wind.

"Booty first, Hannah. You know that. It's our living," Oaks bellowed back.

"But when there are lives at stake?"

Ignoring Hannah, he began to unstrap the harness from the old horse.

"Stop!" Hannah shouted at him against the fierce wind. "Why are you putting him away? He's needed to get help from the lighthouse! Aren't you sending someone to get the lifeboat?" desperation in her voice.

He, weary, wet face crusted with sand, turned at last to look at her, "The wreck's more'n a mile east of here Hannah. Lighthouse is more'n three miles west. Horse needs some water and grain first. I'll send Wood and Jones fer help when ev'ry body's rested."

"But then it'll be too late! The tide will turn full by then! Please! I can hear them screaming for help. How *can* you?"

He kept his eyes from hers as he busily fed and watered the horse. Oaks watched him dig hungrily into the grain bucket. Satisfied, he started out of the shed toward the house.

She saw as he eyed her, not trusting that she'd stay. He unhooked the harness and reins and took them with him as he made his way toward the house.

"Wait! There's *survivors* on that boat. Smith! Don't go!" she cried out to his back as he lumbered away from her.

Terrified and helpless, she turned and scrambled out to the beach. There, Hannah saw the extent of the wagon tracks, dug deep into the wet sand. Booty. He went out for the cargo first. Her eyes tracked the men's footprints accompanying wagon and horse over and across the far dune, toward the spot where he usually buries any stolen property from wrecks. Three years to wait for the statute of limitations to pass, and then its all his, she knows.

This is what she's come to. Nothing more than a thief. And if those on the ship die, a murderess. Her body reacted with the thought. She weakened and fell to her knees, clutching her abdomen, her eyes closed tight. Her inward sight, across her closed eyes, the old cemetery; the secret grave. She violently wretched into the sand. Then, all went black.

63

She woke to the rain streaming down her face and soaking her hair and clothes. Marietta! Hannah's mind cleared to the present. She must be awake and looking for me, she thought. Standing now, and picking up the hem of her soaked dress heavy with sand, she ran all the way back to the house, watching the ground so as not to stumble. There, across the wagon tracks, a sheaf of wet papers became visible near her feet in the grey morning light. Probably dropped off the wagon, she thought. Heavy with seawater, and wrapped with string, a small leather bound packet of papers at her feet.

Mechanically, she picked it up and sheltered it under her shawl, taking it to the house to dry.

Inside, all quiet, no sign of Marietta stirring. The hearth still cold, she began a small blaze first, before going to check on the child.

In her room, Hannah could see that Marietta was still fast asleep.

Making her way to change into dry clothes, she saw the door to the guest bedroom ajar, the room now empty. Jones and Wood probably gone to the lighthouse, she thought. And, in their own bedroom, Oaks, in his wet sandy clothes, lay sound asleep across their bed.

64

As the hours passed into the dawn, hope for a rescue remained high aboard the *Elizabeth*. Young McNulty must have reached shore by now, they reasoned, and would be headed for the lighthouse, whose beacon persisted against the dark storm.

"The lighthouse is not more than a few miles, it seems."

"There must be a life boat there."

"They will come. They must come."

Now, with the weak light of the day emerging, it could be seen from the ship that some islanders began to gather on shore. Those on board were heartened. They renewed their efforts to get their attention by screaming for help. The islanders seemed not to hear.

Reality from the sea to the land was a world away.

The victim's cries reached the shore only weakly, like distant meandering whispered echoes, winding their way, fleeting and ephemeral. Their shouts swirled about, carried thither and around - and then away, like wisps of smoke in the wild wind.

In turn, as seen from the deck in the windswept rain, the tiny forms of the Islanders looked vague and ethereal; as if peering through a dreamlike haze into a phantom world. They seemed to casually wander back and forth on the beach, almost aimless, careless.

They were sometimes stooping and bending, pointing and watching, and moving like molecules on a slide, gathering into groupings, connecting momentarily, and then airily dispersing.

None of the movement on shore was toward the ailing ship.

65

On Shore: Fire Island

The young sailor washed in to shore, rolling helplessly onto the hard packed sand, clothes in tatters, crawling away from the waves that wanted him back in the sea, then collapsing, muscles too weak to carry him further.

He lay there helpless for some moments, soaked in seawater and rain, sand in his throat stinging and choking, blinding his eyes nearly crusted shut. He was grateful to be alive, and aware of his responsibility. All souls on board were depending upon him to find help. To send help.

The beach from east to west was a long lonely stretch, the seas breaking mercilessly, ravaging the coastline. There, several miles to the west he saw the welcoming flashing beam of the lighthouse. Heartened, he got to his knees, spit the sand from his mouth and wiped his eyes, vision clearing. He arose determined, and made his way toward the beckoning beam.

The crashing waves eroding the shoreline forced him up onto the beach where he could see in the distance a lone house on the north side of the island, bayside. He ran for it, finding the way less punishing and the sand more stable.

With hands shaking from exhaustion, he pounded upon the locked door.

"Ahoy! Ahoy, I say!" he shouted hoarsely. "James McNulty, seaman from the *Elizabeth* stranded off shore!" He waited a moment. Then, "Anybody there? Ship Ashore! *Ship Ashore*, I say!"

His wait seemed interminable. All inside seemed dead quiet.

Then the door opened slightly, a warm glow of a fire greeted him, and he was inside dripping sand and sea. A small child sat in front of the hearth, eyes large and luminous, staring.

The house seemed oddly strange. Tension in the atmosphere. The wife's eyes swollen, dark encircled. She like a silent shadow.

"Where? How far?" asked Smith Oaks.

Hannah's gaze shifted to her husband. His natural and easy questions were themselves lies, his demeanor confirming. No one would ever have suspected that he knew. That he had been out there.

Hannah poured the boy some hot coffee. Oaks pushed the young sailor toward the hearth while he looped his suspenders over his shoulders, seeming concerned.

"More'n a mile east," said McNulty, accepting the mug from Hannah. He gulped the scalding liquid sloppily.

"Other survivors?" Oaks asked.

"Yep. I left twenty-three aboard when I jumped. Don't know how many r' left." He proffered the empty cup toward Hannah. "Thank ye," he said.

Steam began to arise from the boy's back; the fire's effect on his wet clothing. He stepped toward Oaks. "How far's the light?"

"Oh, a good three 'n more miles," replied Oaks.

"Thank ye kindly," said the boy from across the room, already at the front door. "Got to get help from the lightkeeper. There's a surfboat?"

"Yep. Selah Strong's the keeper. I'll git to the ship," said Smith Oaks to the sailor's back as he retreated into the storm.

At that moment Hannah understood.

She turned now to confront Oaks, her voice breathy and weak. "You never *did* send Wood and Jones to the light, did you, Smith?"

"Nope. Don' need nobody knowin' I wuz at the wreck first."

"All those hours passed…" Hannah's voice trailed off in grief, knowing the reality of it.

Oaks prepared to go out. He felt no need to reply.

66

Time passed slowly for those on the forecastle of the *Elizabeth*. Knowing there were others on the shore made the wait more excruciating. The passengers and the Islanders across the same expanse of water, it seemed an invisible barrier between the ship and the beach, the way impassable.

"They don't seem to want to help. They don't even look our way!" exclaimed the survivors as the morning hours wore on, now close to noon. "Maybe young McNulty didn't survive. Maybe he was washed away by the sea, never to be found! What of us then?"

The experienced seamen knew this storm was not abating. Wave after wave engulfed the *Elizabeth,* no two alike in force or shape. Some hit them straight on, some came at the ship from either side, and sometimes together, they crashed and crescendoed overhead. The sea churned about them, as if at a boil.

Some of the sailors knew, and decided to abandon their fates to the sea. They stood on the forecastle, and as if from a secret signal, jumped aloft, as birds on a wire who by a mysterious force, decide to lift off into the wind. Better to risk the sea than to wait in helplessness.

The others watched the sailors in the sea. Occasionally a head, or an arm, or torso would break the surface or be seen momentarily in the heave of a wave, or in its frothy foam. They swam, or were pushed and catapulted by the waves, along with debris from the ship. Wooden spars and planks, the ship's timbers, washed to and fro, more a danger from a collision with these than the danger to drown in the waves. The passengers watched until the sailors were far and away and could be seen no more.

One passenger, the young man from Massachusetts especially agitated, hung onto the mast and railed after the sailors. Fear dictated his next action, to impulsively follow them into the deep. Without word or action to the others, he leapt overboard. To struggle against the unknown was preferred than to endure uncontrolled terror.

He hit the water hard. The rest on board watched in horror as the young man sank immediately, like a stone statue. They called out his name. They watched in desperation for some sign of him. They prayed for mercy from God. They watched in shock as he who followed the crewmen was carried downward into the swirling deep, never rising for an instant, to be seen no more.

Clearly, the raging surf was no match for the inexperienced.

By noon, with no help arriving, hope was lost. The flood tide had returned to the full, and the storm showed no sign of subsiding.

"We will never survive if we wait aboard ship!"

"Her timbers groan with every wave."

"She can't hold together much longer! She's breaking to pieces. The hull will give way soon!"

Captain Bangs came forward. "We cannot wait any longer. There will be no surfboat to save us."

His eyes searched the deck. "Carpenter!" he shouted. "Fashion planks large enough to sit upon, with rope handles for each passenger to attempt shore."

They all looked at each other with a mix of horror and hope.

Mixed comments came from the passengers: "No! We cannot survive in this sea!" or, "We must! It's the only way!" Confusion and fear resounded on deck.

Bangs continued, "Each of you on a plank will be pushed and guided from behind by one of the crew who will swim behind. They are strong and know the ways of a storm at sea."

First Mate Davis encouraged Mrs. Hasty to try this method. He would guide her to shore. She looked at the others, at first with fear in her eyes. Then in a moment, she decided. She bravely accepted the offer. After all, she thought, if she did not make it, she would repose in the deep with her dear husband, a fitting ending for them both.

"Hasten them on shore! Hasten the lifeboat to come to us! We will pray for you!" said the others.

She looked to Margaret who held the child. Their eyes met, knowing it might be their last encounter.

All watched as Mrs. Hasty was helped from the ship into the churning sea. Davis firmly seated her on the plank, and he bravely pushed from behind. They both looked like tiny bobbing corks as the sea pushed them to and fro, willy-nilly despite the greatest of efforts by both to remain on a course.

It was not long until they could be seen no more.

Margaret and Giovanni held each other tight, rain soaked and frightened, their fears centered mainly on Angelino, who, exhausted from the wild night, now stayed quiet in a kind of stupor in her arms.

Margaret feared the dangers of the deep, and, despite what the captain said, wanted to wait for help to arrive. "After all," she said, " we can see men on the shore now, even in the windswept rain. I still say there's hope, Giovanni. Perhaps a rescue boat will make it to the ship."

Giovanni strained to see into the thick storm to gauge the conditions against the distance to the shore. "This span, in this storm only allows a small chance of survival for a strong individual. And for Angelino, impossible. A surfboat would be our only chance at all of us surviving."

"Yes," Margaret agreed. "It is our only hope of getting to shore *with* Angelino. Neither of us, and no one seaman, no matter how able, could hold a two year old and swim safely to shore. Not in this storm."

Margaret still felt the pain of the tragic separation of the family during the war. "I could not leave Angelino's safety to any other, Giovanni. We left him to others in Rieti that we thought we could trust. And look how we found him... starving and barely alive when we retrieved him."

She gazed with love at her child, so innocent. Then with resolve, "I vowed then never to forsake him again. No, Giovanni, I could not leave his fate to any other."

Margaret knew this was the turning of their destiny. She added, "If we *were* to separate, Giovanni, and if either of us were to survive *without* Angelino, what of our lives then? How could we go on, knowing our decision cost him his young life?"

Giovanni agreed, "We must never part in this world. Not while we have a breath between us." He embraced Margaret and Angelino, and holding them in his arms, he said, "*Mia Cara*. We wait in prayer. Our destiny is with God. We stay with the ship."

67

As it was, the young sailor who left Oaks' that morning ran the beach from the wrecksite to the lighthouse in the wind and driving rain, reporting the first news of the stranded ship and its survivors.

Susan took the exhausted boy inside and offered him rest and dry clothes while Selah summoned his assistant to get to Dominy's Inn to gather volunteers to man the lifeboat.

"I'll go check the equipment. You rest here," he said to the young McNulty.

Selah grabbed his oilskins and made his way outside, worried. It's a hell of a task in this storm, nearly a thousand pounds to carry more than five miles down the beach, he fumed as he unlocked the door of the relief hut. Hope Dominy's got some strong guests there who'll help.

He surveyed the equipment and what would be needed for the rescue. Doing some quick mental calculations he realized that by the time the men get here from Dominy's and carry this equipment to the wreck, it would be almost noon. Both time and tide were working against them.

Soon, men came from the inn dressed in storm gear, eager to help. When Felix saw Selah waiting, he nodded toward the relief hut. They entered together.

"Look, Selah, not one of my guests has knowledge of the sea. Just men on vacation at the seashore is all they are. Only you, me and your assistant know how to handle a surfboat in a storm like this."

Felix noticed Selah's look of dismay. He added, "These men are here to help. It's not their fault they have no seafaring skills."

"I know that," replied Selah. "It's not them. But this here's what the Lifesaving Service considers a rescue crew," he said to his friend. "Just anyone who'll come."

"We have to go with what we've got," replied Felix.

"A rescue crew should be trained. *Trained.*" Selah spat in frustration.

He went out into the storm and asked some of the volunteers to help haul the surboat out of the rescue hut. Once outside, they all waited impatiently.

"How do we go? How far? When do we start?" came the chorus of husky voices.

They all stood, drenched in the relentless rain. "The sailor who got ashore from the wreck says to go bayside," replied Selah. "It's the most secure right now. We'll take her that away for the first few miles. Then we'll see where it's safest to take her across to the ocean. Let's go, men."

The fierce storm pushed the sea with such force that the shoreline disappeared completely in a hundred places on that slim strip of barrier beach, the sea becoming one with the bay, making the transport of the surfboat perilous and difficult. The would-be rescuers persisted, working against the wild wind and high seas, unceasingly on the rise, the tide increasing.

The men had trouble maintaining a hold. Their feet slipped and sank on the soaked uneven sand. They reached the bay beach.

"From here, men, launch her. We'd be better off to row as far as we can," Selah shouted.

But even the bay had waves that broke over the boat. Men pulled at oars that hit or missed whitewater. The shoreline was hard to discern, impossible most times. "Row her further into the bay, so we don't beach her!" commanded Selah Strong.

Labor spent, men toiled past their limits of physical strength, knowing their efforts could prove the difference between life and death for those on board. "Pull! Pull hard!" they shouted to one another.

Selah recognized the high dune near Oak's place. "Here!" he shouted above the wind. "Here is where we ground her and carry across to the sea."

The task took hours. True to Selah's estimate, around noon, they neared the wrecksite, and could make out the survivor's screams for help carried thither by the wind. And, by then, the rescue crew were not the only ones on that beach.

By then, locals from across the bay had word of the wreck and came to pirate all goods that they could carry. Some surviving sailors who had swum from the *Elizabeth* walked the beach now dazed with exhaustion, searching for their trunks, while the same were being broken in to or carried off by thieves.

Bodies of other sailors washed ashore, drowned and damaged from the floating debris, being dragged in to shore by the helpful.

Exhausted, the morning hours spent, the volunteers deposited the rescue boat near the base of the dunes. It was obvious to all that by then that it was too late. During the hours it took to transport the boat, the tide surge and wind only intensified, and the fury of the sea increased.

The waves relentlessly crested one after the next, high and fierce. "We can't get her out in these conditions," the men cried. They knew then, exhausted and dismayed, their grueling transport of the rescue boat was all for naught. They sat in the sand in shelter of the dune, watching the storm, watching the sea.

Some of the crew who made it to shore alive brought news of the other survivors still on board. "A baby! A child aboard! He belongs to Margaret Fuller of Boston! With her husband, an Italian *Marquis*! She's a *Marchese* now. Royalty aboard, from Italy!"

Word spread among the locals in a flash. Amazement that someone so famous was on their shore. Celebrity. Concern for the baby. A wee child so innocent. How will he make it to shore?

But to many islanders, this news only meant the possibility of higher quality valuables to gather on shore. Riches, maybe jewels! They redoubled their efforts to scour the beach.

By now, Oaks was on the scene of the wreck, busily helping survivors, dragging those who made it to shore from the wreck out of the sea. He seemed the picture of concern and care. He directed survivors to his home on the beach for warmth and solace.

Only he, Hannah and the two journeymen knew how many hours sooner the lighthouse could have been alerted, the rescue boat could have arrived before flood tide returned. Only they knew how much of the passenger's misery could have been avoided had the lifeboat gotten there earlier.

None of these facts impressed Oaks. They did not even cross his mind. He, only pleased with his good luck to have gotten there first to take first pick of the booty.

68

The storm continued, its fury unabated. Oaks returned to the house. Rain and wind entered with him through the open door. Once inside, he forced it shut with both hands.

Soaked and sandy, Oaks stood dripping in the kitchen. Hannah, scouring the kettle, kept hands and mind busy, trying to forget this early morning's scene on the dune. She did not look up.

"Bodies are washin' in, Hannah," he said to her back. "Some alive just barely, we pulled 'em from the surf. Some washed up were dead, pummeled by the planks and wreckage. Storm's jes' splintering the barque into pieces."

Hannah now inclined her head toward Oaks, "What about the lifesaving equipment? The surfboat?"

"Jes' about got there now. Lighthouse didn't git word of the wreck till mid mornin'. Takes time, Hannah. Besides, tide's on the rise now. Prob'nly won't be able to git her off the shore fer the waves."

Hannah stared at him in amazement. He says this all as dry fact; as if he had nothing to do with it. All culpability already has been erased from his mind.

She looked directly into his eyes, knowing.

His glare kept her silent.

Oaks continued, "Git ready, Hannah. Survivors comin' here. Then he added, almost casually, "The sailors say there's a baby on board. A boy. Child of royalty."

"A *baby?*" she cried. She asked again to make sure she heard right. "A baby? *Here?*"

"Onboard the ship, Hannah. Don' git yr hopes up. Don' see how 'e could survive this 'un." Oaks then left the kitchen to get some dry clothes before going back to the wreck site.

Hannah's mind froze. For a moment she could not breathe.

She sank onto a kitchen chair in a moment feeling simultaneously both weak and enervated. Then her mind sharpened. It all became so clear. "A baby! A boy child! Delivered to *me* in this tempest. *My* boy child? Delivered back to me?"

A sudden clarity enfolded Hannah. "*This* is why I am here. This is why I endured here all these years. God has heard my prayers. This is a sign of His forgiveness!"

Her mind flew into a thousand places at once. All of her struggles here now made sense. All of her life seemed contracted into this one moment.

She rose from the chair strong with purpose. With swift hands, she made all ready for the child. Stones by the hearth for warmth, softest warm blankets, a place for him to rest. To revive the child. To hold him and warm him, thought Hannah.

Out on the beach, both those on board and those on shore helplessly watched and waited in the wind and spray merciless and strong.

*****

Aboard the *Elizabeth*, Captain Bangs shouted against the storm to all who were left. "There is no hope here, the storm only strengthens, the tide increases."

"But those on shore…!"

"They will not come. It's impossible in these conditions!"

Then, through the howling wind, he shouted, "You must swim to save yourselves!"

"But what of the child?" cried Margaret.

"A canvas. He can be put into a canvas sack, strong, tied tight, and one of us can swim him in!" He implored her, "You must assess the situation and be reasonable!"

"No!" cried Margaret, "I will not let him go!"

Bangs and the men exchanged glances. They knew her decision was made.

"Very well, then," shouted Bangs.

He turned to all who remained, "Everyone, save yourselves!" his voice hoarse, carried away by the wind.

Bangs, who thought of his own wife and child at home, grabbed a plank and jumped overboard, into the wrathful sea.

*****

The cargo hold, heavy with tons of marble, held the *Elizabeth* wedged tight onto the sand bar while the wild wind and waves battered her hull to pieces.

On shore, bodies of the drowned and those half alive came washing in along with remnants of goods and cargo and splintered timber. Planks, spars and rigging, trunks and boxes of cargo all were strewn for miles westward down the beach as the storm raged.

By now, activity on the beach had become a frenzy. Despite the remoteness of the island, word had spread faster than a whip to the towns across the bay. They knew it was worth the risk to sail across the bay to the barrier beach. A wreck meant riches to whomever claimed them first. From the moment the cry *Ship Ashore* was heard in the villages and the pubs, the townsmen, everyone, even the honest and the hardworking, became thieves.

This ship from Italy carried exotic fabrics, fruits, nuts, olive oil, all tumbled in to shore for the taking. On the beach were stove in casks of almonds mixed with sand and seawater. Juniper berries, flasks of olive oil littered the beach. Silk, braid, hats and fine wools tumbled in with each surge of the sea, now all strewn upon the shore to be collected by the local thieves, "land-pirates," they were called, the goods to be sold openly and quickly. The better booty would be any cash, jewelry, and personal valuables from the crew and officers and passengers.

Trunks that shattered in the surf released all their riches onto the sand. And trunks that came ashore whole were broken into. All that could be had must be taken quickly, as survivors would search the beach for their things; or for the belongings of a mate whose last word was a request to return a wedding band to a waiting wife, or to deliver boon earned on the journey to his children.

Nearby damage from the storm included the telegraph lines that connected Long Island to New York City. The outside world would not hear of news of the wreck until repairs were made. The locals knew that the relatives of the victims wouldn't arrive for days. By then, anything of value would have already been secreted away or sold. If the sea was kind and returned their bodies to shore, the families would at least have their loved ones to take home to their final resting place.

On this island the locals have seen many a wreck. They knew of the aftermath, how to handle both the survivors and the dead. What to do with any cargo, and what to say to underwriter's agents who came too late. They knew their neighbors, their townsmen and their habits. Whom to trust, and whom not to.

They knew the sea and her habits, too. How long she takes to give up her riches, and how far from the wreck she would send the booty and the bodies, depending upon wind and tide and upon the strength and length of the storm that brought the ship into danger.

The locals came with carts and wagons. They came with horses and dogs. Some sailed across the bay with barges. They knew the shallows of the bay and where to swim their horses across. They knew where to wait the tide to return, loaded with booty.

All who lived on the shore knew that sea was the agent of both bounty and of loss. Of beauty and of danger. She gave as readily as she took away. Here, on the shore, only the hearty survive. Or the cunning and the desperate.

69

**On Board The *Elizabeth*
The Reckoning**

Nearing about three that afternoon, few of the crew remained on board the *Elizabeth*. With Margaret, Giovanni and Angelino were Helstrom the carpenter, Sanford the steward, and two old sailors, Westervelt and Bates. Their loyalty to the child is what held them. Angelino's playful cries of pleasure were a delight for all on the long sad passage over the Atlantic since the tragic death of their Captain. These men felt a necessity to make sure the child was spared harm if at all possible. And while they respected Margaret and Giovanni's decision to stay on board with Angelino, the crew knew the parents were inexperienced in the sea, and would most likely lose him if they had to swim for shore. They remained on the *Elizabeth*, Angelino's steadfast guardians.

Margaret sat, wet and numb in her nightclothes on deck with Angelino in her arms, leaning against the mast as the only place left between the arching waves to drink in air, waiting and knowing these would be her last moments.

She kept Angelino snug resting against her breast, their breathing slow and shallow. She almost dozed, and he slept, wet with salt water warmed by mother's body, for him, a familiar warm womb of comfort.

Margaret felt a soft contentment, accepting the storm with all its noise and fury, giving in to its powerful reality.

Giovanni conferred with the remaining crew. He returned to sit with his little family now, wrapping his arms about them both. Margaret's eyes locked with his, silent and knowing. Angelino stirred and Giovanni took his son from her. She looked imploringly. He held a strong canvas bag to secure Angelino, as the time was coming near for the hull to give way.

Margaret nodded her assent, and now alone sat wet and shivering. She wrapped her empty arms around herself, and gave in to reverie. She thought of their plans of a new life back home in America snatched away as they sat almost within reach of shore. She mourned the loss of her mother-joy to have seen her son embracing her own mother. All this taken away by just a difference of some few miles or hours. By a wind gone too strong. By fate, really.

She recalled the days of her youth in Boston, her father a mighty storm, himself a powerful force who had defined her feelings of love, intimacy, connection. Now she knows that on his part, a greedy love it was, determined by his pride. His need to point to her as his, as his creation.

He set her success as his life's task.

She set that fulfillment as her life's task.

It was not until she met Giovanni, who showed her what it meant to give love and to be loved freely; accepted wholly and without reservation or demand. Only then did she know the unremitting generosity, the merging of spirit and soul, of love in its purest form.

But Father? What of those first lessons of love, his unyielding, impossible demands? Even now, in her last moments, that early yearning still troubled her soul. She knew, as she sat in the unrelenting storm, that what she thought, what she wanted, or what she did not want, had been shaped by her father. Her past had been present always, informing her life's decisions.

And now, Angelino…

Her thoughts were interrupted with a sudden shift below. The hull listed, and like an avalanche, the advancing wall of water with wind and spray, rumbled and rushed toward the helpless ship. The very planks on which she sat shuddered as the foremast wrenched free from its bolts, crashed sidewise, slanting over the sea.

The crew acted as one. Sanford grabbed Giovanni who held Angelino and pushed them toward the remaining rigging. The steward grabbed the child in the canvas bag, Angelino's arms and legs sticking out. He secured the child around his own neck and jumped into the sea to save him, swimming as best he could from the wreckage.

At the same time, Westervelt and the carpenter reached for Margaret, but too late. She slid from them by inches, away on the tilting deck, and all were helpless as the wind and spray obscured everything, the sea surging over the ship. Margaret slipped from their grasp and into the deep, as the sea broke off the top rigging by which Giovanni held, leaving nothing but bare mast, and he, too, now swept away into the fury.

The carpenter looked to sea and saw that the child was no longer in the arms of the steward. In a mere moment, he thought, the complete destruction of a family.

He and any who remained, dove into the furious sea and swam for their lives.

70

The violence of the sea shocked her, smacked her body hard, lifting her up and away, then, suddenly, enfolding her, churning her all around. Then, with almost a sudden stop, dropping her, falling as if down from a high mountain, tumbling. Not a moment, but then another wave, suddenly sweeping her upward, somehow into a suspension, as if time had ceased.

Sudden silence. For her, all reality merged. She saw all as simple clarity now; years streaming into the timelessness of the sea. She felt a fresh awareness, an entrance into a newness that was also somehow strangely familiar. Were these seconds, or minutes, or hours she was feeling? Or eternity?

With a roaring push now from below, picked up into the swell, an unexpected inhalation filled her lungs with warm water, salty, stinging but somehow pleasing, like the ending of a long struggle. Then, pushed downward again and dragged, rolling sidewise, her long hair loose like its own wave, streaming past her for a moment. Another force from below, her body churned, tumbling, hair shifting outward and away, like a flag taut on its pole.

Indistinct rushing sounds in her ears. Only a faint awareness of debris streaming by, she among it all. Finally, away from the wreck, her body revolved open, arms and legs wide like a starfish, the surf dragging her down, down. There, a feeling of the most perfect tranquility suddenly occurred to her.

Now, in the silent deep, she could see clearly, could see all around her at once, beyond the scope of ever before. The sea, shimmering walls of softness hypnotic and tranquil to her newly opened eyes. Her hearing exquisitely acute, she felt the blood pulsing in her ears. She perceived all the wash and movement of the sea. All bodily sensation intensified, water, warm and salty all inside her and outside at the same time, womb-like. She felt she could breathe; a clear sweet sensation. She felt effortless and fluid in the warm blanket. Time was all, and all was now, and now was all in a moment.

And now, tossing in the churning sea, I can see Father's face before me. Benevolent. Loving, he smiles as he sees me approaching.

I feel a deep, deep swell gather from the ocean's depths. I see his eyes light up for me as my body floats toward him, his arms opening wide for me. I know now a gentle peace. Father... My loving, dearest Father.

Hair wild and free, she, swept now with the current on an easy journey; flowing and merging with the elements, her arms floating open and wide, outstretched as in ecstasy, embracing the peaceful flood.

71

Fire Island
The Reckoning

Oaks saw him first. A small fleshy thing, tossing in among the wreckage. He waded in, the force of the current nearly taking him off his feet. There he saw a sight that made even him feel a moment's pity. There was the child the sailors had told him about, the baby, now tossing and turning carelessly in the waves as they broke toward the shore.

He reached out to grab the little form, so pathetic and small.

No damage on the body, he thought, but no breath either, as he wrapped him carefully in his buffalo hide. He made his way with the sad bundle down the beach to his house. "Hannah's waitin' fer ye," he said aloud, his words wasted in the wind.

Oaks entered the warm kitchen.

"The baby washed up, Hannah," Oaks announced. "Drowned. Boy. He's perfect; not even a scratch from the wreckage," holding the swathed child in his arms.

"The baby?" she said, stunned. "Bring him in here. *Give* him to me!" She reached and grabbed the child, wet and limp, away from her husband.

"A boy! Aboard that ship," she whispered breathlessly. She took him next to the fire to warm him, and held his naked body to her breast, she, aching with longing. *My* boy? She whispered into the ear of the dead child. Come to me? Come back to me?

Then to her husband, who stood, watching. "He's not dead, Smith. He seems to have color," said Hannah. She could feel he was cold, but still limber.

"No, Hannah. Drowned," he said flatly. He went out without another word, again, into the storm.

Now, Hannah went to work quickly. She rubbed the baby's body all over with a rough cloth to stimulate the blood. She worked mechanically and urgently. The child's young body limp, eyes closed. Her vision misty with tears; tears that fell from Hannah's lashes onto the young flesh, clouding her vision. She saw the child in a blur, his form indistinct and vague.

And in that, a haze of past memory mixed in. Her body felt the fear, the danger of loss all merged, living it all again now. She, Hannah on the muddy bank, limp offspring, does he live, does he yet live? And now then, so you can breathe, she said, as she cleaned his mouth and nostrils.

Clean him of mud and mucus, she thought as she worked. *Clean him of mud and mucus.*

Just then, Marietta.

"Mamma?" Her voice struck Hannah back to the present. She wrapped the boy with flannels while the warming pan and some bricks heated on the fire.

"Yes, child?" Hannah replied but did not lift her eyes.

"Will the baby be alright?"

"It's God's will. Pray, Marietta."

She then gently turned him over...what is his name, she wondered. Despite her efforts, his skin seemed a bluish hue. Nonetheless, she continued.

Instinctively and alone on the muddy bank, she wiped the infant with the skirt of her dress. Clean his face. Maybe he will breathe.

He looks to be about two years old, she thought. She worked while Marietta watched…knowing that the sea had brought her a miracle. … and in slow circles moved the warm pan over his back and spine.

I will revive him, she thought as she moved her gentle, desperate hands. I will revive this child who came to me; my miracle. Warmth can revive. Love can revive.

I will not let you go, little one, she'd said to the lifeless form.

I will not let you go, she said to this baby who came to her from the sea. Not again.

She prayed as she moved her frantic hands, massaging feverishly. Her heart pounded wildly, the sound of her blood like the ocean roaring in her ears. She then positioned him gently upon a buffalo hide, heated bricks on either side of him, and smaller stones warmed his palms and soles of his feet.

She drew a quilt over him, and then laid her hands under it, now massaging his chest to restore the heartbeat. Memory flooded in. *The baby slipped out. Slipped out when I fell. I am to blame. I killed my own. His color was blue, though I rubbed and rubbed. The cord was stuck. I had no means to let him free. I cried. I wept into the mud. My baby did not cry. He never cried. He went to his grave silent and blue. How long did I stay with him? I cannot say. I slept. I fainted. I woke when the shadows had gotten longer. My baby was blue. He never cried.* I must; I must, whispered Hannah, as she worked the young flesh, supple still.

Many a wreck has come to this beach, thought Hannah. But never a baby have I seen brought to shore. To me, he was delivered, she knew, a peace now flooding over her. This is *he* given to me. Beautiful, perfect his features and shape. Needing so much to live out his years.

Oaks soon returned to the house with some of the surviving sailors, bruised and battered, clothing shredded from their backs, wrapped in blankets dripping, looking for the warmth of the fire. Their eyes wide, wild and lost, as only the sea can make a man. They stood a moment on the parlor's threshold, searching the room, vision adjusting, seeking the hearth.

When they saw Hannah and the baby, tears sprang from their eyes, and rolled down their wet cheeks. "Angelino," one whispered. They turned their faces away, toward the fire.

She saw, and silently worked her hands with even more urgency, her pleading prayers now turned to sobs audible.

Oaks saw her. He knew.

"No more, Hannah," he said, stepping forward. "No more." He now stood above her, gazing down at his wife and the dead child. "He's gone," said Oaks flatly. "Drowned."

She looked up at her husband with desperate eyes.

"You can be of some use to these sailors here," he said, gesturing toward the men's backs, their faces hidden, ashamed of their tears.

72

That night, Hannah, in and out of a doze, though uncomfortably upright in a chair, held a funeral vigil for Angelino, watching over him, laid out, dressed all in white, candles burning all around him, angelic glow.

Hannah sat, exhausted, mesmerized by the candlelight, the quiet, the deep darkness of the night. She thought of the past. Her childhood home. Burdened by responsibility too young. Mother, beset with illness.

Then that day that her eldest brother called her down to the cold cellar. He was strong and handsome. He had been an idol to her, but distant. He never paid her much mind, as she was just a child, many years between them. He, a man really, helping to support the household. She, Hannah, the only girl child, was there to clean up after the family. Laundry, cooking and cleaning; household duties, her lot since mother took ill.

One afternoon, while mother had a visitor in the parlor, he called Hannah to come down to the cellar. She felt so complimented that he wanted her. That he showed interest. That he needed her for something, she, the stand-in woman of the house.

Her eyes searched for him in the dim light. She thought she heard a snickering. Were they not alone? The town boys maybe? She did not know why. Seeing her confusion, her brother beckoned her; coaxed enter the half dark of the cellar.

He said, "Go inside. Into the storeroom."

Puzzled, she hesitated.

He said again encouragingly, a strange smile, "Go. Go to the back storeroom. There's a surprise."

Curious, frightened, trusting, she obeyed.

She wanted him to like her. This was an acceptance, she thought. A recognition.

She was afraid. She heard snickering. But her brother said to go. She made her way in the dark.

She stopped in the rough entrance, a hewn out doorway. She could barely make out a movement in the empty space before her. She could not see.

Did she know who was there?

Then voice from the dark said, "Come in. The surprise is in here." She was afraid. She did what she was told. She obeyed.

She was suddenly taken. One arm held her, searching her body. Rough. Skirts pulled up. All her private places. The hands hesitated a moment to position himself against her. She struck out with her free arm, tried to scream but he held his hand over her mouth. She could hardly breathe, so he let go, held her head still by her hair, pushed her down, now against something wet on her mouth. "Open," he said. She choked. She fought. Tried to cry out. Struggled in the dark. He let go, laughing. She ran.

Out through the front room. Her brother. Now others. They all laughed.

Tears streaming now. Weeping.

Up the cellar stairs, into the house, to the parlor. To mother who sat with the visitor. Mother and other. Parent of one of the town boys.

Hannah stood silent in the doorway. "What's the matter, Hannah?" she was asked. She stood disheveled, face wet with tears. She went to Mother, sidled up to her quietly.

"What's the matter child?" she was asked again. "Why so strange?"

Hannah could not speak. She could not say. She had no words for what just happened to her.

The visitor said, "Oh, probably the boys roughhousing. They're just too wild."

The visitor's words took possession of the event. Her explanation stood.

Mother said, "Stay here, then, Hannah."

Later, Mother, half blind and weak, was guided back to her bed. Exhausted from the neighbor's visit, she slept. Nothing else about this event was ever spoken. The horror and fear of the day became a void for Hannah. She could not define what happened. The happening became a feeling.

Fear had been seeded into the mind of young Hannah, defining her as she grew up.

*****

He had a name. Jessup. Older than the other neighbor boys, but by how much? Stronger, too. A farmer mostly. His hands were rough with work, his skin browned. Friend of her brothers.

In years to come, he would watch her come into town. He appeared from nowhere it seemed when she had bundles to carry, or the day was late. He was awkward; had not much to say. She did her best to avoid him. The event of the past buried in her mind, a blur of darkness and danger, but the fear remembered sharply.

On this day he approached Hannah as she came from the dry goods store.

"I can handle the bundles, Jessup. I don't need your help. I have the cart today."

Jessup stood stubbornly, not moving from the spot. He stared. He watched her go. He mounted his pony and rode him hard and fast, passing her in a cloud of dust as he sped down the road toward her house.

She's mine, he thought, rage mounting. Giv'n t' me by her brother all'as years ago. Been watchin' her. Been waitin' too long. She's growed. She's ready fer me now.

That day.

Then after, her child, unwashed and unblessed, lay in an unmarked grave.

73

Hannah passed that night in the glow of candlelight, watching over Angelino. This motherless child arrived to her shore, to her alone. Hannah's life streamed before her mind's eye. The losses of her life all piled together.

I watch over this child, alone, she thought. Only I can mourn this child for his lost mother, and for myself. Hannah waked the child through the night.

Angelino, his face, his skin, perfect, beautiful, whole. Hannah kept watch. She felt comforted, seeing this child in sweet repose. Cleaned gently with loving hands, with honest tears that fell from Hannah's eyes upon his cheek. He, in peace, as if asleep.

With this child I mourn my own son taken from me unborn.

I with the duty of love to have held them only briefly, then to let them go. I only. I was chosen to be their comfort for their brief time on earth. Now, returned safely to heaven. Peaceful rest be granted, at home above.

A strange softness enfolded Hannah, now a quiet in her heart.

PART IX

74

Aftermath

In the small towns across the bay, women wore silks from Italy; their dyes spoke of faraway places sunny and bright. Men wore wools too smart for these rough shore towns. Children played in frocks too fine.

Felix and Phebe strolled down Patchogue's main street on errand day. There they ran into their old friend Gregory, who always had the latest news.

"What brings you into town?" asked Felix of this old friend, offering a friendly slap on the back.

"Same as you, prob'bly," Gregory retuned with a grin.

He graciously took Phebe's hand to kiss in gallant greeting, but Phebe was distracted, her eyes following a woman behind Gregory who strutted proudly in a splendid large-brimmed hat with fine Italian trim. "They don't even try to hide their ill-gotten gain," she declared with disgust.

"The townspeople here are so open with it all," Felix replied. Both men turned and followed Phebe's focus on the lady with the hat as she haughtily crossed the street and walked on.

"Ha! That's nothin'!" declared Gregory. "Yestidday I saw a man with *six* hats on! You shoulda' seen that! He walked oh-so-slowly to balance 'em all." He mockingly tried to imitate the man's stride. "Ye could see he thought he looked kinda' natty, showin' off his wares. 'Course they was all Italian felt. Hats was smooth and sharp, they were. Prob'bly sold them pretty quick, too."

"Awful!" declared Phebe. "Just here after we docked today, we saw a man hawking wicker olive oil flasks for six cents apiece. Then, his wife just a few paces off selling buttons and coats, cuffs and brocades for practically nothing!"

"Wa'll, that sure don't help calm the publicity on this wreck!" added Gregory.

"Of course!" agreed Felix. "It's all good stuff to sell more newspapers! First, the baby dies. That's a heartbreaker right there! Then Fuller and Ossoli's bodies don't turn up. *That* story's all across the nation. People *love* to read about a tragedy. Then, the people out here, showing no remorse, just interested in selling their stolen goods. Long Islanders' looking pretty bad. Papers' all covering that, too!"

"I never seen so much publicity on a wreck with so few victims," declared Gregory.

After Phebe and Felix said their goodbyes, they continued their walk to the dry goods store.

"What about the Marshal's investigation into the pirating?" she asked.

"Seven of 'em were charged."

"Smith Oakes among them?"

"Yep."

"Why's he still around then?"

"All those guys 'r thick in with each other. One lies and the other swears to it. Booty moved around t' houses and hid so many times, befuddled the Marshal. His investigation yielded practically nothing! His men searched their homes and found goods from the *Elizabeth* altogether worth only about a hundred and fifty dollars. And most found miles from the wreck. Like this stuff here on the street. Small stuff. Too incidental. Don't know yet if they have enough to pursue."

"But I'll bet anything worthwhile having is still on shore. Buried probably. Waiting for statute of limitations to pass."

"Yep. No doubt."

"How is Hannah, by the way?"

"Haven't seen her much since the wreck."

"Life as usual, probably," he surmised.

75

Early morning on the barrier island. Smith made the boat ready for a long day of errands across the bay. Good southwest wind t' sail across, he thought. Can make it early t' Islip, then make a run downwind t' Patchogue. The longest leg 'l be beatin' into the wind to git back here 'fore sunset.

"Hannah! Git a move on!" he shouted from the deck of the small craft.

Finally, he saw her approaching.

Hannah handed him her bundle of sewing to be delivered to Mrs. Johnson. Then she gingerly gathered the hem of her dress as she stepped aboard.

Oaks untied the line and pushed away into the bay. "First stop's t' Johnsons."

Hannah didn't respond.

He added, "An' don' fergit t' get paid fer it t'day, Hannah. They's rich 'nough so's no need t' make us wait fer our money."

"Mrs. Johnson is always prepared, Smith," she replied. He just has to make a contest of every interaction, thought Hannah distastefully as she settled in the prow.

"An' be quick about it while y'r there. Got a long way t' go t'day, too."

She didn't bother to reply, already lost in the beauty of the day with its wide blue skies.

Hannah had been going more and more often across the bay to the estate of Mrs. John D. Johnson with her sewing. Mrs. Johnson, a lady of good heart and much kindness, married to a family of wealthy Louisiana sugar plantation owners. The family's wise patriarch, Captain Johnson came north and opened up a whiskey distillery in New York City.

"The city's growin'. Men git thirsty," said he.

Wise indeed, for a distillery is a natural outlet for his own sugar crops. He bought property on the west side of Manhattan, on the Hudson River, so the cane could be easily delivered in ships from the south. He made a large fortune.

Now, his son John, rich in inheritance, built an estate on Long Island's south shore just east of Islip Village on a tract of land on Champlin Creek, a cold, freeflowing freshwater stream that empties into the Great South Bay. Here he could indulge his passions for hunting, fishing, and boating. The Johnson family, churchgoers and bastions of the community, stable and secure.

Hannah disembarked after Smith tied up to the dock. Brackish water splashed against the hull of the small catboat. Smith handed her the package of sewing tightly bound and secure.

"Don' overstay," he warned her again. "I'll be waitin' here fer ya'." He tied up to the private dock.

"I'll stay as I am needed," Hannah replied. "You'll wait as you please. If it's a dress needs fitting, takes time. Money's too good to walk away from something like that."

Inside the sprawling home, Hannah was escorted by a servant to the private parlor of Mrs. Johnson. She was greeted warmly, and was welcomed to sit while her work was inspected. Mrs. Johnson's eyes sparkled when she saw Hannah's fine needlework.

"You have quite a talent," remarked Mrs. Johnson, "and much patience to produce such beauty in stitching."

"Thank ye kindly. That's what Mama left me," added Hannah shyly. "She taught me all she knew about sewing and making."

"She must have been good and kind, as you are," remarked Mrs. Johnson. "I am sorry she passed to the next life so young. That must have been hard for you."

"Yes. I still miss her," Hannah's eyes lowered.

"Did your Papa re-marry?"

"No, ma'am."

"So you did the chores and took care of the home?"

"Yes, ma'am. And four brothers. Until they grew up and went away. Then took care of Papa 'till he died, too."

"Poor Hannah. Life has not been kind to you."

"I just do what is needed, that's all," she replied.

"Come with me into the sewing room, now. I have some fabric I would like you to see."

Up until now, Hannah brought mending home to sew for Mrs. Johnson, to return on her next visit, a simple transaction. She had not been invited into the sewing room before.

But now she was taken to a room on the third floor, spacious and bright. Shelves on the left were filled with all that is needed for sewing. Needles of every size lined up just so. Threads of every hue arranged in colors descending in tones. Then shelves on the right held the fabrics, just waiting their turn for service. Linen for household use, then warm wools, then fine crepes and silks. Then in the center of the room, work tables, a pressing board and iron. And pins, pins, pins galore.

Mrs. Johnson's eyes followed Hannah's as she took in the room, enjoying her look of amazement. She said, finally, "There will be a gala in a few weeks in the city. It's the opening ball of the New York Yacht Club, and Mr. Johnson is one of the founding members. I must make an impression. Turn some heads. Show those city ladies that we out here in the country have some finery, too."

Hannah stood, intrigued.

"I would like you to create something special for me to wear."

"Of course, Mrs. Johnson. I am flattered that you entrust a gown of such importance to me."

"My dear, I see a talent in you as I have seen in no other. I trust your eye for color and shape, but more, I think you truly creative. Make me something unique. Adorn me with something none of the other ladies will have never seen."

Her arm swept the perimeter of the room, "Pick from any fabrics, trims and laces you see here. This will be your workshop. How soon can you return?"

Hannah could not conceal her delight to work with such finery, and in a room filled with such treasures. Possibilities were all around her here.

"I have a tea to attend now, but just have enough time to take you through the silks. Silk is so lovely for this time of year, do you agree Hannah?"

"Of course, it is quite lovely ma'am," she replied.

"And when you work here, bring Marietta. She gets along so well with my little ones. They will find lots to do here while you sew."

*****

Smith waited impatiently for Hannah on the dock.

"What! No sewin' to bring home this time?" he asked seeing Hannah's arms empty as she arrived from the house. He put out his hand to receive the money Hannah had collected. Silently, she complied. Counting it quickly, he secured it in the pocket of his overalls. He then looked expectantly at Hannah for the answer to his question.

"No, no sewing to bring home this time. But Mrs. Johnson would like me back. I am to stitch for her a new gown for a special occasion. She offered that I work in her sewing room. Marietta can come too."

A grunt was his only reply. Hannah boarded, then he pushed the catboat from the dock, sailed her down to the bay and pointed her east toward Patchogue.

There, Smith had his errands. Guns and ammunition. An old sail that needed repair. But the day was much too nice for Hannah to wait in town.

"I will walk a bit, maybe down to the old house," she told Smith.

"What ya' gonna do there? House don't belong to ya' no more."

"I know. You sold it as soon as we were married."

"Husband's right, Hannah," replied Oaks.

"Well, I'll take a walk down there, anyway."

Hannah, lost in her thoughts, wended back through her old walks, down paths she remembered. Now the trees have grown, filled in, she thought.

Although the property sold, no one came to occupy the house since she left. Now she could see roof half collapsed, wallboards full of rot. The house, disintegrating from neglect.

The back is still open land, she observed, and the small family plot she had tended still lies in solitude, overgrown.

She surveyed the small graveyard, untouched and unkempt. Her past came flooding back. Father, Mother and baby brothers and sisters. The rosemary and rue are still here. I can pull out these weeds to let in some light and air, thought Hannah, so the sun can shine on them and warm their bones. She knelt to clear away the overgrowth that had crowded out her plantings made carefully so many years ago.

Hannah's mind revolved with all she had lost in her young life. Now, on this visit, no sadness. Only a restful acceptance of all that went before; all that brought her to this time and place and understanding.

And just away, the unmarked grave, the secret one. There, the bayberry still blooming. She pulled the weeds, her deft hands loosening the soil around his small grave. She snapped the ends of the bayberry to shape it, keep it in trim.

The memory of her unborn still clear, but now has taken on a different cast. The destiny of this child was never mine to determine, she thought. Even our children are not truly ours. Each soul has its own path.

Her hands now still upon the soil, upon her child. And you, my boy, given to me, a soul not ready to be born into this world. You favored me. You chose me to be your bed, your soft couch for the weeks I had you in my womb. I thank you, my child, for choosing me to be your restful place while on this earth.

I know you are at peace now. Flesh of my flesh, but destiny onto your own.

The sun shone upon Hannah and on the soft soil.

*****

"What's 'at in the bag then?" Oaks said to Hannah after they'd set sail for home, heading across the bay against the long last rays of the late day.

"I spent time weeding by the graves at my father's house. Pulled some plantings for the garden at home. Not much grows on the beach unless brought from the main island."

Hannah settled now in the boat, Oaks skillfully at sail, tacking away toward home.

Hannah looked toward the west, the sun lowering in a cloudless sky. She felt dreamy and calm. She felt a settling, a peace for her child unborn, a surety in her love for him. She'd released him, let him go, he now safe from all sin and tears, forever blest.

Hannah put her hand into the bag to touch the cutting she'd taken of his bayberry bush, one that she knows will grow in her garden sturdy and strong.

76

Hannah appeared at the Johnson house faithfully. The gown she made was a perfect cut to flatter Mrs. Johnson's figure. Last fitting, now she would begin her embellishments. Her design of fine embroidery. Her work, delicate. She adorned the gown with stitching. The motif, her unique vision.

Hannah loved working with the hand-woven silk, textured, the color of the palest sand upon the beach so pure. And from her mind's eye she embroidered a scene of beauty seen so often by her of the Atlantic shore.

A sparkle was added using thread of silver, woven, nearly hidden, seen only as glimmer, as when the sun lights up the sand, aglow a moment like diamonds.

Then, she added softly flowing lines of green, like the dune grass that seemed to wave in the breeze with the wearer's slightest movement. Blue sky and clouds woven behind; delicate, like a whisper.

Shading subtle, scene exquisite, Hannah knows this landscape all in her memory. Now she captured it onto the cloth, and here the scene came alive in the soft silk.

Nothing like it was ever seen by Mrs. Johnson, or among the ladies of the New York Yacht Club.

77

Smith Oaks was truly spooked this time. Worry pervaded his sleep and disturbed his waking hours. There have been too many inquiries. Too many questions. Even after the Marshal's investigation fell apart and the suspects were released, he felt the pressure. Never before had an inquiry into pirating on this shore been covered so closely. Publicity brought speculation. Curiosity brought onlookers from near and far and kept the incident alive in the minds of all.

Last trip t' town was rough, he thought, remembering. The owner of the drygoods store, usually friendly, was curt. Oaks resolved to make his purchase quick, when who should walk in but Daniel Jones and Benaja Wood, looking to buy cigars. Jones, sloppy, and a little drunk.

Smith gave but just a nod, left the store, and waited outside for them. When they saw, he tipped his hat to signal them to follow him down the alleyway.

"What the hell's *a' matter* wit' you two?" he sputtered into their faces. "Didn't I tell ya t' split up an' not be seen t'gether? An buyin' cigars? That ol' nosey storekeeper'll be knowin' ya' have some extra change around somewheres!"

Wood stepped aside to stand apart from Jones, who sobered up quick. His eyes darted between them, mouth working nervously, saying nothing. Oaks took them both in. Jones looked like he was falling apart. "Stay off the streets ya' two jackasses… and stay away from *me*," he hissed. "An' stay *low*." He quickly left them and hurried back toward the dock.

Oaks normally worked alone when he pirated wrecks. The isolated position of his house usually afforded him that. But, he thought, that morning it was too easy t' get these two involved. Picked up more an' got it hid faster wit' 'em t' help, fer sure. But now I'm stuck with 'em. Now I got t' worry over both of 'em that they don't do anythin' stupid.

He knew that under pressure, nobody's reliable.

*****

Next morning, tending to chores, Oaks sat out in his horse shed cleaning his guns. A solitary place for a solitary task, and one that had always given him a calm sense of security. Alone and quiet, he would rub and polish and think and plan.

But now, he could reach no ease in his mind, anxiety mounting. He knew the danger of that. His aggressive attitude and deft actions had always served to keep others at bay long enough for him to strategize. To stay one step ahead. But the fear that was creeping in is an easy thing for an enemy to sense. A chink in his armor could lead to danger.

Involuntarily, his hand jerked, spilling the linseed oil onto his workbench, a spontaneous reaction to a disturbance in his quiet surroundings. Someone on my property, he thought. Instinctively, he reached for his pistol. Then he heard a voice, familiar but not welcome. It was Benaja Wood calling out to him from his bayside dock.

"Ye out here, Oaks?"

"In the shed," he replied. "You alone?"

"Yep."

"Come on back."

Not trusting anyone, Oaks pointed his loaded pistol toward the doorway. When he saw that Wood was alone, he relaxed, laying the pistol on the workbench.

"Wha's a' matter with you? I *said* I wuz alone!" cried Wood, annoyed.

"Can't be too careful now. Too many people snoopin' these days."

Wood now settled now in the shed, Oaks mopped up the spilled oil and applied it to the stock of his rifle.

Oaks was irritated. "I told ya' like I told Jones not to come round here. Whaddaya want?"

Wood began, "Came t' bring ya' the papers." Wood handed the *Daily Tribune* to him, folded to the headline. He pointed, "*Still* talkin' 'bout the wreck."

"Newspapers goin' crazy," said Oaks. "Usually wreck reports r' just one-liners on page three." Oaks glanced at it, then tossed the paper aside. "Page one fer nigh two weeks now."

"Yep. Here it says folk's mad cause the government wastes money on a rescue service that didn't rescue nobody. Sure makes Selah Strong look bad," Wood said wryly. He hoped to get a rise out of Oaks, whom he knew hated the Strong family.

"Yeh," muttered Oaks, not taking the bait. "S' why *you* here?"

Wood continued, "Marshal's not givin' up. Keeps askin' round. Never got so close before."

"Yer sure Jones didn't blab nothin'?" asked Oaks.

"He swears he didn't. But he's drunk a lot these days."

Wood shot a conspiratorial look at Oaks. "Mebbe' we should dig up the booty an' move it, eh?"

Oaks saw Wood's eyes focused on the dune where the booty lay buried.

"Nah. Nope. Let it be," replied Oaks. "Movin' it could mean trouble. I'm watchin' it outtn' my windows ever' day." He put aside the rifle he was working on and looked directly at Wood. "I kin' tell if somebody's around. Can't nobody git past *my* eyes."

Oaks was firm. He picked up the rifle again and continued oiling the stock. Wood had no choice but to accept his answer. An awkward silence filled the shed.

"Dominy gave the underwriter's report at Atlantic Dock," said Wood, eager to gain back favor. "Him an' the big man, the underwriter's man, brought whatever washed in later."

"Yep. That should end that. Family'll pick up belongings there. Finally mebbe they'll git off'n my beach."

"And that nosy reporter from the *Tribune*'s gone home too. Sez he worked with the lady writer on the paper before she left fer Europe. Sure asked a lot o' questions, he did."

"Lot o' publicity around this Fuller lady. Family came to fetch the baby. Was askin' bout some papers too."

"Yeh, so was the feller who says he 's a writer friend o' hers from Boston. Was keen on her writin' papers and her personal belongings. Searched the beach for five days, and followed up leads for her stuff in Patchogue and Sayville."

"They're all gone home now."

"Anybody else comin' now's jes' too late."

"Family left word in case her body comes washin' in."

"Shark's prob'ly got 'er by now."

"Yep. Sharks got 'er fer sure."

*****

In the weeks that followed the wreck, curiosity seekers streamed to the beach by the hundreds. Some hoped to pick up any remaining items that the sea would wash in. Some wanted just to say they were on the beach where Margaret Fuller died.

Rumors of her remains were various. Some had it that her body never washed up. That it was trapped under the timbers, held by the cargo of marble. Some said that her body came ashore and was stripped of valuables by locals and secretly buried. Others claim that she washed in, half eaten by sharks, was taken by a local captain by boat to New York City to the editor of the *Tribune*. He refused to see the body, and in a panic, the captain didn't know what to do, so he buried her on a deserted barrier island just outside the harbor.

It seemed the talk of this wreck would never end.

It didn't help that salvage attempts were underway for whatever was still in the hull. Tons of Carrera marble sat on the ocean floor. And, of widening interest, still wedged into the sandbar, was a work of art. A marble statue carved on commission by Hiram Powers in Florence of John C. Calhoun meant for the South Carolina State House.

All this helped to spread curiosity, and kept nourishing the rumors associated with the wreck. This was bad news for Smith Oaks. He counted on life to return to normal and for people to forget.

What's more, it impinged on his livelihood as sportsman guide. Activity on the beach kept the game away. If hunting and fishing suffered, the sportsmen stayed away. Smith Oaks' business fell off in this, his busiest season.

Time on his hands made things worse. Too many people around on my island, he thought. Too many prying eyes. Too many questions. He became obsessed with protecting his boundaries; protecting the booty, trying to manage his environment.

And as gossip spread, mysteries resurfaced around Smith Oaks' past. Talk about him swirled in the towns from one curiosity seeker to the next.

"Wasn't he the guide who took out that poor boy, Judd who was killed?"

"Yes, I believe that was him. That was a mystery never solved."

"And was it the same summer that his brother Andrew suddenly died at his house?"

"Yep. Poor man. Nice feller, too."

"This Oaks was the guy named in the missing trunks of the *Louisa* wreck, too. Wasn't that him?"

"Yep. But whatever happened to that investigation, anyways?"

His name was on the lips of the locals in the pubs and in the streets. He remembered from his days as a drifter... he knew that talk only leads to trouble.

He realized then that this might have been his last haul. All he could do was lie low and wait.

78

Hannah worked in the rays of sunlight that filtered in through the lace curtains of the sewing room. She could hear Marietta and the Johnson children playing happily on the expanse of lawn outside. This is so good for Marietta, she thought, away from the isolation of the island. Suddenly, a servant appeared, and Hannah was asked to see Mrs. Johnson in her parlor.

"Please sit." Mrs. Johnson gestured toward the chair next to hers.

"If I may be so bold, Hannah, I have a delicate question to ask."

"Of course, ma'am," she replied.

"My dear, what is your situation?" Seeing Hannah's look of puzzlement, she realized the vagueness and awkwardness of the question. Mrs. Johnson clarified, "I have heard some rumors that are not flattering."

"Oh?" Hannah was speechless. She looked around the room uncomfortably.

"About your husband. About your situation there on the barrier beach."

Hannah became afraid. Just a few days before she had been stopped by the Marshal on her walk from the dock to Mrs. Johnson's.

"Excuse me, Mrs. Oaks. Have you a minute?"

Hannah's eyes nervously searched for Smith, to see if he was watching.

He registered her concern. "Don't worry, ma'am. He's in the pub on Main Street. I saw him go in after he dropped you off on the dock."

"What can I do for you?" she asked nervously. "The last time I agreed to talk to you didn't go well for me."

"Yes, I'm aware. I'm sorry Mrs. Oaks. But I must ask about Daniel Jones, yer husband's friend. Been to yer house lately?"

"No. I have not seen him," she replied. "Why?"

"Gone missin.' No one's seen 'em of late."

Her interview with the Marshal was brief. Oaks, already suspect, the pieces of the puzzle were not hard to fit together.

Hannah was afraid now to be questioned by Mrs. Johnson. She, uneasy, rose from the chair, saying, "Excuse me, ma'am," and started past her for the door. Her eyes cast down, she said, "I must go. I have work to finish."

"Do not be afraid my dear." Mrs. Johnson stood and with a gentle touch on Hannah's arm, detained her. Her tone calmed Hannah. She waited, still facing the door, her head down, eyes averted. But she stayed to hear what Mrs. Johnson had to say.

"I ask because I merely want to offer you an option. An alternative for you, and for Marietta…"

Hannah had known it was only a matter of time. And here was an opportunity. Unbidden and unsought, it came to her to act. Perhaps now, she could be free. She and Marietta.

"Mrs. Johnson," she stammered. "The Marshal. He stopped to talk to me on my way here," she began, uncertainty in her voice. But it was a comfort to be able to confide. Soon, all her fears came tumbling out.

"Just be honest with the Marshal," encouraged Mrs. Johnson.

"I know it's the right thing to do," agreed Hannah. There were others who could help, too, she thought. The Dominys were always by her side when needed.

"The timing must be perfect, said Mrs. Johnson. "All must be set accordingly."

*****

Back at her house on the beach, Hannah went through her personal things in her bedroom. Her few clothes, her mother's comb and brush set, and her locket. A prayer book, and a bible. And among these things is where she'd hidden the packet, damaged from the sea, although now long dry. Having found it during the storm the morning of the *Elizabeth*, she'd hidden it away during the turmoil. And so it had sat, salt stained and brittle among her things, so few.

Hannah had kept the packet of notes, written by the mother of the child she'd found, loved briefly and mourned fully. She held the packet as a connection to the lost child, hoping to know more of the woman who bore him.

Since the wreck, she'd cracked open the folio and found pages browned at the edges, paper and ink remarkably preserved by the tightly wound leather cover.

From this she would read in her quiet moments. She had never known thoughts like these before. Here this woman wrote of truth, thought Hannah as she read. Of right. She writes of duty and of the brave. Of what we owe to the life we have to live. Of what we owe to our selves, and others.

"I stand upon this earth," thought Hannah. "I now take my place, my rightful place."

She remembered, and carefully placed the pages among her things as she packed.

*****

Oaks was making his way down the shore from a day of ocean fishing. Slung over his shoulder was a string of striped bass whose dappled scales shone in the late afternoon sun. As he approached the house, he saw the parlor windows open wide, unusual for that time of day. He saw footprints in the sand, large and small, and marks, as if something heavy had been dragged.

Immediately suspicious, he dropped the afternoon's catch, and reached his right arm over his shoulder for the rifle that hung across his back.

He approached with caution.

"Hannah? You there?" he called as he entered the house.

"I'm here," she answered. She knew that now is the time. Now it is right.

When Smith saw Hannah, he was surprised at her appearance. Dressed for town, she stood waiting for him in the parlor. She looked upon him, and spoke in a voice assertive and confident.

"I *can* no longer..." said Hannah to Smith.

He stood, puzzled, sandy and disheveled, the rifle still in hand.

"What'r you about, Hannah?"

She continued, "I can no longer stay here. Marietta must grow up on the main island, near neighbor, church and school. We are to be part of the household of Mrs. Johnson. I, her personal dressmaker. Marietta will be schooled with their children. She will be educated. There we will have a life of peace."

"What are ye sayin', Hannah? I'm yer' *husband*. Yer took a oath before God!"

"Don't you *dare* say that to me! God cannot have blessed this union, Smith. You who are so wicked and deceitful. All these years I spent here with you...." She trailed off, finding it all too much to express.

He looked stunned. Automatically, he fingered the rifle.

She saw the threat and looked out of the window toward the bay. His eyes followed hers and saw Dominy there, helping Marietta onto his boat. When she was safely below, he stood and kept a watch on the house, waiting.

She motioned toward Oak's rifle, "You can't use that on me with a witness right outside."

Through the open door, Hannah could see over Oaks' shoulder the fleeting forms of the Marshal's men scurrying over the far side of the dune near their house. She stepped forward assertively, toward her husband, to draw his full attention upon her.

"And I *know* you won't come after me. It isn't three years from the wreck yet. You must stay and guard your wicked gains. But more... this time, there's blood on your hands for this haul. And I can't be part of that."

His face now gorged red with rage. Like a trapped animal, he attacked, grabbing her throat with his free hand. His fingers, long and strong, held her in his grip. She, choking, went to her knees, tears streaming, eyes bulging, weakening.

"*Who ye been talkin' to?*" he ranted, bending forward into her face. He recovered his rage enough to remember that Dominy might hear, so he released Hannah, letting her fall to the floor.

"Stupid, stupid woman." He looked down upon her supine figure. "It's the same as allay's. Booty along the beach is there for the takin'. Comes from the sea, 'at's all. Same as anythin' that washes up." He stood over her.

Hannah, gasping, rolled to her side to recover her breath. When she could speak, she looked up at Oaks. Slowly rising first to her hands and knees, then upright to stand, she said, "This one's *not* the same... It's not just stealing."

She stopped, coughing, then managed to inhale sharply, regaining control. "In the time it took you to bury the booty, you could have notified Selah Strong. But no, instead hours passed until that boy from the wreck showed up. If you'd sent Wood and Jones like you said, they all could have been saved."

She saw clearly his bedraggled form, his body wiry and tense, his eyes darting. She knew what he could be like when confronted... this, and Dominy waiting outside... His mind was surely in a spin.

She knew she must continue. Coughing, again, sharp pain reported from her neck. "Those people *died* because of you, Smith. That's on your soul."

Smith stared at her in wonder, as if she were a stranger.

"And there were others," she added, "Before. When I was too weak."

Hannah glanced out of the window toward bayside to see Felix, his eyes trained on the house.

"No, Smith. I can no longer stand by," repeated Hannah. "And I will not have Marietta exposed to your ways."

Smith turned to look again toward the bay. He saw Dominy waiting to take his family away.

His defensive instinct took over. His lips curled back into an involuntary snarl. He reached forward, grabbing Hannah's hair gathered at her nape and forced her head close to his face. She could smell his sweat, his foul breath, as he growled, "Yer *mine*. An' that's mine *kin*. Ain't nothin' gonna change that." With that, he thrust her head back with force and released her. She toppled backward like a small child.

Oaks saw her stumble, then thought again of Dominy waiting outside. He forced himself to focus on what's most important. Booty rested in his dune, awaiting the day. His choice was a simple one.

Once more his cold gray eyes took her in, but the treasure was his real concern. "Do what ye will Hannah."

He stood with his legs spread wide, defiant, his rifle held sidewise between his crossed arms. He said, "Jes' don' go askin' me for *nuthin'* when the day comes."

She, confident. "There's nothing from you that I could possibly want," stated Hannah, locking him with her eyes. She turned, head high, and strode purposefully over the threshold for the last time.

*****

She was helped aboard by Felix. Marietta below, now emerged onto the deck. Relieved, she embraced her mother tight around her knees.

"Let's go," Hannah said to Felix. "The Marshal will take care of him." She and Marietta made their way to the prow to sit together for the sail across the bay.

Hannah afforded one last glance toward the house. She saw activity on the far side of their dune… sand being tossed high, rhythmically, shovelfuls one at a time, the Marshal's men digging.

They sailed away, the small boat swift and sure. Hannah and Marietta, heads inclined, their arms encircled. The air smelled sweet. The horizon beckoned.

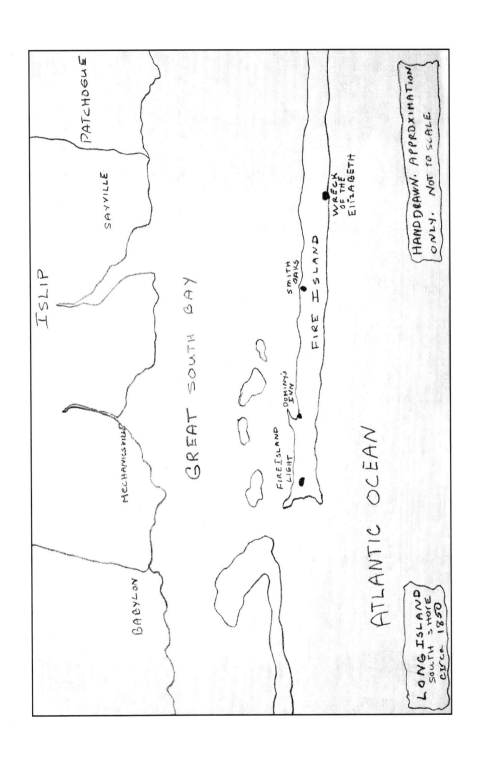

PATCHOGUE

SAYVILLE

ISLIP

MECHANICSVILLE

BABYLON

GREAT SOUTH BAY

FIRE ISLAND
LIGHT

DOMINY'S
INN

SMITH
OAKS

FIRE ISLAND

WRECK
OF THE
ELIZABETH

ATLANTIC OCEAN

HANDDRAWN. APPROXIMATION
ONLY. NOT TO SCALE.

LONG ISLAND
SOUTH SHORE
CIRCA 1850

Made in the USA
Middletown, DE
15 June 2019